11/22

# THE

# DECEPTIONS

# THE
# DECEPTIONS

———— ✦ ————

*A Novel*

✦

## JILL BIALOSKY

Counterpoint
Berkeley, California

This is a work of fiction. All of the characters, organizations, and events portrayed in this novel are either products of the author's imagination or are used fictitiously.

THE DECEPTIONS

First Counterpoint edition: 2022

Grateful acknowledgment is made to the following for reprinting images: p. 270: Cubiculum (bedroom) from the Villa of P. Fannius Synistor at Boscoreale: Installation view, photographed in 1964. Rogers Fund, 1903; Gift of J. Pierpont Morgan, 1917. p. 124: *The Castration of Uranus*. Engraver: Giovanni Battista Galestruzzi, Italian (1618–c. 1669). Etching. Gift of Belinda L. Randall from the collection of John Witt Randall. Polidoro da Caravaggio (1490/1500–1543).

Library of Congress Cataloging-in-Publication Data
Names: Bialosky, Jill, author.
Title: The deceptions : a novel / Jill Bialosky.
Description: First Counterpoint edition. | Berkeley, CA : Counterpoint, 2022.
Identifiers: LCCN 2021059505 | ISBN 9781640090248 (hardcover) | ISBN 9781640090255 (ebook)
Classification: LCC PS3552.I19 D43 2022 | DDC 813/.54—dc23
LC record available at https://lccn.loc.gov/2021059505

*Jacket design by Jaya Miceli*
*Book design by Wah-Ming Chang*

COUNTERPOINT
2560 Ninth Street, Suite 318
Berkeley, CA 94710
www.counterpointpress.com

Printed in the United States of America

1 3 5 7 9 10 8 6 4 2

For Isabel Elizabeth

✦

But what else
can a mother give her daughter but such
beautiful rifts in time?

—EAVAN BOLAND,
from "The Pomegranate"

Leda and the Swan

A sudden blow: the great wings beating still
Above the staggering girl, her thighs caressed
By the dark webs, her nape caught in his bill,
He holds her helpless breast upon his breast.

How can those terrified vague fingers push
The feathered glory from her loosening thighs?
And how can body, laid in that white rush,
But feel the strange heart beating where it lies?

A shudder in the loins engenders there
The broken wall, the burning roof and tower
And Agamemnon dead.
                              Being so caught up,
So mastered by the brute blood of the air,
Did she put on his knowledge with his power
Before the indifferent beak could let her drop?

—W. B. YEATS


Now goddess, child of Zeus,
    tell the old story for our modern times.
Find the beginning.

—HOMER, *The Odyssey*,
translated by Emily Wilson

# THE
# DECEPTIONS

Harriet Rothman
Feminist Press
October 15, 2023

Dear Harriet,

I am thrilled that you've acquired *Vindication*. I'm eager to dive into this new project. I've been looking for some contemporary examples to support my thesis, and I've come upon a new discovery concerning the poets Abigail Frost and Justin O'Donnell. It may seem like a footnote at first, but it radically transforms our perceptions of their work. As you know, Abigail was my neighbor growing up and was the first person to encourage my own writing. The work is fueled by an episode that happened during my first semester in college, and has given urgency to my academic path. As well, I want the project to further the conversation I began in my book *The Female Voice* and I'm grateful for the opportunity.

Best wishes,
Amelia

Amelia Finnegan
Assistant Professor of English
Stanford University

## DAY I

Dark clouds threaten all day and break loose. Sheets of water slash the windows. Fill the sill to its breaking point. Water gurgles in the gutters, drips down the spine of the building. Trees bend to the wind. Branches keen. A crack of thunder, as if the sky is breaking in half. Ribbons of lightning. Trees falling in Central Park. No one predicted the storm's strength. Something terrible has happened and I don't know what to do.

Earlier I scrubbed the floors. Spun a few loads of laundry to push away the sense of dread that is like my shadow. In the afternoon, graded a handful of less-than-enlightening papers on an aspect of Odysseus's multifaceted character in *The Odyssey*. I've taught the poem for more years than I can count and still I don't know how I feel about our hero.

My husband's fixed in his loyal spot on the old Pottery Barn couch watching a football game. The reclining arm wears the shape of his long runner's body. His T-shirt is soft, wrinkly, thinning at the collar, shadow of sexy beard already turning to elegy. Monday morning it will be gone. I'm reading a long review of a new Plath biography in *The New Yorker*. I've been obsessed with reading reviews. One's been assigned at *The New York Times Book Review* for my new book of poetry due to come out in two months. It's made me jumpy. I haven't told my husband. I don't want to jinx it. Another downpour. The window blinds shudder. Shadows from swaying trees dance across our wall.

My eyes wander from the review to the swivel chair my son used to slink into, making it his own, sticky from sweat, rotating like a god on his throne, exhausted after a run at the track, slurping a Jamba juice he picked up on the way back. Now his ghost shape in its leather form. Without needing to cook his dinner, to clean his jerseys and school uniforms, his sweaty bed linens, to get him out of bed for school (a task I typically failed), I'm at loose ends. Eighteen years and, poof, it's gone.

I wish my husband would turn off the football game, suggest we go out for dinner or a glass of wine to obliterate my dislocation. Does he not know that my mind spins and spins with nowhere sensible to land? On the weekends, he lives for the games, football in fall, basketball in winter, baseball in spring and summer. I don't mind. I hold my obsessions dear and therefore must let him hold his, and yet I don't know how to reach him. What's wrong with him? Why doesn't he need more? I turn back to the piece on Plath biting Ted Hughes's cheek the first time he kissed her at a party.

What do you want to do for dinner? I ask. Are you fucking kidding me? he says. Ah, apparently, the receiver missed the pass. Shall we go out? I'm restless, I say, his eyes glued to the screen.

When we were first married, we used to take a golf umbrella to Riverside Park in the rain, our arms linked. Sheltered on a bench underneath the umbrella, we listened to the relentless patter while looking at the hundreds-of-years-old elms enveloping Riverside Drive and beyond the ripples of the Hudson River. Watched the raindrops slither down the slender portal of a soon-to-be-dying leaf. Tasted the rusty rain. In a downpour, we dashed into one of the tunnels. Then, dripping wet, off to the pub for a pint, at the bar, our wet thighs touching, his soft-whisper-tickle in my ear.

Go out? It's raining. For Christ's sake, he says. A fumble. Someone's hurt. The emergency team brings out the stretcher. We have wine here. I can make us something.

The open room extends to our galley kitchen. To the pitchers and bowls on the counter. To our son's hockey equipment in the hallway. (He hasn't played hockey in years.) My failing hosta plant my mother gifted to me eighteen years ago when I gave birth. It is in need of tender revival. A painted vase my husband and I bought together on a trip to Italy on the bookshelf. The color fading, chips and cracks that can't be restored.

This mealy couch I've been meaning to slipcover. I can barely stand to look at it all.

The crowd screams. Another fumble on the twenty-yard line. Make the goddamn pass, you idiot, my husband says. I turn back to the page where the reviewer quotes from Sylvia Plath's *Johnny Panic and the Bible of Dreams*: "What I fear most, I think, is the death of the imagination . . . If I sit still and don't do anything, the world goes on beating like a slack drum, without meaning. We must be moving, working, making dreams to run toward; the poverty of life without dreams is too horrible to imagine." My husband stands up and grabs his ears. Get him, you fucking coward, he says.

"What a game! It looks like the kicker is actually three children stacked in a football uniform," the sportscaster roars on the television. Rain continues. At the bottom of the screen more reports of falling trees, flooding. The game is interrupted by a weather report and photos of Manhattan. It isn't pretty. Every other street is scaffolding. The overcrowded subways incubate disease. Homeless shelter from the rain underneath dripping store awnings, garbage strewn on the streets and sidewalks. When I picked up bagels and lox at Zabar's for brunch, a man was eating out of a trash can. I love the city, but its extremes are widening, the heartbreaking poverty that borders the grotesque extravagance and freakish wealth. I still wake up startled when a siren blares, or I hear screaming fights, or drunken wails out the window.

I get up to water my hosta. I can't sit still. My mind is a running stream of anxiety. What's wrong, I say, touching her long green fingers. I sprinkle an ounce of water from a glass into her vortex. Why are you suffering? I dust her leaves. Some are burned at the edges. The rain bleats. A fire truck rages down the avenue. Trees career from ferocious wind. My husband's at the edge of the couch with his hands covering his ears. For Christ's sake, he says. Are you out of your mind? What, I say, and turn back from the plants to look at him. What have I done now? I wonder out loud. Not you. The punter missed the kick. He looks up at me. I'll start dinner soon.

He grew up in the basement apartment of a crusty row house in Queens, longing for light, he once told me, so that light became all that he wished for. His father, the building manager. His mother washed tenants' cloudy windows for extra cash. Now that his father's dead, his mother's taken over as manager. His father drank and gambled on horses. His sister, a drug addict; the last time she came to dinner she stole my mother's blue pearls and the first edition of *The Great Gatsby* that I found in a used bookstore in Paris. She's no longer permitted in our home. Now my husband looks after his mother and her depleting funds.

The storm hasn't stopped. Red sirens on the police cars keep turning, blinding as they stream past. The rain is streaming down the window. Some loose wires dangle from their poles across the street, twisted and exposed.

Unable to settle, I go to the bedroom, perch on the iron bed we found at a thrift shop. It was the first bed we owned together. Until then we slept on a double mattress on the floor, sometimes found ourselves, after a restless night, half on the wood floor. The mattress sagging, the once-royal-blue satin bedspread that looked to me like a romantic bedcover in a Victorian estate, faded to a color I can no longer identify. It's been fifteen years since I've bought a new mattress and bed linen. A working mother, poet, an oxymoron in itself, who has the time? I go back to my husband. Sit on the other side of the couch under the neck of the standing lamp and pick up the review again. My mind drifts. That day at the lake. The swans preening. The sun burning my skin. It's strange he hasn't written. I don't know what to think anymore. My mind loops from anger to nostalgia. After he packed up and slunk back home to Ohio, I waited for his emails. I was afraid of myself, and so I told myself it was better to wait. I didn't want to have to sit with it. What he'd done. What I allowed. No, I mustn't think about it. I turn back to the review, but it isn't working.

My husband stands. The quarterback throws a pass. Everything's a game. This inventory of our home. Every object, the painted vase from Rome, the Matisse cutout prints from a surprise birthday weekend in Paris, the engraved Tiffany clock I gifted to my husband—he's obsessed with clocks—artifacts from our twenty-year marriage. Like the curator of a historical museum, I can chart each year of purchase.

The rain makes it impossible to see out the window. The light descends. The building's panel of bricks has withstood decades of weather and wear. The facade charcoal black like the walls of a prison. I must stop dwelling. Move forward, pull out of this funk. Each day, a new journey, blah, blah, blah.

My husband stands up and raises his hands. Touchdown. The ugly TV in the center of the bookcase. Some days I'd like to smash it. Beside it the Lego gas stations and Harry Potter scenes of the magician's dungeons my son built. Tiny miniatures of a past life. Have you heard from our son? I don't remember how many days since I last spoke to him. I just want to hear his voice. To know he's okay. My mind carousels to wild drunken parties, to worrying he isn't eating, to piles of dirty clothes smelling up his dorm room. To disorganized papers and books. Haven't you? he says. No, he doesn't pick up my calls. I know the dean said we should let them settle, but it's hard. Didn't she also say we shouldn't interfere with his courses. His overzealous mother did not abide. You told him he should consider Intro to Philosophy and Classical Civilization, he says, raising his eyebrows. Those classes are important. I pause, and nod. Yeah, I fucked up.

It turns out that the reading alone is beyond the capability of any reasonable athlete and social animal with raging hormones whose constitution is not meant to be kept in the library for more than a few hours on any given day. My son is a good student, but he is prone to distraction and procrastination. I don't mind. I read that procrastinators are more creative. He texted me, I said, a thumbs-up. I can't remember. Was it yesterday? Or a few days ago?

Long, lean like his father, both over six feet, dark hair and eyes the color of bark, in a certain light the green of an unripe acorn. Recruited for track and field, I shamelessly boasted, to the parent next to me at orientation. It's been almost two months since he left. He's also a dreamer. Head in the clouds. He'd catch snowflakes on his tongue. The call of a bird distracts him. He once almost got run over by a bus, watching a flock of pigeons descend on a smashed sandwich in the street. He can never find anything in the storm of his room. His teachers and school counselor told me to institute daily planners, checklists.

It wouldn't be the end of the world if he couldn't run track at college, would it? I test. Why do you say that? says my husband. Has he told you he's quitting track? No, but can he handle it and keep up his grades? I inquire. The kid's been at the bar since four this afternoon. The charges pop up on the app on my phone. Don't they know that more than half the students have fake IDs? As long as it's money in their pockets, they don't give a fuck. He looks back at the TV screen, shaking his head.

Sports, track, music lessons, private high school—to keep him from trouble. While the goal was obtained, student loans procured, there are excesses we had not predicted. Students drink quantities of Gatorade, vodka, 100-proof grain alcohol concocted from the frat pantry and poured into a trash can slipcased with a garbage bag where they dip their party cups. The goal, to black out. There are other concerns. Ecstasy, Molly, Candy, unknowingly or knowingly spiked in their drinks. The spread of germs and infectious disease from party cups. Unprotected or nonconsensual sex. At orientation, the dean of students gave her spiel on safe sex and consensual sex practices. Afterward we took our son to a farewell dinner. I told him to make sure if he's with a girl that he asks for permission, even if he's sure. Women are complicated, I said. Mom, stop, he said, and rolled his eyes.

The college is in a small blue-collar town in Maine. Charmed by the Tudor buildings, grand towers, austere library, Olympian pool, state-of-the-art athletic center and track, industrious-looking students when we visited, how did we fail to notice the meth houses, white supremacists, and churches of the Nazarene settled on wide green lawns in the surrounding town, or to predict that on this small campus there is little to do but drink, party, and run sprints?

The self-portrait my son painted in high school art class is framed on the wall. It bears his perfect nose and dreamy eyes. It looks like he's winking at me. I wink back. I miss how he makes me laugh. His enthusiasm. I'm pumped for that grilled cheese sandwich, he'd say with delight in his eyes. A-maz-ing when I asked him about his day. I can't bear to see him sad, suffering, lost. I miss how when I ask him to empty the dishwasher, I find him, pondering drops of water cascading down a glass or halfway in, making a peanut butter sandwich with the dishwasher door half open, only the plates put away. Why was he at the bar at four in the afternoon? Did we overprotect him? Is he too young for freedom? I don't like the term *helicopter parent*. I don't hover. I stand beside him, as a mother does. Take care of yourself. Stay strong, don't drink so much, I say to his portrait. An *all good* or a thumbs-up in a text carries me for nearly twenty-four hours. *I love you* with an emoji heart makes my week. Why doesn't he text me? Ghosted like the other girls.

My husband rises to start dinner. He casts his eyes on the mounting stack of student papers splashed with coffee I left on the dining room table in the afternoon, trips over my books in a tower on the dining room floor. (Where else might I put them when every wall in our small apartment is covered ceiling to floor with overflowing bookshelves? Soon we'll have to rent a separate apartment.) He picks up my copy of Edith Hamilton's *Mythology*. Do you need this? he says, raising the book in the air. Is there a reason why it's next to our kitchen sink? Sorry, I say, and get up to retrieve it. I was looking something up. Since when has our dining room become your office? he says, and gives me one of his "mischievous" smiles. He prefers not to have his dining room table crowded with books, papers, pamphlets, stacks of still-ungraded papers. If he had to read the incoherent and clunky sentences in the papers some of my students turn in, he'd forgive my procrastination. He keeps the research he brings home to read in color-coded files. Where else am I going to work? I almost say. For years I've been telling him that a poet needs a room of her own to write. As if he reads my mind, he says, Now you have a room of your own, referring to our son's bedroom.

I can't write in there. With all his stuff. It's his room. It's not like he isn't coming back home. The prodigal son, my husband says, and sighs. He misses him too. I move the gold heart on the chain of my necklace back and forth. It's wobbling. Heavy. I hear him in the kitchen chopping vegetables. I come to join him. Let me help, I say. Once we delighted in making all-day pot roasts and splendid layers of potatoes au gratin, tomato pie. Long mornings in bed. He's a kind man. Generous. When I'm sick, he makes me cups of tea and strains the chicken pieces from the chicken soup. When we grocery shop, he carries the heavy bags home. When I travel, he plants a set of earbuds in my carry-on so I can listen to films on the airplane screen. On the weekends, he gets up early and goes to Fairway for fresh muffins. He splits the household chores, brings home tulips for our table. This week they're bright yellow, they've opened slightly, revealing delicate black stamens and dusts of pollen like a shedding of blood at the end of the month, fallen to the table. There is no map to follow. Marriage is a geological problem. Two forces of competing desires create instability in a rock formation. I must step carefully, watch where I tread. Don't start anything. We haven't learned how to be alone together again since my son's been gone. I've got it, he says. Go finish reading your article.

The rain falls down the windows, leaving puddles overflowing on the outdoor sill. Cars on the street slosh through flooding water. The window, a dark kaleidoscope. Streets damp and dark. Like a madman, Poseidon continues to wield his rage, tumbling trash cans, hurling garbage into the streets, forcing rats underground. My mind won't quiet. The impending review. The Visiting Poet. The work it requires to repress. My mind grinds through it all.

My husband checks out the scores on the TV with a dish towel tucked into his pants. Boyish, with nerdy black glasses that leave indentations on each side of his nose, hair tousled and a sheen of sweat on his face from the game's excitement. He points at the screen, raging at the quarterback for making a terrible pass like he does to the pundits on CNN who won't confront the political spin. He's become an alarmist. He listens to the news at night and shakes his head. It's a zoo out there, he says.

I look from the review to see my husband staring at me. He does that now, as if he knows something I'm not telling him. What, I say. Nothing, he says. He goes back to the kitchen and stops at the dining room table. Are you planning to clear off your work, he says, raising his eyebrows, so we can eat? He picks up the advance reader copy—ARC—of my new book. *The Rape of the Swan.* A sonnet sequence that ends in violation and loss. In her email yesterday, my editor said it's the first book from the press that the *NYT* has deemed worthy of review. Why would they review a book from a small press only to trash it? *They wouldn't give it to Hugh Pynyon, would they?* I feel sick.

I tuck my papers in my tote bag for Monday and bring the rest into the bedroom. Put down my ARC on the dresser. Wander into my son's room, collapse on his bed, thrust my face in his pillow, smell the Axe shampoo he insists upon. He has a touch of vanity, something new I have noticed in this generation of boys. I long to smell the top of his head, to see him flash me his smile.

I go back to the bedroom, to the ARC of my book on my dresser, and flip through it. All the years of tinkering that went into each sonnet. All the years of rejection before my first book was taken. *The Bell Jar* was rejected by Plath's poetry editor, until it rose from the ashes to become a sensation. Published only a month before she died. A poet who never knew the depth of how she was admired. It doesn't seem fair. I roam back to the living room still holding the ARC. In graduate school I sometimes questioned whether I had a gift or was just wasting time, whether my desire to write—my need—was stronger than my voice. Even after publishing in established literary magazines, two critically acclaimed books, the doubts still creep in.

My husband attacks vegetables in the kitchen with a paring knife. He does everything with force. I stand on the other side of the counter. I can no longer contain it. I heard from my editor on Friday. My book is going to be reviewed by *The New*

*York Times Book Review*, I say. That's great, my husband says. Isn't that what you've always wanted? I nod. So what's wrong, then? he says looking up.

What if it's bad? Mehta can't wait to humiliate me in our department meetings. Did I tell you what he did last week? He accused me of treating the boys like my children after a scuffle in the hallway. Said that I'm not tough enough. He thinks he's teaching at a military academy. Do we have to talk about him again? my husband says, going after the carrots now as if they will run away. He looks back at me. That's great about your book, he says again. Really.

I retreat to the bathroom, slam down the toilet-seat cover. Sit. Lean over and put my head in my hands. How can I tell my husband my hope is that the review will elevate me, a minor poet, into the limelight? How would he understand how important this is? If it's good, I might win a prize. Leave my institution for something bigger, grander. No. I shake my head. But *he* would understand. I steel myself before wandering back into the kitchen. What's happening to me? I take out the plates, wineglasses, and silverware to set the table. Our best linen napkins. Why not celebrate?

My husband uncorks a bottle of red while the sauce in the pan simmers. I put *Swan Lake* in our CD player on the counter. Why not? I love Tchaikovsky's opening. I've heeded to the magical story of the water nymph, visualizing her long, welcoming gestures waiting for something grand and magical to happen while composing my long poem.

This is my prince, my husband, with his dish towel tucked into his waist, his uncombed hair pushed back. He has beautiful hair, thick with little gray, and a cleft in his chin. He bears a scar on his left cheek that runs from the corner of his ear to his cheekbone. A tussle with his good-for-nothing father (his words), when his mother asked him to fetch him for dinner from the bookie who lived in one of the neighboring apartments in their building. His drunken father pushed him away, my husband fell, gashed his cheek on the corner of a table. It's raised and bubbly from never having healed properly. I'll never forgive his father.

I set the table. Fold the napkins into little pockets I learned waitressing in college and place the fork inside. I put the yellow tulips in the pitcher in the center of the table, fuss with their arrangement until I'm satisfied, then stand back to admire them.

That cover of your book. What is it? I left the ARC at the other end of the table. He picks it up. *The Rape of the Swan*, he says, that's what it's called?

Five acts. Each act a crown of sonnets where the first line of each sonnet repeats the final line of the preceding one. The poem is meant to realize the music and destruction of romantic love. Its relentlessness. Its repetition. Its agony. In an early draft, I composed it in free verse, but it felt like it needed to be reined in. And then I thought of Shakespeare's sonnets of love, tried it in blank verse, and it spun to life. One slant rhythm allowing me to find another. How to explain. How when I'm composing, I sail into the ether of my imagination. Places where desire, loss, anger, confusion reside. Dark, raw, dangerous. I sometimes don't like what's revealed. The painful abduction in *The Rape of the Swan* left me blanched and quivering. Two swans are a strong team when together, but if the male is away, the female will often stop eating. Male swans are loyal, they help to incubate the eggs and care for their cygnets for eight to nine months after they're born. Male swans vigilantly guard their nests, preventing their mates from being with another male. If another male threatens the nest, the male swan will busk, flaring his wings, grunting and honking in agitation. When the perpetrator threatened the female swan, I felt her fear, as if it were my own life threatened.

How relieved I used to be to hear my husband come home from work, the jangle of his keys dropped on the wood counter. I'd go into the bathroom and take a shower like a guilty lover, embarrassed by the smell and deceit of my mental labor, and out of the shower, while I listened to him chop onions to the sound of the NewsHour I'd feel calm again.

It's an engraving by Cornelis Bos I saw at an exhibition of drawings and prints at the Met a few years ago, I say. He made it after a painting by Michelangelo. It inspired the earliest version of the poem. It's an image of the myth of the rape of Leda by Zeus disguised as a swan. So, your book is about a rape? he asks. I pause. Possibly. Or a transgression. I pause again, draw my finger to my lips. It's for the reader to decide, I say.

He looks curiously at it. Leda naked, the swan ecstatically curled into her abdomen, fanning his wings. He's not literary. At dinner parties with my faculty, nodding through debates over David Foster Wallace and whether it was fair to release his unfinished novel, if Roth deserved the Nobel, fair enough, with his colleagues from the research institute, I'm treading water, with little to say. Suddenly, though, through my husband's eyes, the cover's suggestion of rapturous, bestial lust makes me uncomfortable enough to want to hide it under the sofa. What does he gather when he reads my poems? He has secrets too. The Russian bride he corresponds with on his computer. He thinks I don't know.

If it's bad, will the academy want to fire me? If they think my work betrays the high standards of our institution? Why are you going there? He shakes his head. There's a touch of gray along his hairline. He's still in his T-shirt and sweatpants. Veins of tension throb in his neck. What does he think?

You can't control what critics will say. You must stand behind the work regardless, he says, impatient with my doubts and concerns. I know he's thinking about the reception of his own research, which he agonizes about, testing and retesting before he publishes a paper. Still, it doesn't make me less anxious. Look at you. You don't see it, do you? he says. I wonder what he means. I reach for my hair. It's pulled up with a clip at the top of my head. I look down at my yoga pants. Touch my chest. What does he see that I can't? What don't I see? You're in your own world, he says.

I've never been reviewed in a major venue, I say, going to the refrigerator for the Parmesan and putting it in a small bowl for the table. This is important to me. How does that make me in my own world? I bump my hip on the edge of the counter and let out a gasp. He gives me that look, joins me in the kitchen, plates our dinner. How childish we are.

Our plates in front of us, across from each other, my husband pours me a glass of wine. To your review, he says, and clinks glasses. And your new book. Thank you, I say. I take a bite. The broccoli is overcooked and the sausage too spicy.

Nevertheless, I'm grateful I have a husband who has made us dinner.

The cover, he says. It doesn't look like rape. It looks more I don't know. Sexual, he says. What are you saying? Is it too much? It inspired the poem. That's not what I'm saying. He takes a bite. It's just a little strange, he says. That's why I like it, I say defensively. It certainly makes a statement, he says, and gives me that look again. A cover *should* make a statement, I say. I bite my lip. He cuts into a piece of sausage. Shakes his head. You sound like your mother. Always obsessing. Never standing behind your instincts. Always second-guessing.

Please let's not talk about my mother. Why is he doing this? You've done your best, he says. Have I? I'm not so sure. It's awful, the care home where she's living. They give it five stars. I didn't go to see her this week. Sometimes it's too hard, I say. And I'm not sure she notices how long between visits. Are you going to take care of her? my husband says. It's around the clock. You couldn't do that. He's right. I had no choice. She could no longer feed or bathe herself, or do her business on her own. My husband is the practical one. He doesn't question. He waits for the right answer and doesn't look back. It's one of his many traits that I admire.

I bring my wineglass to his and clink it again. Cheers, I say, to divert. To cheer us up. What's going on with you? How's your new assistant working out? Another crack of thunder shakes our glasses and plates. Not tonight, he says. There's been a new strain of virus. Some new pattern in the disease his lab's been researching after an outbreak in a rural community in the South. When he comes home, he doesn't like to talk about work. After he unloads his pockets, he turns on the faucet in the kitchen sink, pumps soap into his hands, and scrubs them until he's washed it all away. So what's it about, your long poem? he inquires.

Threats to our civilization . . . the fear of the loss of belief, of loyalty. Of encroaching danger. You know those two swans in Central Park? On the way to school, through the park, I started watching their courting dance. They inspired it. I pause to take a bite. It's not for the poet to know what her poems say to the reader. Will you read it? Of course, he says. I always read your work. When it's finished. Do you? You never tell me. I don't know what you think, I say. That's just the way I am, he responds. But why? I ask. Do I have to have a reason? He puts down his fork. Do you want me to tell you how much I love your poems, how brilliant they are? Is that what you want? I thought we were past that. He shakes his head.

My eyes fill. Why should I expect him to understand? Doesn't he know what I've sacrificed in our marriage? That yearlong fellowship in Rome I had to decline. International conferences, summer residencies I frequented before we were married. What dreams I've deferred. I didn't mind so much when my son was little. I drew strange comfort when I trailed behind my husband and son deep in conversation, on the way to a restaurant or store, as they walked ahead taking long strides. I sometimes lingered just so I could stay behind them, still not quite believing I was part of a family that did not include only my mother. But now it's different.

Your work comes first, he says. The sky cracks and the lights go out. Across from each other in the dark, I want to disappear. Doesn't yours? I say. What does he want from me? The tension has been nesting there, since our son's been gone, and now that we can't use him as a buffer, I fear our pent-up anger the last few years wanting to let loose.

My husband fetches the candles in the cupboard, moves the pitcher of flowers to the end of the table, lights the candles. Takes a sip of expensive wine that should be drunk for a celebration and, after savoring it, looks at me as if attempting to read the unspoken in the candles' shadow.

I'm sorry you feel that way, I muster. It may seem to you like I'm in my own world . . . I stop myself. How can I presume my husband understands? I move the sausage and broccoli around my plate. He's tapped into my constant debates on what I should and should not say in my work, what to reveal, hide. I can't eat. I take a sip of wine.

*The Iliad* and *The Odyssey*, the two greatest poems of ancient Greece, inspired me and fueled my love for books at an early age. Who would I be without poetry? Books saved me. Reading on a bench in one of the changing rooms of the dress shop in Hoboken where my mother worked when she wasn't at home making decoupage boxes she sold at craft fairs. Our living room, her studio. Littered with her wooden boxes of antique postcards, ribbons, glitter, and trinkets she used to create her miniature masterpieces, it smelled of glues and adhesives. There was no money for babysitters. Reading in those changing rooms crammed with undesired dresses hanging on racks, I understood that the characters in novels, extremes of emotion in poems, are more engaging and profound than life itself. How to explain that the imagination flourishes under the poverty and synthetic smell of retail in a secret chamber of a dress shop? How can I expect my husband to understand that I'm a captive? Writing is like a dream. You have to stay inside it, but this I cannot say for fear he'll think me self-serving. I quail with my deviance. My anger roils inside me.

We haven't had sex in months, he says. Maybe a year. Ah, this is what it's all about. Has it been that long? Maybe it isn't so bad, I say. After twenty years. Maybe we're allowed a period of exile. He raises his eyebrows. Is that what this is? he says.

I rise for a glass of water, bump the table. The pitcher with tulips pushed to the edge falls to the floor and breaks. Sex . . . I don't know. I don't want it. I can't. Not now. Not yet.

Now look what you've done, he says, and peers as if he can see inside me, all I try to hide from him. He shakes his head. I pick up the pieces, severed like two sides of a heart. The small head of one of the tulips broke from its stem. I cup the head in my hand, and its soft and tender petals fall loose. I mop up the water from the floor with a paper towel, throw the broken pieces of the pitcher into the trash. The remaining tulips have gone limp. Frigid. I try to bring them back to life by cutting a bit of the stem and putting them into another vase of water, but they remain flaccid.

I return to the table. To the half-eaten pasta on my plate. A beep. My husband looks at his phone, flashing on the table. It's his app, letting us know more money has been spent—I don't want to know—and that our son is still at the bar. My husband shakes his head again, rises. Are we finished, then? I ask. Yes, he says. I'm done. I don't know if he thinks I meant us or our dinner. No more words are spoken. Fantastically, the lights go back on. It's too bright. I blow out the candles. The smell of burning wax lingers. My husband retires to resume his sports.

I tidy the kitchen. Dregs from dinner refuse to go down the drain. I scrub the cracks on the linoleum of the counter. Then the ancient stove, sinking into the wooden boards of the floor. The refrigerator shakes when the motor starts, and startles me. I put down the dish towel. It's not all me. He's been absorbed in his work, in our son. I go to the bedroom, my hands dry from the ammonia in the cleaning products. Ammonia, named for the Ammonians, worshippers of Amun, Egyptian god of sun and air. I get some lotion. Rub it into my hands and around my ring finger and its thin gold band. I want the ruby-and-diamond engagement ring my husband had given to me when he proposed twenty years ago. It cost him his savings. It was stolen from me. I worried the theft was a terrible omen. I want it back.

My husband's sportscast presses through our thin walls. More turbulence. A play has been challenged. Rain batters the windows, moisture slips through the crevices and fractures. I search for the flicker to drown it out. Flip through dramas on the screen, one of lovers in some made-for-TV drama in the throes of passion, and turn it off. If only sleep, but my mind won't stop, all that was said and not said travels through my brain. I turn to the digital clock. Midnight. The door to my son's bedroom shuts, the last remaining light of reconciliation blackened. The room holds our son's fake gold trophies, stuffed animals, books, old baseball mitts. *O love, how did you get here?* creeps in from Plath's "Nick and the Candlestick." Who has given him permission to sleep in our son's room? A fissure and then a sound—grief, heartache, woe, like the cries of a creature who has lost her way—buries itself in my pillow.

Something terrible has happened and I don't know what to do.

## DAY 2

My son hasn't texted me or picked up in more than a week. I try again. Direct to voice mail. Still in bed, my eyes swollen from crying through the night hurt to open. Dishes clank in the porcelain sink. My husband's breakfast completed. I stay in the master bedroom—it's mine too—until the door shuts. Lock clicks, and I know he's left. Off to lift weights. The gym, his refuge. Sweat pouring down his brow, grunts and groans, and a surge of testosterone, like a kind of human Heracles, building his body as if to thwart the inevitable. Then he'll go on a run.

Words from last night sit hard on my chest. Yes, I've been lost in my own world. It's been a hard year. Tension between us over our son. Senior year, all those late nights meeting up with friends, god knows where. Playing beer pong, which I understand he's very good at. Sleeping at Olivia's, and missing practice. All-night skateboarding, running his board down slides in playgrounds. Jumping curbs. The alcohol consumption. Partying. Laziness and preoccupation. It drove my husband crazy. Feared he'd lose his scholarship. He pushed him to run laps, take the stairs in the bleachers to stay in shape. Sprints, hurdles, relays. Interval training. Runs up and down our co-op stairs. His shrill whistle. He was a runner too. Laps around the park. Strength training at the community gym. The place he went to escape his family and his psycho sister, his words, not mine. My husband ran track in middle school. High school champion in track and field. *Discipline is the key to success.* A hoarder of motivational phrases. *Most people never run far enough on their first wind to find out they've got a second* is another favorite. It is attributed all over the internet to William James, which most likely means it's a fake. Taken out of context, it sounds like an ad for Nike, of course the Greek goddess of victory. One of our pleasures, mine and my son's, is making fun of my husband's attempts to engender competitiveness and motivation in our son.

My son's a gifted athlete, but you can't really push him. He's the same with everything. He'd get lost in the details when working on an English paper, annoyed that every paragraph had to link up with the paragraph before it. I'd lean over his shoulder and see that for hours he'd been sketching the vase of flowers on the table or playing a game on his phone. At a track meet he tripped and missed the gun. It's because you were out all night getting trashed, my husband said, loud enough to turn heads. I was humiliated. I couldn't stand next to him. I wandered to the side of the track. Who does that? Humiliate his son in front of his team? Afterward, before we got in the car, I asked my son if he was all right. I don't give a fuck, he said. The ride home he slept in the back seat with his earbuds in. When I tried to tell my husband later that it was humiliating, he wouldn't hear it. The kid made a commitment to his team, he said.

Before a big cross-country tournament, he got our son up at five in the morning. Dawn or after sunset were the best times for a cross-country runner to train without distraction. It was dark and our son was not exactly happy. He crawled out of bed half-asleep, put on his running pants, tied his laces in the dark, groaning. As he ran through the narrow underpass in the park, on the side of the street, a driver sideswiped him. He broke his wrist, fractured his shoulder, and suffered a concussion. I blamed my husband—of course it wasn't his fault, but it had come to represent a new chapter with our son. His expectations, intensity, pushing and judging, pacing the floors at three in the morning waiting for the click in the lock. Unable to get out of his own head. There had been anger in him, and our son had touched it, broken him in a way I had never seen, and I could do nothing about it. Nothing. It was as if there was an irrational animal inside my husband that feared for our son's well-being. One night, when we were sleeping, my husband shot up in bed. It must have been two or three in the morning. He trailed into our son's room, and under the covers our son had built an image of himself with stuffed animals. He was gone. My husband told me years before that once his sister began using, she'd stuff her bed with clothes. My husband was a teenager then, and his mother sent him to bring home his sister because his father was out gambling or drinking. My husband found her in the high school baseball field, shooting up. My son, however, had snuck out of the house, we found out later, to sleep at his girlfriend Olivia's. When he came home at six in the morning, my husband was on the couch waiting for him. I saw him leap up, this fear turned to anger, and he grabbed and shook our son, until I had to pry him away. There were times in those months when, so anxious I couldn't sleep, I slipped into my son's room and slept on the rug on his floor.

While they were training or at a meet, I retreated to the library or a café, tracing the vein of an argument, the scratch of a thought. It was how I coped. Escape into books. Words. Detach. My modus operandi, to get relief from my mother's obsessiveness, her constant need for approval, her half-finished decoupage boxes all over our home, her requests. Her less-than-average suitors—it haunts me, what we do to prevail.

For the first time in our marriage, I fear we will not get through this. I put my phone on the nightstand, lie back in bed, stare motionless at the painted ivory beams on the ceiling. I peer at my phone again, willing it to ring. Nothing. I make a pot of coffee, the sound of the water gurgling against the grinds as it brews. In the cabinet next to the coffee mugs, the hand-painted egg cup we bought together on a trip to Rome. We had suffered several miscarriages and worried about whether I would get pregnant again. The trip, serendipitously, was timed to my injections of Clomid to stimulate more eggs, to increase the likelihood. My husband found the egg cup with its delicate yellow and white flowers along the rim, at the little china shop near the Colosseum. Our good-luck charm, he called it, then patted my abdomen where I'd gotten the shot and kissed me. The miracle drug worked. Weeks later, I discovered I was pregnant with twins. Now it's chipped along one edge.

Odysseus seems to be the ideal man of the Greeks. He's strong, brave, with a sharp mind. He's also capable of strong emotion. His strategies, along with the help of Athena clench victory for Greece and result in the fall of Troy.

In the end, Odysseus is a hero because, war, courage, and sacrifice were considered high virtues during the time in which The Odyssey is set in.

But Odysseus is not without faults. The greatest of which was his conceit.

Like many of the male characters of Greek literature, he too has his egotistical pride.

I'm too distracted. In the stack of papers, a handful I've already graded, culled from CliffsNotes (do they think I don't know?), my proofs, thin in my hand. I flip through the pages. The first sonnet I open to reads without the power and passion I felt when it was conceived. I can't stand the sound of my own words. Out the window passersby on West End Avenue are wearing sweaters and jackets. Walking their hounds. Running to keep up with their toddlers. Maybe the first cool day in October after all that muggy rain. I want to be a part of life. Get out of my head. I grab my raincoat off the hook in the foyer, find my bag and throw in my iPad, my phone, my keys, sunglasses. When I'm like this, there is only one place to go.

The minute I'm out the door, turning the key in the lock, I see my neighbor on the stairs taking out the trash in a shopping bag from Bergdorf's. It's too late to avoid her. I put on my sun-glasses so she can't see my puffy eyes.

Where are you going so early? she says. I don't want to tell her where I'm going, but I don't know what else to say. I'm going to the museum. The Met, I say. Really? So early? she responds. Is there a specific exhibit you want to see? What gallery do you like the best? she says, and on she goes with the questions.

It is where I go to be alone. To think and restore. But I don't say it. My mother brought me to the museum every Christmas when I was a girl; each time we explored one specific gallery. It got so I knew which gallery to go to in a particular mood when I was on my own. Lonely, to the impressionist wing. I'd imag-ine myself in a Bonnard courtyard, or bathing on the grass in a painting by Seurat. When I longed for love, those statues of Rodin's lovers. Yearning for a child, off to view the Renoir or Degas portraits of young girls and Mary Cassatt's *Young Mother Sewing*. The Temple of Dendur was where I went to mourn my babies. Sometimes in my greed, I believe it belongs only to me. My first kiss was in front of the Jackson Pollock painting that takes up an entire wall. I can't go into that gal-lery without thinking about it. Someone, maybe it was me, said one's first love is the key to the heart. But that is another story.

To honor the tradition, I took my son to the museum when he was little; he loved the shining knights, the Egyptian tombs, and the temple. My husband had the gym and the track with him. I had the museum. Beauty, it is dangerous. It consumes. It perpetuates. It leads us to desire. Reveals our darkest emotions. I took my son to the museum when he was against my chest in a Snugli and the top of his head hit my chin; I could simply tilt my head down and kiss him at will. People used to stop me to marvel at his long eyelashes and dark hair with a violet ring around his crown when the light hit it. I brought him when he was interested in touching all the objects, and he was not allowed to touch them, and we learned this lesson. Then I brought him to the Temple of Dendur when he was learning about the Egyptians and was required to write a report for school on mummies. To celebrate my birthday, we'd always end our time at the Temple of Dendur strolling around the walls until eventually he felt free enough to tell me about Olivia, his girlfriend, or the first time he smoked weed. The only way I can get him to tell me about personal stuff is when he doesn't think he wants to talk about it. I've long deemed the museum my second home, but I don't want to tell my neighbor.

Can you sit for a sec? she asks. Her eyes are red. She clings to my arm. I can see the strap from a thin negligee under her silk Japanese robe. On the cold marble stairwell steps, she locks her arm in mine and tears puddle in her eyes. What's wrong? I say. Her body is warm; I feel her tentacles attaching to me like a prickly bur. I don't know how much I can take, she says. The bloke has no time for me. Marriage is not for the fainthearted, I say, and shake my head in conciliation.

My son always liked her Aussie accent. He had a crush on her as a little kid, liking how she fawned over him, asked him questions, flirted with him like she does with everyone. At times I wished I was more like her. Not so tightly wound. Protected. My son adored her twins when they were little, a girl and a boy, two years older than he is. They were so sweet with him, though sometimes her son would get angry if my son beat him in a game and he'd send him home and he would sulk until I could distract him. He should have been a twin, too. He was, he is, but our daughter, his twin, died shortly after birth. His sister's now only a ghost. Once I caught my neighbor's daughter brushing my son's hair while he sat very still.

Over the years, I became close with my neighbor's daughter. She's introverted, awkward, a reader, the brightest in her class at Emily Dickinson, my son's sister school. She was valedictorian when she graduated. She read my poetry, came to my readings, and we discussed literature together, books we both were reading when she was in high school. My neighbor worried that she shut herself in her room too much. She complained her daughter was critical of her. My neighbor wanted her to be more social, worried that she rarely went out. Even as a young girl she kept herself apart when my son came over to play.

I long for those days when my neighbor and I lounged on her Italian velvet couch drinking chardonnay while our boys trashed her apartment, which was three times the size of mine. My son wolfed down his Cheerios so he could dash across the hall to their place, to play Nintendo. Sometimes, especially on Saturday or Sunday, my son was gone for an entire afternoon. I missed his shiny hair, his warm fiery cheeks after hours of intense play and pondered ways to lure the children back to my apartment by baking chocolate chip cookies or Rice Krispies bars, but the minute they finished their baked snack they went back to my neighbor's. Sometimes her daughter lingered, ran her fingers over the spines of my books, and I'd give her something to borrow. My neighbor initially resided in a one-bedroom. Until their upstairs neighbor put their apartment on the market and they bought it, broke down the walls, and created a palatial home inside the dreary walls of our co-op, whose outside hallway is desperately in need of a new coat of paint. If you walk into my neighbor's apartment, is it is like you've entered a house with two floors. Instead of warped wood floors, marble, and the sleek furniture straight from *Architectural Digest*. Contemporary art on the wall bought from many of the stylish galleries in Chelsea. My neighbor has a good eye and great taste. She was an art history major in college. It puzzles me that she doesn't take herself more seriously. The children, when they were little, liked to play in this apartment because there's a playroom and, unsupervised, they had no one to tell them when to turn off the Nintendo. Her husband manages other people's funds.

✦

I like my neighbor's husband, but I don't like how he treats my neighbor. It's as if he's harboring anger that has nothing to do with her. I see this sometimes in people who are unexamined. Of course, all of us are capable of self-delusions, even when we think we know ourselves. He's pale, with hair the color of a Turkish apricot, rosy cheeks, tall and fit. Wears large black-framed glasses; possesses a cutting sense of humor. Extremely bright. Content to eat his crisps or watch telly and read his book, or so I am told, by my neighbor. I am not privy to his internal life. He dislikes the work he does. Complains it's too stressful. Says he plans to retire early. He is an avid reader, and when the kids were little we used to have dinner and talk about books. His favorite authors, not quite my cup of tea, are Pynchon and Joyce. His daughter and I were more aligned in our tastes. My neighbor sometimes grew impatient when her daughter asked me questions about when I started writing, what graduate school was like. She doesn't like to be left out of conversation. Her daughter wears her hair short and side-parted. She bears intense brown eyes that don't miss anything; a surprise tattoo of a peacock running down her arm nearly caused my neighbor to faint. She reminds me of myself when I was young. My neighbor says her daughter has become a stranger to her. I tried to explain that books are her way of trying to make sense of a strange and confusing world that, for a young woman of her age and intellect, would be especially complex. I've grown close to her daughter and was glad she felt she could confide in me. I love how her eyes brighten when she tells me about a book or a paper she's working on. My neighbor doesn't understand. She hasn't had a boyfriend, my neighbor said. Don't you think that's strange, at her age? Not really, I say.

He's a selfish prick, my neighbor continues. Always thinking about himself first. I'm sorry, I say, and shake my head. Can you believe it. He's planned a hunting trip with chaps from work on our anniversary weekend. He didn't remember. I had to buy my own engagement ring, she says. He didn't have time to pick it out. I look at the light catching on the yellow stone the size of a dollop of fresh cream in a cup of coffee. I automatically bring my thumb to my ring finger searching for my ruby engagement ring, but there's only the thin wedding band.

I shouldn't complain. He's not like those cheap kangaroos loose in the paddock I once dated. But I can't help it. He drives me crazy. Do you know what he said to me? That he needs to be serviced. This is what I'm living with, she says. Did he really say it that way? I ask. It's what he meant, she says, and rolls her eyes.

My husband and I call them the odd couple. She's extroverted, and he's mostly unsociable and withdrawn. On occasion we enjoy their company, but she has the habit as soon as we sit down for a meal to bombard us with questions. What did we do on the weekend? What movies have we seen? Where are we going on holiday? I'm stunned into silence. Listening to her chat about where they've been, the people they've seen, I'm reminded that I don't have much of a social life, there's so little time with teaching, writing, my family, but this is not something I'm willing to disclose to my neighbor. My husband likes her husband's cutting sense of humor, and they enjoy talking together about sports. He has affection for my neighbor too, but behind her back calls her a chatterbox and wonders how her husband puts up with it. I remind him that it is impossible to know what goes on between couples behind closed doors. Since our children left for college, we don't have as much in common, and see them less.

I have to go, I say. I'm sorry you're so upset. Do you think it's just a bad period? You know. A lapse. I don't know, she says. It feels different. She squeezes my hand and thanks me for listening. You're the only person I can trust. I recoil. I do not want to be that person. Even in her anxious state, my neighbor's hair falls to her shoulders in soft coiffed waves saturated with sun-lit highlights. Her nails are painted black, too dark for this hour of the morning. My head aches. I smell the scent of her musky cologne. It makes my stomach lurch. I don't want to tell her that something has happened that I can't undo. That she's not alone. I pick up my bag from the step. The weight is so heavy with one or two books I always carry with me, my notebook and iPad, forever concerned that I might want to make notes on something I'm working on, or have something to read on the bus, I can barely get it over my shoulder. And then I hear him, her husband, through her half-open door. Is the missus going to make breakfast? he calls. The missus? She has a name.

I shake my head and cringe. He hasn't yet discovered that the patriarchy has failed. That money isn't enough to please his wife. That he can't lock himself off with his books and sports. That relationships are malleable and need attention.

## SALON ON BROADWAY AND
## EIGHTY-SIXTH STREET

I step out of the elevator and through the foyer. I nod hello to Arturo the doorman, who stands outside our building with his hands behind his back, stalwart and formidable, and slip quickly past before he can engage me in conversation. Not because I don't like Arturo, but because today I've lost my ability to make small talk. I pass by the salon on Broadway on the way to the bus and linger at the window. Creases from my pillow are pressed into my cheeks. My hair is a tangled and knotted bird's nest. I can't remember the last time I washed or brushed it. There was a time when certain men found me beautiful. Lament washes through me. I can't go to the museum like this. A flash of my neighbor and her long coiffed locks. I too need more protection from my despair. I open the door to the salon, and the bell, as if to offer assurance, rings in welcome. Inside the salon I take off my sunglasses. My swollen eyes barely open; the light hurts. I put them back on.

Once a week my mother took me with her to the beauty shop, her weekly splurge. Her hair in big curlers, we sat side by side under the hair dryer with its motorcycle-helmet-like cover over our heads. My ears burned from the heat. My mother's mantra: *You don't get to look beautiful without pain.* She slipped off her heels, and her nude stockings revealed her crowded, overlapping toes. Her makeup bag overflowed with mascara wands, lipsticks, eye pencils, and powders.

On a bench I wait until it is my turn. Mirrors everywhere, so you can't help but look. I strain my neck to find a scribble of wrinkles. I cup my hand over my neck in horror. Is one of my eyelids sagging?

Next to my chair, a stylist is blow-drying the locks of a wig on a mannequin head. A woman twice my age at the sink, getting her roots dyed. It's only the beginning.

My turn. I move into the seat and the stylist slips her long painted fingernails, extensions, as if there is no aspect of the female form left to nature, through my hair. Beautiful, she says, and shakes her head, pumping me up to attention in the chair like I'm at the dentist's office. Why don't you take better care of it? Where's style? You're not a teenager, she scolds. No, I am not. Embarrassed, I sink into the chair while she puts her foot on the pedal and pumps me up farther. Look at those cheekbones, she says. You need a little makeup. Right under here. You know. Blush. It will make them pop. Why so sad. You'll get frown lines. You have a beautiful smile.

She performs a blow-dry called In and Out, as if she's the maestro of an orchestra, in miraculous precision wielding the round brush and hairdryer to create a blow-away look like an ad in a fashion magazine. I barely recognize myself. Looking at my coiffed hair, my impulse is to want to mess it up, but I refrain so as not to insult the stylist, her own hair ribboning in a symphony of different shades of blond. Disguises are the key to my sanity, I tell myself, but I'm not sure I can carry this off.

## M86 BUS

Assaulted by passersby licking ice-cream cones, panhandlers, shoppers balancing their Zabar's or Fairway grocery bags, one in each hand, on Broadway, I run to catch the bus. A wave of shame washes over me. I forgot to tip her. What's wrong with me? I almost trip over my own feet, go back in the salon, and press a twenty-dollar bill in her hand. It's all I've got, and I'm too embarrassed to ask for change. The crosstown buses are lined up, two deep, waiting for their scheduled departures. The drivers drinking coffee from a donut cart. One interrupts his conversation and gives me a friendly, appraising look. "Hello there, Julia Roberts." I flush. It's my hair. I smile at his gallantry. Trying to make a middle-aged woman feel good.

A new system on the crosstown bus. You take your Metro-Card and insert it in a vendor machine at the bus stop, and the machine gives you a slip of paper that has the time and date and the fare, which once again I've forgotten to do. A wave of heat washes over me. I rush toward the front of the bus and attempt to get off and almost trip over a teenager's long legs crowding the aisle. The driver motions for me to sit down and lets it slide. His kindness makes me want to cry.

I slip into a seat near the window, anxiety abating, and look at my reflection. Who is this woman with shiny dark locks flowing below her breasts? I run my fingers through my hair in an attempt to mess it up, to add just a little kink, but no matter what I do, the blow-dry holds its shape. It's as if I've been transformed into Aphrodite. And suddenly I'm assaulted by an image of the Visiting Poet at our school, when I've pleaded with myself to forget him. His solicitous intrusions. The smell of alcohol on his breath. I blink and shake my head, forcing the image away. I hear the chorus in my head. *Forget*, the chorus says, *you're not alone*, and I am briefly comforted.

And then suddenly I remember riding through the park on the bus when I first moved to New York, Sunday mornings, eager to escape my roommate and the sounds of wake-up sex through our thin walls. The museum was my church. That seedy SRO with its damp and germ-infested brown carpet; I never took off my socks. The mini fridge that hummed all night. The Ziegfeld Follies ladies with blue or purple hair who sat in the lobby all day, as if waiting for an audition from the underworld.

I'd met my roommate in grad school. She was more adventurous. She'd sleuth out the parties and drag me along. We'd inevitably run into Ruth Marvin and Mark Shepard, who never remembered our names. Both had MFAs from Columbia and already had their first books taken. Their epic fights, as if timed, sucked all the air out of the room, and later in the night they'd be on top of each other making out. I met Jules Sacks at one of those parties. Even with his pockmarked face, he was weirdly attractive. A scholar of German translating Ingeborg Bachmann. We slept together a few times and then it trailed off. My roommate and I scavenged the basement vintage store on the corner of Columbus Avenue and Eightieth Street searching for faux fur jackets and sexy party dresses. She'd do this little shimmy in the mirror. On Saturdays we went to see the latest foreign film at Film Forum and rode the subway to the East Village for cheap chicken tikka and parottas in Little India near St. Marks Place. Afterward we'd venture to St. Mark's Bookshop and browse lit quarterlies. The first time I had a poem published in *The Paris Review* we celebrated at Fanelli's on Prince Street clinking glasses of prosecco. Her manuscript was a finalist for the National Poetry Series, it didn't win and she wouldn't leave her bed all weekend. Yes, we were jealous of each other, when one of us got a poem accepted or wrote something so stunning we wished we'd written it, but we were also attached to each other and close. And we laughed together, sometimes about how pathetic we were, two lonely poets trying to sort out a life in the big city. I suppose I was jealous of her less inhibited nature and felt lonely when she didn't come home some nights. And I think she was jealous of me too. She always said I had a focus she lacked. Of course, she had more frequent boyfriends than I did and I was envious of how easily she could open herself to men. She mooned over a Puerto Rican poet who performed at the Nuyorican Poets Cafe. Then it was a New Formalist, but as far as I could tell, he was a young Republican who wrote an erotic villanelle that we figured out, after he dumped her, was about me. I got the job at Academy Preparatory first. Even though I had a master's degree, I hadn't yet published a book and so I wasn't able to get a university teaching job, only adjunct positions that didn't pay well. She was temping the first year, and then when a spot opened on our faculty, I put her forward and she joined us. We were timid at first in faculty meetings, dressed in our vintage dresses and sweaters and knee-high boots, eager to please, adapting to the curriculum of an institution founded on the literature of white men, and of the predominantly male faculty in their buttoned-up preppy attire bearing degrees from Princeton and Yale who assumed their words were the only words that held meaning or authority. Outside faculty meetings, they expected us to listen when they spoke; it happened so often it felt like the order of life. We'd meet at the school cafeteria on our breaks or on a bench around the corner from school and share a clove cigarette to escape. The mansplaining, a word not then coined, was intolerable at the academy, but the salary was decent and we needed jobs to support our writing. I miss the camaraderie, dishing Matt Brodeur, disguised frat boy and hockey jock underneath his frayed Brooks Brothers suit eying us in the corridors, his hands covered in chalk dust (the boys claimed he once fell asleep writing a math proof on the chalkboard), or poor Miss Reynolds, straight out of a Dickens novel, worships the academy like a nun to her parish, always at every athletic event, recital, school play. During breaks we'd edit our poems together, hers language obsessed. Mine more meditative. In the evenings, we'd rail about Mehta, former chair of the English Department, who is long past retirement, and his misogyny, the way his eyes looked to the ceiling when either of us spoke. Or poor Fitz and his boring stories about his time in the Peace Corps. We complained we didn't have enough time to write. Still, the poems came late into the night or in the early hours. It was like a muscle linked to a synapse in the brain that fired when emotions, discontents, desire built into a storm cloud and eventually released in cadences of verse. There was a time when I imagined a different, more independent life. Living in hotels in Paris or a studio in Rome. Getting grants and fellowships. Living solely for my art. Was it because I wanted a child so badly, a family I never really had, that I sacrificed my dreams? Or maybe those dreams had already vanished. I don't understand what happened. We were supposed to do this thing together, be poets in New York, but after years of teaching and being broke, she fell in love with a man who owned a string of luxury hotels she met sitting at the bar at the Royalton (by then we had decided to up our game, splitting a glass of wine on our less-than-modest salaries) and eventually moved with him to Los Angeles and had babies. We're still in touch, but we only see each other maybe once or twice a year. On occasion, we still trade poems and help each other edit them, but it's less frequent. Sometimes I wonder why I never pursued getting a professorship at a university once my first book was published. By then I was married, and we had settled in New York City and there were few appointments available in such a competitive teaching market. At least that is what I told myself. But now I think it's because change frightens me. It always has. And I love teaching the boys at the academy, even when they disappoint me or get on my nerves. My imagined future; on days like today it cries hot in my ear.

Fifth Avenue already? I quickly gather my things and nearly twist my ankle in the rush to get off the bus. And there it is, the grandeur of the museum with its slabs of ivory marble and large, elegant windows. That racy feeling of excitement, of discovering something new, overwhelms.

## MUSEUM

In line, I wait to get a new membership card. The young man who takes my information has a lovely smile, thick tortoiseshell-framed glasses, and short dark brown hair with locks that fall to the middle of his brow. His face bears a resemblance to a portrait I've seen in the museum, but I can't quite remember it. My guess is that he is committed to art because people who work at the museum—the man who signs up new members, the museum guards who stand like stoic pillars before each gallery—must be afflicted with the need to behold. One must be a certain type of being to subscribe to passing one's days in the solitude and service of art.

May I help you find something? he asks after he's finished with my details. Do you have a favorite gallery? I ask, and color. He probably hates that question. What did you come to see? What do you like? He jumps and fidgets when he speaks. I don't know. I should know. You're right. The gods. I'll go to the Greek and Roman rooms, I say. Or perhaps the Temple of Dendur, he says, brightening. How does he know that I worship in the temple?

It's the place I used to take my son, I say. But today. I don't know. I want tragedy. I can't wash away the disdain on my husband's face. I must live with it as my punishment. The gods will understand. Then you're right. Off you go. The Greek and Roman rooms, he says. Why not start with the Greeks? There's this incredible marble statue of Heracles. I'll look for it, I say. Thank you. I wind the scarf around my neck to hide my creases.

Anything else I can help with? he says, and I jolt, aware our transaction has ended and people are waiting behind me. Is he flirting with me? I wonder, before remembering I'm too old to be flirted with. And he's barely older than my son. Yet his deep, wide brown eyes like the light reflected in a dark pond carry me far.

Marble statue of Herakles seated on a rock
(1st or 2nd century A.D., Roman)

I enter the gallery and go right to it. Oh my god. Heracles. He's right. That muscular chest. The curve in his waist. Years ago, before I was married, I went to the Prado on a trip with my roommate. We stayed in a hostel and explored the museums. Zurbarán's Heracles cycle. That one painting where he swoops down, arms outstretched, each hand on a grip bolted to the boulders separating the Mediterranean and the Atlantic, one of his twelve labors after he murdered his wife and children. What labors must I endure for what I've done? Why do I blame myself? But I do.

He looks so vulnerable. I want to hug him. Speak to him. Those feet barely visible on the rock floor suggest the ghost we can't see. I mourn the rest of him. Even his cock is cut off. His torso so beautifully incomplete, the shoulders slightly caved by an eternal longing for what he can't have. Is this what the boy-man at the membership table sees? I take a photo on my iPad. I have a cornucopia of photos of the gods and goddesses, and as of late they've taken on new meaning. I sometimes scroll through them admiring their power, their cold beauty. A guard taps me on the shoulder, tells me to step back. I'm too close. Yes, I'm too close. This statue so vulnerably realized. Or is it that he represents what I've deprived my husband of? My husband has a voracious appetite for sex. It is sadly a congress of which I am no longer a member. I have lost all desire. The libido isn't the life force, it's a fragile, fickle drive. What is it about the curved chest that moves me so? Without desire it is impossible to make love. My husband does not understand that my yearning is without limits. Nor that I am not a vessel. That though I long to reconnect, I don't yet know how, or if I can anymore.

A colleague told me recently that he is divorcing his wife. When I asked him why he said that he was constantly telling his wife he was insecure but what he meant was, Why can't you touch my dick? I burst into laughter and then recognized that he was serious. I'm sorry, I said. So, you're getting divorced because you're not having sex? Yes, he said. We expect too much of marriage, I remarked. Or it expects too much of us, he said.

Marble statue group of the Three Graces
(2nd century A.D., Roman)

Three headless women beckon from the hard bench where I
sit. Look at them, what blissful friendship, one leg kicked up
flirtatiously while the others bear the weight. I wonder if these
lovely beings were to service the gods. The gods are entitled to
any mortal they claim, even if they have to turn themselves into
bulls or swans to mate. The Three Graces are handmaidens
of Aphrodite. Cronus castrated Uranus and threw his genitals
into the sea, and lo and behold, lovely Aphrodite emerged from
the sea foam. In every story, she is beautiful and sought-after.
Her beauty concerned the gods, who feared that those in desire of her would come to war. Clever Zeus married her off
to Hephaestus—the god of fire, who was born lame and grotesque—to protect her from rivals. What did Zeus think?
That he could stop her. Beautiful Aphrodite, she did what she

pleased. Surely, she did not worry about pleasing her husband, or hate herself for her acts of infidelity. Those gods and goddesses, they have no shame.

The Swiss-British philosopher Alain de Botton postulates that we marry the wrong person. He believes we must abandon the Western notion of marriage, perpetuated for more than 250 years, that there is someone out there who can fulfill all our needs and desires. He claims marriages survive the romance period when the less desirable traits and insecurities are still submerged, awash as we are in the attraction of two opposite forces coming into contact. Before we marry, we rarely have the time to fully know each other. We're still in a state of bliss, when we believe we have found that perfect other that will counterbalance the things in ourselves we dislike. It isn't until much later that our true selves emerge.

A gang of teenagers rushes in. The kids can't keep quiet. Can't keep their hands off one another. Can't stop talking, pushing, and shoving in their attempt to be heard and noticed. Their energy makes me think of my students. I can't quite make out if one is a boy or a girl. She has short-cropped hair, boy jeans, and a tight T-shirt, and from the neck down her torso is square and boyish and yet her face with two pierced earrings in the shape of buttons stamped into her ears is that of a girl's. She reminds me of my neighbor's daughter. We email and text since she started college; she's asked me for advice about courses to take, professors I might know about, an editorship at the university literary magazine. If I'd read a paper of hers. Her freshman year, she wrote a feminist paper decrying the representations of desire and self-destruction in women through the texts of Flaubert's *Madame Bovary*, *The Age of Innocence* by Edith Wharton, and Kate Chopin's *The Awakening*. The paper was so brilliant that her professor accused her of plagiarism, unable to fathom that a freshman could have written it. Their fight went viral. She called me weeping on the phone, traumatized and humiliated that people would think the accusations were true. She was exonerated after the university put her paper through plagiarism software, but it had left her vulnerable and hurt. I told her that she needed to turn her hurt into anger. Anger is good, I said. To succeed as a writer, she'd have to push through the cronyism. I liked being able to support her; I wished when I was younger that I'd had a mentor. She made me wonder what my own daughter would have been like, what kind of relationship she and my son would have had. I was sad he didn't have a sibling. I asked him a few times what he thought about losing his sister. He said it was hard to know, but that sometimes he feels her shadow with him, and it touched me that he said it.

A broad, large-boned girl among the group surrounding the Three Graces has hair dyed blue on one side and pink on the other. And an Asian boy, small, has delicate features, hands, and body. I wonder whether the sexual fluidity in this new generation is a result of the evolution of the constraints of marriage, and the ultimate incompatibility of the sexes. Or perhaps more simply that now there is freedom to be oneself. A woman, their teacher, comes into the gallery to attempt to harness them.

My phone vibrates. A text is coming through. Maybe my son. I take my phone from my pocket. It's my neighbor. *I can't take it*, she texts. *He's been in the theatre all afternoon watching soccer.*

The "theatre" is in their apartment. It houses four recliners for the family and a television the size of a movie screen. I text back and tell her to go to yoga or take a walk. She texts back, *Shopping.* That's what she does when her husband ignores her. Why she purchases expensive bags from Prada and Louis Vuitton. Retail therapy, she calls it. The way in which the privileged delude themselves into happiness! How can they keep track of it all, their luxury items? When I've indulged, once on an expensive designer clutch purse, I've noticed how quickly these objects lose their appeal.

*It's like living with a corpse*, she texts me. *Ta.* Even though my neighbor is sometimes a nuisance, she makes me feel less lonely. And she makes me laugh. I need her to judge against my own motivations, jealousies, peculiarities; otherwise I am ambushed in my own head. I don't know when my need to quarrel with her in my mind about her behavior, her flouncy clothes, her selfishness, her inability to see how others view her, her lack of ambition, her inability to recognize her daughter for who she is became almost an obsession. Sometimes I can't help but wish I was like her, unburdened of striving. Of wanting a meaningful life.

Marble sarcophagus lid with reclining couple
(ca. A.D. 220, Roman)

And there it is. A sarcophagus, which means "flesh-eating" in Latin. Those Romans. The care with which they bed the deceased is admirable. The description reads: "The couple are shown as semidivine personifications of water and earth . . . The bare-chested man holds a long reed, and a lizard-like creature crouches beside him. The woman holds a garland and two sheaves of wheat, attributes of Tellus, goddess of the earth. At her feet is a furry-tailed mammal with a small Eros on its back." Hoping Eros will reunite the lovers in heaven? My mother's wish. She's ready to die. She wants to go up there, she says, and points to the heavens when I visit her. She thinks she'll be miraculously united with my father. We don't even know if he's dead. Lately, I'm wondering if he ever existed. My poor mother has dementia. Another word I cannot abide. Latin for "out of one's mind." A hideous word. It does not adequately describe the state in which a person forgets how to boil water for tea or gets lost going to the corner grocery store but can remember her favorite color of nail polish, Raven Red, and her daughter's seventh-grade performance as Jo in *Little Women*.

The man's head is carved so that we can see his expression, stern and dominant, but the woman's head is featureless. Did no one think that carving her likeness was warranted? He looks at her, his arm around her shoulder and the woman's head is tilted up toward his face. Was that what started it: that he looked, when I had forgotten what it was like to be desired? How stupid and careless. Once the limbic system is triggered, all judgment disappears.

*Meet for a cuppa?* she texts, a few minutes later. My husband ignores me, she confessed on the stairwell. I was so used to it that I didn't recognize how alone I'd become. How can I make love to him when he can't see me? Of course, I'm going to stiffen when he starts wanting to touch me. Wouldn't you? He'll come in the bedroom and press up against me. Does he care that I don't get off? Does he even know I'm angry, that I don't want him? Maybe if he would only utter a few words.

I flinched in the tumult of so much information. It sounds awful. But I'm not sure I know what she should do. Can't she find something else to keep her occupied? You need more distraction. Maybe start those design classes you've been talking about, I said. You're talented. You need to take yourself more seriously. Not everyone has your confidence, she said. We've had these talks before, and each time they go nowhere. I need to stop. She's like the featureless woman on the sarcophagus. Or perhaps her husband is angry at her too. It is impossible to know what two people share. Yes, at times I wish to be more like my neighbor. Less encumbered, less in my own head. More fun. But more it's the inner, imaginative life I count on. *The death of the imagination.* At heart, I'm a loner. I'm contrary and difficult. I can't stop the flow of thoughts. The constant questions. The self-berating. The need to push further in my work. To take more risks. Or maybe she's always reminded me of my mother, kind and warm, though constantly needing to be fed, and for some reason I've never been able to identify, without inner resources. Maybe that's why her daughter's critical of her. I text back and say coffee today won't work. I'm not in the mood for senseless distraction. There are more pressing questions that need answers.

I spot the boy-man at the membership table. I begin to sweat and feel dizzy. A panic attack is coming on. This happens now for no rhyme or reason, tittering just at the edge of consciousness. He wanders into the gallery and as he passes me, he stops. We say hello and then I watch him circle back to Heracles. To want more is to test the gods. To want less is to decompose. I take some long breaths to calm down. Sit on a bench. Search my bag for my bottle of water. Then I continue my exploration, avoiding the glass cases so as to not see my reflection. The blow-dry makes me feel as if I have no self, as if I have morphed into a being I don't understand. I pitch my fingers through my hair and toss my locks.

Farther north in the gallery is a statue of an Amazon woman, depicted in Greek art as often battling with Heracles, Theseus, and Achilles. Her hair looks as if it is shaped into a helmet. She bleeds under her right breast from battle or self-mutilation. I'm not sure. I clutch my own breast. My wound.

Marble statue of a wounded Amazon
(1st–2nd century A.D., Roman)

Strong calves and broad shoulders and the strength of a man. Her one cup-shaped breast is soft; the other, in one account, has been self-mutilated so that she, as a warrior, can use a bow and spear. Her features and slight curve, in contrast to her girth, give her a girlish vibe. Despite her wound, she remains steadfast. She almost looks coy in that pose. The Amazons used men for procreation. Otherwise, they lived in their own society and were thought to be equal to men in strength. Heracles's ninth labor was to steal the belt of the queen of the Amazon. Knowing the strength of the Amazon women, he brought a ship full of men. Hippolyte, the queen, eager to be friends, threw a dinner in his honor. Maybe she wanted to bed him. At dinner she promised him the belt. But Hera disguised herself as an Amazon and told the other Amazons that Heracles meant to capture Hippolyte. The Amazon women armed themselves and stampeded the ship. Heracles killed Hippolyte and took her belt. Did he feel remorse? Did he *really* believe the labors would free him from his guilt? I want to ask him, but I refrain. *I didn't mean for it to happen. Do you ever mean to care for another? Don't scold yourself*, the chorus says. *You're not perfect. No one is. You're a mortal. Why are you afraid of your desires?* Yes, the chorus is right. I have an appetite. It's unquenchable. Everything I do, teaching, writing, reading, looking at art, at these gods who feed on the vulnerability of humans, is to tame it. Maybe the Amazon women were onto something, living without men. What freedom! She cups her head in her hand, like a pose we do in yoga to allow more space in the neck. Or a pose you'd see in a Marilyn Monroe poster. No one is telling the Amazon woman to make more space in her neck. She is taking the weight off her wound. But mine is still bleeding.

I don't know what came over me. I had friends, I had colleagues, but none of them seemed worthy of me, or I worthy
of them. It was selfish. My husband had begun to disapprove
when I went out with my writer pals to book parties or bars.
He thought they were egotists, always talking about their
work or gossiping about other writers, and I couldn't blame
him. Those of us who see the world through books, we're in
our own secret society. I know that he also respected them
on their own terms, as long as they did not take my attention too far away from him and our family. I was hungry for
someone to see me differently. To see the things in me my
husband disliked. I couldn't control it. It may seem naïve,
but I was out of the game. I didn't know what was happening or what I wanted. Maybe I was never in the game, but
suddenly I wanted to be. The Visiting Poet awakened in me
the thought that I missed having the kind of relationships
I'd had in grad school, with other poets, with my old roommate. It wasn't my husband's fault. I admire who he is. It's
just that I felt so alone. Perhaps we are meant to feel alone,
perhaps feeling alone and safe inside oneself is the greatest
achievement, but I didn't know it then. The Visiting Poet
stirred in me too, that I hadn't taken enough risks. Been
dangerous enough, that I had withheld myself too much out
of fear, that I hadn't explored my sexuality in a way that perhaps you could only do by being dangerous. I look at the
gods and goddesses in the hall. Which one cast the spell and
took away my reason?

## THE VISITING POET

We gossiped about him in the teachers' lounge. Some of us had read his poems. Others had seen photos. We were desperate for a new member to share our too-familiar halls. The first time I laid eyes on him, he was wrapped in an overcoat with a lilac scarf draped from his neck bringing out the shape-shifting shades of the sea in his eyes. Does he dress like an aristocrat, even in Wittenberg, Ohio? Dark blue cotton shirt with a pocket over his breast where he carries his pen. Dark jeans. Tweed jacket. It was last September, at the beginning of the school year. Our institution each year hosted a visiting poet, funded by a former student donor, who had abandoned poetry for law. He sauntered into my classroom, where I was grading student essays, as if he owned it. Broad frame; wide nose; large, penetrating eyes. Refined, yes, but there was also a feral quality about him that he had learned to cover over with education. At last we meet, he said. The academy's poet-in-residence. I welcomed him. Yes, I was concerned that he'd overshadow my presence as the only poet at the academy, but I was glad to have a co-conspirator among the self-important academics in my department who did not consider contemporary poetry literature.

He towered over me. I pulled my shoulders back. I needed to stand up to shake his overwhelming hand twice the size of mine. You're one of the reasons I accepted the invitation for the year, he said. I've read your work. My cheeks grew hot. I perched on the window ledge and crossed my ankles. His face was honed. Something magisterial about it, in contrast to his pale skin, pallid, almost funereal, and large, brutish hands, on his left a silver wedding band embedded into his finger, almost strangling it, as if it had grown too small over the years.

Welcome to the academy, I said. Of course, I had read his work. I was jealous of it. Of his ease with language and daring posturing. Of his many accolades. A few days later he scooted next to me on the olive leather couch in the teachers' lounge, freshly brewed coffee in a paper cup that looked like a child's cup in his big hand. Close enough to smell his well-worn blazer, an odd mix of cologne and damp wood. There were hairs embedded in the wool. It's weak, I said. But you get used to it.

He held a copy of my first book, *The Erotics*, in his hand. Said it was impressive. Sparrow Press First Book Prize. Mentioned what he called the fancy blurbs and asked me if I would sign it.

It was early in the morning, and I was not prepared to be flattered with attention. My eyes traveled to the framed map of the world above the coffee cart; I had studied it so many times over the years, it had been burned into my consciousness. So much to see, to digest, to know. It's not like it was the Yale Prize, I said modestly. He seemed solicitous. But maybe I was misjudging. My body began to twitch inside. I can't remember what was said; the many encounters revolve in my mind like a carousel. Not enough time has passed to make sense of it. I sensed he was attracted to me. I could feel invisible tentacles reaching out as if he were touching me. He was ostentatious, presumptuous, compelling with a cunning intelligence radiating in his eyes. The Adam's apple on his thick neck terrified me. His eyes were seductive and haunting. I feared they would engulf me the longer I looked. I told him I would sign the book later. I was late. I stood up and gathered my things to get to class. As I walked out of the teachers' lounge, he followed me.

Will you lunch with me, he said, later? Since when did teachers use *lunch* as a verb? It was oddly compelling. Of course, I said. He was new to our institution. I must be cordial. I remember my heels almost slipped on the newly waxed floors.

We dined on slices of cold pizza tasting of cardboard at the school cafeteria sitting at a table in one of the last rows, and remained there talking and sipping burned coffee once the cafeteria had cleared. I kept noticing little things. The hair on his arms when he rolled up his sleeves to eat. The shape of his thick fingers, hard nails, hands that seemed too large in proportion when he hugged the coffee mug. He dug into his satchel and pulled out my book again, a paperback worn and yellow at the edges. A first book is virginal in its purity. All those years that went into its creation, but in his gluttonous hands it seemed small and strangely not my own. Heat rose to my face as he flipped through it. He recalled the title of one of my poems, "The Erotics of Time," and quoted a line from it. *Who are we but ghosts of many selves, / unfinishable roots of our desire.* My face warmed. You're blushing, he said, and I touched my cheek. This is how it started. With words. Words are powerful. We must use them carefully. I felt uneasy about how I looked. My hair was tied up in a bun at the back of my head. I plucked out a few wisps around my face. The shift I was wearing seemed too tight and made me uncomfortable. I unbuttoned the top button. My bones froze.

I admire your work too, I said. I felt stupid. Speechless. I looked up at the clock, that big white circle of time, and then gratefully the bell sounded, and we both rose and carried our trays to the dish room.

Before I left that day, I walked past his classroom and peered through the door's rectangular latticed window. It was four thirty. The boys had long cleared out. He sat beneath a small desk lamp. Alone in the classroom, he took up less space. His reading glasses were balanced on his nose, his head moved this way and that following the page in the book he was reading, his dark hair in the light glossy like black stones on the beach, the lilac scarf draped around his neck. He looked up from his book and stared out into the empty classroom, deep in thought. Out the window the light was dwindling, and a shiver of it reflected on his silver wedding band. In that moment, I saw that it was my book of poetry he was reading. I quickly ducked and skulked away. That impression of him with my book, the poems written before I was married, full of erotic longing, met with heat and prickly irritation. The image became sealed in my memory, and even now, a year later, I still recall it, in all its vanity, nakedness, and excitement.

A week later, he overtook my classroom, leading with his magnanimous spirit. His arms stretched out to embrace me. After we briefly hugged, he put his two hands on top of the desk like a large dog with its tongue out, begging for attention, and hovered over me. I put my pen down. He took my hand. I was trembling. Look, he said. Your pen is leaking. His hand, big and rough with hairy knuckles; mine felt childlike and vulnerable in his palm. It always does that, I said, slowly taking my hand away. I'm addicted to these pens, I hardly notice it anymore, I said, rubbing the ink away from the smudge on my middle finger with my thumb. I was suddenly conscious again of my stiffly ironed dress and my hair in a tight bun on the top of my head. For a moment, I thought of taking out the barrette. I felt goose bumps form on my bare legs.

I've been thinking, he said. Your work deserves more attention. I picked up your last book in the school library, the other day. *Divinity.* A book of poems that has nothing to do with religion. Have you tried for a bigger publisher? I could talk to mine. When you have a new manuscript. I was taken aback. I told him it was kind of him but that I was attached to my press. I didn't trust him. I don't know why. I felt as if I needed to assert my authority. I lowered my head to my desk and my stack of papers still in need of my attention. I couldn't really take in his presence. It was too much. He leaned over. I understand, he said. Loyalty.

Our eyes met. He was smiling at me. I was uneasy again. I nodded. I had lost my confidence. But he kept looking so that I almost felt as if I stood naked in front of him. I crossed my arms over my bosom. You look very pretty today, he said. I admit I was flattered. Are you flirting with me? I said, realizing I had to take some control. Of course, I didn't trust him. Who could trust a poet? In graduate school I had seen what some poets would do to gain ground. But I liked him. I liked his sparkle and dazzle. His arresting presence. And he made me laugh. Oh how I longed to laugh. I had forgotten what a release it is. It was as if I had been living underground, covered with layers of mud, and now I was beginning to shake free and breathe again. He made me feel young. How useless to be a woman in the cloak of middle age, when the soul and consciousness is of a much younger creature knowing soon, in a matter of years, she would step onto the next precipice. I didn't want it to happen. I would do anything to stop the clock, but it was ticking and my body, I don't know, it wasn't my own anymore. It was reacting. My face blushing. My clumsiness.

Maybe, he said, and gave me a half smile that lit up his eyes. He took a tour of my classroom, as if in a gallery. Stopping to look at the posters of Virginia Woolf, Gwendolyn Brooks, Elizabeth Bishop, Sylvia Plath, Lucille Clifton, Emily Dickinson framed on one wall from the year I was finally able to get the funding to host a reading series of women writers. Then to the bust of Keats I had on a pedestal, a gift from a student. Over to the bookshelf. On top was a bowl of heart-shaped stones I collected one summer when we rented a house near the shore. I saw him pick up a white stone, hold it in his palm, finger its crevice and then put it back. It was as if he was taking inventory.

## MUSEUM

I awake to a racket. The pounding vibrates through my walls as if it's coming from next door. More construction. Amazing, this prewar building filled with families, couples, inhabitants who make their meals in their kitchens, do their business in the bathroom, people from all walks of life living in these close quarters. We're like rats hiding in our domains and, on occasion, peeking out and saying a gruff hello in the elevator. My mood is dim. I dress haphazardly for school. No use in dressing up. I don a pair of black pants, a T-shirt and a navy blazer, boots, my new teacher costume. I have given up dresses. Tight shifts. Heels.

I decide to walk through the park on the way to school to revive. My phone buzzes and further interrupts my need to be restored. It's the aide from the care home. She calls to say that my mother has been asking about what happened to her wedding ring. I tell her that she never had a wedding ring, tell her to say to my mother that love transcends a ring and that she has beautiful blue eyes, and that should calm her. I ask if she had a bowel movement. If she drank her Ensure. If she had her pineapple slices for breakfast. My poor mother. Now that she has moved from assisted living into full-time care she can no longer call me.

Her brain has forgotten how to match a number on a phone pad with a memory of a phone number. Now I am the vessel for all her numbers. I ask to put her on. Hi, Mom, I say. How are you? Is that you, she says in a crackly voice, my darling daughter? When are you coming? Then she drops the phone. The aide comes back on. Give her a hug from me, I say before we hang up. After talking with my mother, I'm left in a trance of sadness, guilt, regret. I'll go on the weekend, I tell myself. In her honor, I decide to make a quick detour to the museum. The academy and the museum are only eleven blocks and two avenues from each other. One of the job's special perks. On my walk, I notice the trees have their own way of dying, yearly shedding, falling as variously as generations, some wanting to hold on longer than others, some more quietly, though today it feels as if I'm already wandering in an afterlife. So much decay, so many ghosts. By winter the lawns will be sealed in like a corpse in frost.

Every Christmas, we rode the bus from Hoboken to the museum. It was our ritual. My mother always trying to catch a handsome man's gaze in the museum's corridors. First to the big tree with the golden angels and the manger, then to the cafeteria for a croissant and a hot chocolate with a swirl of whipped cream on top, and then off to explore a new gallery we hadn't seen before. Each room with its hidden treasures to discover. We'd sit in the Astor Chinese Garden Court, a replica of the scholar court in the Master of the Nets Garden in Suzhou, with its rocks, stones, and greenery, and imagine we were dressed in silk frocks drinking tea; view the *Standing Ganesha* in the Asian Wing, the elephant-headed Hindu god who "controls obstacles"; visit the African wing filled with masks and ceremonial figures. In the Egyptian wing, one of my favorites, a miniature coffin, sized as if for a dollhouse, found buried with Queen Neferu. Among the European paintings, the brilliant clarity of the Vermeers *Young Woman with a Water Pitcher* and, a favorite, *Allegory of the Catholic Faith*, the girl's hand at her bosom and her foot on the globe. What inspiration! It's as if they're all there, waiting for me, just when I needed to behold them. Before we left the museum, it was off to the gift shop, and if we could afford it, sometimes she bought each of us a replica. I still have my pair of Vermeer's pearl earrings and my Byzantine lapis gem drops. This morning in my mother's honor I venture to the ancient Greek and Roman jewels.

## CORRIDOR THAT LEADS FROM THE TEMPLE OF DENDUR TO THE GALLERIES OF EGYPTIAN ART

Gold armband with Herakles knot
(3rd–2nd century B.C., Greek)

The gold is inlaid with garnets and emeralds. A Heracles knot was thought to heal wounds and ward against evil! Of course! A common feature on jewelry of the Hellenistic period, I read. It's something my mother would covet. I used to explore my mother's jewelry box, trying on her pearl necklaces, clanging bracelets, and earrings when she was out with one of her dates. I worried about her when she was gone. She produced in men pity and desire, whether it stemmed from her own childhood exile as a daughter of immigrants, or the loss my father left her with, I can't be sure. When I stayed home from school with fever or a cold, she let me sleep in her king-size bed and made me tomato-and-butter sandwiches. Together we feared the Old Maid when boredom forced us to a deck of cards. It was only when I got older that I grew frustrated with my mother's belief that a man would save her from her growing financial difficulties, loneliness—the men she was drawn to did not seem worthy. I hated watching her coat her face with makeup. Spending hours on her toilet. Her hopefulness, and later despair after one of her dates, gave me a stomachache. I couldn't separate her needs and behavior from my own. You will be a different person, I would tell myself in the mirror, looking at a face that seemed to change from ugliness to acceptability depending on my mood every time I looked. The glitter from my mother's decoupage boxes, in my hair, stumbling barefoot over the beads and charms that had fallen to the floor. Her obsessive need to make each box perfect, an obsessive trait I'm afraid I've inherited, her anxiety when we ran out of monthly funds, the shame when she'd put on her cheery voice to get the super in our building to fix what was broken.

My father, I'm told, was a brilliant philosophy professor. Two decades older. My mother was twenty-two and a recently graduated art major at Rutgers when they met. Her parents had died in a car accident. It was the beginning of the woman's movement, the pill, Warhol, *Playboy* magazine, Gloria Steinem, and my mother, a free-love hippie with a touch of Doris Day, her long hair parted in the middle, wearing love beads and peace signs dangling from her neck. She knotted macramé curtains for our living room, strung beads that hung from the corridor separating her room from mine. Forever that sound of the beads moving against one another when I passed through. She met my father at an antiwar demonstration. They married at city hall, and she moved into his apartment in Princeton, their love nest, she called it, when she was three months pregnant. I was conceived out of wedlock. The apartment wall-to-wall books. Papers and pamphlets everywhere. To the sound of the typing of his speeches, essays, and antiwar propaganda, his communist denunciation of the American ruling class, she made her art. Shortly after I was born, there was some sort of scandal related to his communist leanings. He told my mother that he needed to decamp somewhere in Europe, packed a suitcase and said he'd send for us. My mother always held out that he'd come back, but he never did. To admire her optimism was to believe in illusion. She tried to track him by reading articles on microfiche in the library. Eventually she came to believe he was in the witness protection program or in the CIA and that the cause was more important than us, one day all would be revealed, and we'd be reunited.

When after twenty years Odysseus returns to his family, Penelope recalls a dream of geese feasting on her corn in her house and an eagle who kills them. Odysseus explains that he is the eagle who has returned to slaughter the suitors that have ransacked his home. But unlike Penelope, my mother worked in a dress shop in Hoboken; she never got a homecoming, and none of her suitors—one was a pharmacist, another lived in his van, one a guitarist with unpleasant, dirty hair—were sacked. I think of her now with her decoupage crudité all over our dining room table, sometimes working late into the night if she had an art fair coming up. It was the best of times when she wasn't in bed for weeks suffering from migraines. What amounts to a life, decoupage boxes, taking your daughter to the museum, longing, loss, despair, and in the end your days asleep in a wheelchair? I look at the Heracles knot again. The garnets shine with brilliance. And suddenly I see a vision of Heracles wearing the belt buckle, his massive breadth, and then the Visiting Poet's hands; in mine they seem monstrous, groping at my thighs. *You must stop*, the chorus intervenes. Yes, I must move on, I tell myself.

I find a small corridor in the museum and plant myself on a bench. My head is bursting. I need to stop thinking. I look up. I am no longer alone in the corridor. A young woman has also come to seek refuge. On a bench across from me she's planted, tall and big boned, with a long neck like an orchid, short-cropped blond hair and a lovely blue shawl covering one shoulder and naked breast. If I were a painter, I'd want to paint her. I look again, transfixed by her youthful elegance; she's breastfeeding a tiny infant. Our eyes meet, and she smiles. I hope you don't mind, she says. I feel a sudden ache in my abdomen. It's as if seeing the woman nurse elicits hormones. It wasn't easy for me to have a child. The first time I miscarried, shortly after we got married, the grief was like a rope threatening my neck. There were more miscarriages. Every time I saw a pregnant woman walking down the street or sitting on the bus, my longing made me want to scream with rage, or bury myself to absolve my private suffering, or worse wish the same pain of loss upon her. I'm not proud of it, but there it was.

In ancient Greece, mothers had to nurse their babes in a specific part of the house, I say. It was where they did their weaving. Those were their only duties. Can you imagine. Girls were married when they were fourteen, passed by their fathers to their husbands as if they were a piece of property. What is wrong with me, talking to this stranger about whatever pops into my head? Unbelievable, she says, raising the blanket to peek at her daughter's face. It was only when a girl gave birth that she was deemed a woman, I continue.

It's so quiet in this corridor. Through the window the sight of the narrow plane trees, their branches linked. I can't imagine being a mother at fourteen, she says. I can barely handle it now, and I'm in my thirties. We laugh.

She smiles and kisses the top of her baby's fuzzy head. The others are waiting for me, she says, reluctant to leave. She removes the baby from her breast, pats her on her back, and then attempts to strap her into her buggy. And just then recognizes she needs to be changed. An entire day and night pass this way, twenty-four hours of feedings, diapers, a bath, a push of the buggy for a stroll. And then the next day the ritual begins again, unaltered. I miss those early days of motherhood. I couldn't take my eyes off my little boy. I couldn't believe he was mine. It's religious, this practice of taking care of a baby. Those were the days when time ran its own course, when I felt as if I were serving a higher purpose, hours marveling at the tiny, closed eyelids, the perfect little fingers clutching a finger, quelling the night terrors. Straight off maternity leave, I went to teach my class covering the spit up on the shoulder of my jacket with a scarf and after class sprinted home to see my boy. If the subway was delayed, I panicked. Now god knows what my little boy is doing.

The young mother finishes diapering her baby, her face bearing a look of satisfaction and contentment, as if caring for her baby is the best aspect of herself, and then lifts the baby from the bench and places her gently in the buggy. Eighteen years ago. The feel of her inside me, with her other twin—further on in my pregnancy, I felt that when I held my expanding stomach I knew which one was moving, our girl twin or our boy—persists as if it has been planted in my DNA. I remember vividly the small pink-and-white hospital cap on her head, swaddled in the pink hospital blanket when the nurse handed her to us for the last time. She was perfect, not yet cold like the statues, but the same milky white. On some days I can't believe she's dead. That all of it happened. And on other days, the loss seizes me and for moments I'm nearly paralyzed. So many days I've imagined her sitting at our breakfast table squabbling with my son over the last piece of toast, her knee socks falling to her ankles. One baby alive, the other dead. What were the gods telling me? What sin had I committed?

Good luck, I say to the new mother as she pushes the buggy away to find her companions. I look down to my hands, clutching my coat and my bag. Blue veins make raised rivers and tributaries in my skin. I walk back to the Greek and Roman gallery to find the marble girl I've come to know over all these years.

Marble grave stele of a little girl
(ca. 450–440 B.C., Greek)

She clasps her doves—are they love birds?—before she must say goodbye, presses her mouth against one dove's beak in a kiss. The other she must let go. Gentle head bowed in sadness. Her hair is gathered up, but part of it falls past her shoulders in waves.

## GALLERY 171: GREEK AND ROMAN STUDY COLLECTION, FIFTH MILLENNIUM B.C.–A.D. 313

In this room are sixty cases filled with study material from the art of late prehistoric Greece through late Roman art. And as I look at the vases, there it is. Right in front of me. A swan in a shard from a terracotta vase. My breath quickens. I want to stab myself to stop the pain. Tears flood forward.

Terracotta relief from a lamp with Leda and the swan
(Roman)

Here Zeus is disguised as a swan pecking at Leda's neck and raping the living daylights out of her. Why? Because he spotted her beauty from his throne on Mount Olympus and wanted her whether she was married or not. Whether she wanted him. In Ovid's *Metamorphoses* she is characterized only as lying under a swan's wing. In many versions of the story, she is raped by Zeus on the same night she bedded with her husband, King Tyndareus, and hence two eggs were laid, in one the children of Zeus sprang forth, and in the other the children of Leda's husband. In this rendition of the myth, Eros is perched on the swan's back, to what? To suggest that Zeus is helpless against his desire, unable to control himself, that rape is inevitable? In another version of the myth, Zeus turns himself into a swan and is violated before he abducts Leda. In another version, she enjoys the flirtation, but, married, she refuses to betray her husband with another man. Hence, a swan! It is said that the image of Leda and the swan is depicted in art of the sixteenth century because it was more acceptable to view a woman raped by a swan than by a man. A rape or a seduction? The Visiting Poet of course argued for the latter that day at the lake, watching the swans preening when I mentioned Yeats's "Leda and the Swan," and we argued about its intentions.

I take one last look at the swan lost in the moment, as the enveloping Zeus sucks her dry. Did she want it? I shake my head. No. I can't think about it. I walk quickly through the corridors into the busy lobby, straight to the gift shop and jewelry counter, like I used to do with my mother—and lo and behold, there it is. A reproduction of the armband with the Heracles knot. I take out my credit card, happy for the membership discount. I would give it to my mother, but the care home reminds us not to leave any meaningful possessions out of fear that one of the floaters might steal it. And besides, I need it to protect myself. I slip the bracelet on my wrist. Glance at my watch. It's half past eleven.

I rush out the building, and thankfully there's a bus waiting. It's suddenly so bright outside the dark museum corridor, my eyes ache. The bell of the sun rings out its shiny glory. I lift my head to drink it in. The bus. It's titanic with its accordion in the middle; whenever it takes a turn, my stomach flips as if I'm on a ride in an amusement park. An annoying fly, perhaps the last of the summer, buzzes against the window. *Closer than a dream, more alive than a buzzing fly.* A fragment from one of the Visiting Poet's poems comes into my mind. Why? Because it had been a long time since I'd had a friend at the academy. Because I was lonely. I must remind myself that it began in friendship.

## WEEK 3

My husband in his haste to get to the lab has left his computer on rest. It's sitting on our dining room table when I walk in the door from teaching. I can't resist. My husband does not know that I know that his password (as is mine) is our son's name. Both of us so predictable. I look at his history; he's been corresponding with the Russian bride in a chat room. What does my husband say to the Russian bride in these chat rooms? He wants to lick her cunt. Wants her to wrestle him to the ground. Who knows? It is his secret world, and if I have mine, he's entitled to his.

I close the computer. I don't want to imagine any more of what my husband would like from the Russian bride. Is she even real? I whip out the Cuisinart, quickly shred onions, peppers; once they are sautéed, add tomatoes from a can. I add basil and salt and pepper and let it simmer. Tear a head of lettuce into bite-size pieces for salad. It is soft and buttery. While I am grating fresh Parmesan cheese and boiling water, my phone buzzes.

It's my son. My body races with excitement until I discover he's failing one of his classes and has not finished a research paper that is due in the morning. Will you help? he says. I know that I should not help. That I should be the kind of mother who allows her child to fail, but I am not that kind of mother. I know I have pushed my son too hard, wanting him to go to a private college, wanting him to have the things I did not have growing up. And because I have pushed him beyond his comfort zone, I feel complicit.

You made dinner, my husband says when he gets home. He goes into the bedroom to change and reappears in a T-shirt and sweats. Seated at our oak table, that because it once bore wood bugs is riddled with tiny holes but bears a beautiful grain of honey, my husband meticulously twirls the whole-wheat pasta on his fork using his spoon in a superior wielding of cutlery. I think of something I might say to break the silence, to breach the weight hanging over us, but as I continue to watch my husband twirl his pasta, I know there are no words. I try not to slurp the noodles into my mouth. All okay at work? I eventually muster.

He nods. He doesn't like to talk about his work. Nor does he like to listen to me talk about mine. He does not want to know whether Ethan turned in his assignment or whether James is getting into Yale or whether Marco will get suspended for smoking weed in the boys' bathroom. At the end of the day he's tired. If I mention a concern for Annie, one of the art teachers, and the way in which her partner is depleting their retirement money with failed businesses, he says, Why are you telling me this? Tell her, my husband says to me. It isn't our problem.

Any new developments? I ask. He shakes his head no and takes a sip of wine. His great anger, like Poseidon's, resides in his clenched jaw, in his quick-to-react outbursts. I've learned how to move around them. It is the raging sea rising inside him, as another sea of longed-for tranquility resides in me.

The clock strikes in the hallway. He has a collection. He says it's the hands he likes, Roman numerals are his favorite, or the sense of being able to control all things, the ticking away of minutes, hours. He has a clock he saved from boyhood. It stands on two feet like an owl with a push button on top to press after the alarm rings. A drawer of antique watches. While I shuffled through a gallery, at the Musée d'Orsay on a trip to Paris, he sat on a bench fixated on the big clock and the turn of its fingers. The grandfather clock he inherited from a maiden aunt strikes in the hall at the top of every hour. He listens for it, puts his plate in the sink, and begins the dishes. There is no question that I love him. Perhaps I love him too much. Like a good soldier I submit to his authority. I want him to submit to mine. But I also know that a certain man, the kind of man my husband is, may feel that a woman's authority means the erasure of the man's. We are both willful. And I do desire him. These days we are estranged, I long for him to surprise me in the middle of the night. To press his longing against me. Words are inadequate when love has been interrupted. My chest hurts. I wonder if he's already decided what he wants to do, if he's just biding time.

After dinner, I work at the kitchen table helping my son with his paper via email. My husband occasionally looks over my shoulder. Grading, I say. I fear if my husband knows I am helping my son he'll either worry that he's failing or explode. I tell myself that it's okay. The Greek aristocrats were helped by tutors. You give them too much of yourself, he says, shaking his head. What does he mean? That after dinner I should sit with him while he watches the news? That I should cuddle with him and lay my head upon his shoulder. That was another century ago.

When our kitchen is spotless, my husband retires to our son's bedroom. Sounds of sport and the little bleeps on his phone from texts coming in—his associates text him from the lab late into the night, or maybe he's texting with another woman—permeate the walls until I see the light underneath his door go out.

Two in the morning, my computer, papers, books on the side of the bed where my husband once slept, I wait for my son's final draft to show up in my email. He needs to turn the paper in by 9:00 a.m. Trying not to fall asleep, I scroll to my students' evaluations stored on my computer. I have avoided looking, I don't want to hear praise; it makes me feel as if I have failed. *I think our teacher is slightly insane. But that's cool because it makes the class fun and open.* Who has written this? I wonder. Tyler, Jerome, Mohammed? My eyes are heavy. I'm half inside a dream. Heracles towers over me, as large as his stone-colored physique in the museum. His tears cause rivers to flood. I want to comfort him, apologize—*I'm sorry, I'm very sorry*—but I can't reach him. Each time I get close, the waters send him farther away from me. I awake in a sweat to a beep coming from my computer. I turn to the clock. Five in the morning. For a minute, I forget what I'm waiting for. It's as if I'm programmed to wait as long as it takes. For what? For some clue? Some way to undo it? And then I remember. It's my son. I'm proud of him for staying up all night to finish his paper. I read it and note that with my help, it's strikingly coherent.

### WEEK 4
### MUSEUM FIELD TRIP

We're reading *The Odyssey* in fifth-form English, so off we go to take the Homer tour at the museum. Today's guide is Ms. White. Short, round, with glasses dangling from her neck, rosy cheeks, cloud of curly white hair, a cotton ball on her head. The boys flock around her in their identical school uniforms of khaki pants, white shirts, and navy jackets, wearing name tags above the school emblem, an *A* for *academy*. An *A* for excellence. Our school motto.

Marble statue of a youthful Hercules
(A.D. 69–96, Roman)

What's draped over Heracles's arm? prods the guide, in a Queens accent. She searches the boys' name tags and picks Jerome. Jerome is hesitant, afraid of being wrong. In class, he gnaws at his fingernails. He's doing it now. I look at him and make a gesture for him to stop, then realize what I'm doing. I'm not his mother. It looks like a claw? Jerome answers. That's right. A lion's claw. His first labor. See the face of the lion on the skin draped over his arm? Heracles finished him off with the lion's own claw.

I'm a little uncomfortable looking at Heracles with a stance that seems to show off his excellent naked body in front of my boys. They're now riveted. I too am riveted by his endowment. Heracles, a man with brutal strength and yet the vulnerability of a woman. The Greek males were trained for war, and it's as if the male species has adapted the characteristics of the warrior. Superior. All-knowing. Commanding. Stalwart, stoic, never to appear weak. I see it developing in the boys I teach, in my son. I remember that in-between period just as he was approaching adolescence, before his armor went up. He, like me, is a watcher. Sensitive. Lagging behind his friend group, who in sixth or seventh grade had the heft and bodies of men, while my son was tall and so thin his ribs looked like a birdcage. A follower, not a leader. But an anxious follower. I found him crying into his pillow one night. I rubbed his shoulder and back, asked him what had happened. A girl from school he liked (weeks ago he had asked me what he should give her for her birthday) was going out with someone else. A broken heart at thirteen. He cuddled into my body and fell asleep. The next morning, he grabbed the box of Cheerios and milk from the fridge, wolfed down his bowl, put on his backpack, and gave me a kiss on the cheek before he left for school, his armor up, though I saw him hesitate at the elevator, biting his lip. Does anyone know why Heracles had to execute the twelve famous labors? Ms. White asks. Jason hunches over and flexes his muscles like Heracles. The boys laugh. I snap out of my thoughts and give them my stern look that means behave.

Hera made him think his wife and sons were enemies. He went crazy and killed them, says Justin. But why did Hera do this to Heracles? the guide asks. Because she was a jealous bitch, Hamilton interrupts. Rolex watch, slicked-back hair, a mini of his father, Hamilton Hallberg of the Hallberg Fund. The kid that's always testing the limits to get attention. A few of the boys start ribbing one another.

Hamilton, language, I scold. Yes, she was jealous, I add. But she had claims too. A woman doesn't always have to adhere to her husband's commands, I say. Ms. White looks at me strangely. Heracles was born a bastard from one of Zeus's affairs. That's why she was jealous, Ms. White adds. Does being a bastard make him any less? I wonder.

Heroes like Heracles are better than gods because they must endure courageous suffering, James concludes. He's tall and bright with a jubilee of curly hair and a smile that stretches to his ears. We're not supposed to have favorites, but of course we do. I look up at Heracles. We assume the heart is smaller in such a hero, but it isn't. It means a man must live up to such strength. I shake my head. It isn't quite fair.

Zeus's wife, Hera, wanted her own son to become king of Mycenae and was afraid that Heracles would steal the title. She tried to strangle him in his crib with a snake, but Heracles killed it. After he murdered his family, after being driven temporarily insane by Hera, he was tortured by grief and guilt, and pleaded to Apollo to help him. Apollo proposed that if he completed the twelve labors for King Eurystheus of Mycenae, he would be free of his guilt and achieve immortality, James explains. He's an old soul, the other boys don't quite know what to make of him, but he is too good to be bullied or ignored. When James was in kindergarten, his grandfather, a partner at Cantor & Fitzgerald, died along with more than six hundred employees when the towers collapsed. We offer an academic scholarship in his name.

The guide nods, ushering the boys closer as another group of students enters the gallery. Heracles is the embodiment of what the Greeks call pathos in tragedy, a figure who elicits existing emotion in the viewer or reader. He's a tragic hero, says the guide. In Euripides's version he's more nuanced, his complexity heightened by his conception as both a god and a mortal for the Greeks. His suffering gives him agency.

James's eyes sink into Heracles. I gaze too. *Tell me*, I say to him. *What was it? What happened to me?* I don't know anymore. I don't trust myself. Is that what my dream was trying to warn me? I'm staring up at Heracles, and as I move back I bump into Mohammed and apologize.

Heracles's struggle was made virtuous by his actions to rid himself of his guilt, says Ms. White. Shame and guilt are complicated psychological emotions. The Greek poets and philosophers employed them to consider human nature.

I crane my neck to look at the huge breadth of Heracles, a spectacle of strength and arrogance. Guilt is a form of mental anguish. Heracles, strong, arrogant, and punished, the proud thrust of his pelvis and the nothing where his sex had been. As if he'd been unmanned as punishment for mistaking his wife and children for his enemies. I wonder whether his sexual instinct, subverted, is part of what gives him his godly power. The only thing I am sure of is that Heracles is a fine specimen of pathos. And that I am a coward. Wanting my freedom when I was not free to want. There is no freedom in love. I clutch the Heracles knot bracelet on my wrist.

The guide leads the group away from Heracles; I follow and sense Heracles's gaze on my back. I don't want to leave him. There is more to learn, I know there is. There must be. My husband and I haven't talked in weeks. Only texts, mostly about our son. It's awful to live together in a house of silence. To wake up some mornings and lie in bed and remember, even when I don't want to. That day at the lake. Look, you're shivering, the Visiting Poet said. Your arms are covered in goose bumps. Here, come closer. Let me keep you warm. The old feelings come back. Everything comes back. Even when I fight against it.

The guide stops in front of a statue of a Greek aristocrat with its arm broken off. She peers at Mohammed's name tag and asks him what he imagines is missing. What he thinks the aristocrat might be doing. Mohammed thinks for a moment before he reaches out his own arms in a pose. Like this? he says, pointing his index finger in the air. He's posing like he's ready to give ideas, to speak or give a speech. The guide nods. Bro, let's hear it, Fidel says. The boys break out in laughter.

Can any of you boys think of an important Greek speech? the guide asks. "The Apology," Plato's dialogue of the trial of Socrates. We read it last year, says James. In "The Apology," Socrates brags that he's more heroic than Heracles because he seeks self-enlightenment, while Heracles hopes for redemption through acts of physical strength.

That's right, James, absolutely. Boys, who do you think is more heroic? I ask. Heracles, they say, almost in unison. Wrong answer. This will be your essay assignment for the week. To define *heroism.* They groan.

Let's go, the guide, says. She leads us to a room of glass cases.

Glass gladiator cup
(ca. A.D. 50–80, Roman)

These are gladiator cups. Gladiator games were hosted at the Colosseum. Sometimes forty to fifty thousand people attended. Gladiators were often slaves or prisoners. Anyone guess why?

Because during the contests people died, Mohammed says. He's a descendant of a prince of Saudi Arabia. His father works for a bank. He shared aspects of Muslim culture at assembly. He told us—and a mixed cheer, great but so late?—that recently women in Saudi Arabia have been permitted to drive. He is one of our stars on the debate team. That's right, says Ms. White. The gladiator fights were a gory spectacle, a sort of cold-blooded theater. Rarely were aristocrats gladiators. They were not going to risk their lives. Unless they were bankrupt. But if you were a prisoner or a slave and you won the contest, you were granted freedom. Some gladiators became famous and were worshipped by women who flocked to their contests. Women wore jewelry dipped in gladiator blood and sweat, and some mixed the combination into their creams and makeup. Sick, Hamilton says. They considered the blood and sweat to be an aphrodisiac, says Ms. White. The boys break into more laughter. They're getting restless. I fear soon they are going to lose it and go tearing through the gallery or do some other stupid thing.

Now look here, Ms. White says, as if she too senses she must rein them in. The cups in the glass case were given away as souvenirs at the games. The depictions are of gladiators fighting, and the Latin bears their names. If they wanted people to root for them, they gave them out at the games. Like hat day at Yankee Stadium, she says. In ancient Greece sports were revered. In every city, there was a gymnasium. Greek men liked to keep in shape to prepare themselves for war. The body was their weapon.

All those cross-country competitions. Longer strides, faster, my husband would say. In the hallway, I'd hear them jumping rope. Lifting weights. He needs to take it more seriously, my husband said, as if, like the Greeks, he was training his son for war. Ms. White leads the group to another wing. I tell her that I'll meet them at the information booth in thirty minutes. I sit down again near Heracles.

Heracles gazes at me when I look into his eyes. I bluster amid his greatness. I look deeper. My eyes sting. Must anguish always bring us closer to what we've disregarded? My husband's disdain of me is painful. I want him to love me, even when now I don't know how to love him back. A young girl walks into the gallery. Converse sneakers without laces; statuesque, with legs longer than her torso by two; long hair shining under the museum light like the glossy black of a mink coat; olive skin with several piercings in one ear. Deep into her phone, wearing earbuds, oblivious even when all eyes turn to her. I remember what that was like. That show of obliviousness—that learned absence. To be gazed at, taunted, leered at, even just walking down the street to buy shampoo at the drugstore. When I moved to New York City from graduate school I carried my keys in my hand when I walked alone at night. I look at this girl again, and a smile has crept into her face. She hugs her shoulders and does a half pirouette as if a boy is whispering into her ears through her earbuds.

As I leave to meet up with my students, I bump into this awful creature perched on a pillar.

Bronze statuette of a reclining satyr
(6th century B.C., Etruscan)

A satyr with his long goat-like beard holding a phallic drinking horn that looks like a dagger. I have no trust for his self-serving gaze forever cast in bronze wagging his member, satisfied as if he's just conquered, bedded, and left to boast. And those monstrous, out-of-proportion hands! No. I can't. I won't think about it. I turn and walk briskly away and meet up with Ms. White and my students at the entrance to the museum near the information booth. I look for the boy-man at the membership table. Our eyes connect; he gives me the raised chin and a smile. I look at my students laughing and chatting, white, yellow, black, brown. Girls from their sister school have now made a ring next to them and whisper close together, in an excited mating dance, while my boys huddle, looking at something on one of their phones, occasionally glancing back at the girls.

My own phone buzzes. Another text. What does she want now? My neighbor has been texting me at odd moments for days. *Will u pick up salmon on your way home?* It's my husband. Warmth expands my chest. My husband has invited me to pick up salmon.

## WEEK 5

I take out flour, sugar, vanilla, almonds from the cabinet. Open the refrigerator for the butter, then the eggs, and—whoops—I slip on a grease spill from last night's dinner and hurt my hip. The egg crate falls out of my hand, and the eggs splatter on the floor. The yolks running, the translucent membranes in little blobs, the cracked shells.

My husband trails into the kitchen. What's all this? he says. I tell him I'm making my almond cake, swatting a lock of hair from my eyes and then wiping away the flour on my blouse.

Why the trouble? There's nothing to celebrate, he says. Because I want to, I say. Isn't that enough?

To make yourself feel better, I hear him mumble. Why don't you pay attention to what you're doing, he says, looking at the smashed eggs on the floor. You're always somewhere else. His eyes drive into me like nails. It's not a big deal. It's just some broken eggs. I'll clean it up. Why is he scolding me? Nothing's a big deal, he says. I feel his disdain like an awful yeast rising inside me. Don't bake the cake for me. I'm going to the lab, he says. On Sunday? I say.

And then his phone buzzes. He picks it out of his back pocket. Slowly it becomes clear that the person on the other end of the phone is our son. What do you mean you may drop philosophy? I hear him say. What's the matter with you? Get your work done and stop hanging out at the bar. What's the matter with *you?* I say, when the call ends. Have you forgotten what it's like to be a teenager? Maybe he needs some help. Maybe he can't manage all his classes on top of track and field. I was never a teenager, he says. You deal with it. He picks up his backpack and slams the door behind him. I'll make dinner, I call, but he's already gone. Why do I even try? I wet a paper towel. The egg whites adhere to the floor like sticky glue. There's yolk on my sweater, egg in my hair. It's no use. There's no way back. I'm tired. I scoop up the shells, mop the floor, put away the rest of the ingredients I've taken out from the shelves. My elbow knocks the carton of sugar onto the counter and it rains down onto the floor. I give up. Maybe it's impossible to return to the period of our marriage when our love settled into the current of our lives, when just baking a cake, waiting for it to rise, to cut into it and taste its sweetness was enough.

I go into the bedroom, fall onto my bed, slowly sink into sleep I've been needing for weeks; it's leaden, deep, as if I've been enveloped in a thick fog so that when I awake, I'm groggy, headachy. Lethargic. I don't want to get out of bed. I want to sleep for a thousand days, but I can't let down my guard. It's almost two in the afternoon. I go into the kitchen, finish cleaning the mess, the tiny granules of sugar sticking to the bottom of my bare feet. Had he caught the uncertainty in my face? My brief bursts of happiness? These moments come back to me as if suddenly lit like lights in a dark garden.

## MUSEUM

I take my keys, my sunglasses and put on a fleece. It's a cold afternoon. My stomach is in a knot. What am I going to do about my husband? My son? I sense he's overwhelmed. He never knew how to rein himself in as a kid. Always the last one out of the playground. Staying up all night texting or on his computer when he needed to get up early the next day. Saving his work until the last minute. Raised by a single mother and with no siblings, I have few role models for boys other than the boys I teach. They are fidgety, need more wiggle room, rarely ask for help if they are stressing, instead act tough to gain attention. I need to find out more about the transformation of boy to man, the key that so abruptly turns and childhood ends. When young men begin to withhold their emotions. Blow up in rages. Act out of control to escape themselves. Become impulsive and do stupid things.

My son, out with his teammates one evening, blew off curfew. I didn't understand this change in him. Why he was moving away from us. Becoming secretive. What we might have done that stopped him from obeying the limits. My husband finally tracked him on Find My Friends at 3:00 a.m. (Now you can find your friends, and your sons, even if they don't want to be found, at a bar on the Upper East Side.) I didn't know bars in the city stayed open so late. Or that my son had a fake ID. Or that athletes are capable of consuming enough beer that one could be so drunk he peed in his bed. When I don't hear from my son, this is the image that prods forth.

My son's late nights tortured us. I worried he'd get so drunk or high he couldn't find his way home. That he'd get in a cab or on a subway and someone would assault him. Why do you do it? I asked. Because it's fun, he said. I couldn't fall asleep unless I heard the lock turn in the door. If our son was still in bed when my husband came home from the gym on an early Sunday afternoon, the veins on his head throbbed, nostrils flared, eyebrows lowered like the face of the Minotaur trapped in the labyrinth, the one I've viewed repeatedly on a marble sarcophagus, in Gallery 162. I doubt my husband's aware of his Minotaur gaze, but he can't fully control it either. I don't understand my husband's fury. I don't understand many men. The sexual drive and its intense need to be instantly satisfied. The desire to dominate. To hold forth power. The way the male professors at my institution claim territory just by their very sex. Or their height. Broad shoulders. Suit and tie. The uniform of entitlement. Perhaps a new dress code is due. Maybe men should be required to wear skirts. My neighbor claims it is all testosterone. She too believes I overthink. But it's what I teach my students. To question. To observe. To not always follow the status quo. I must investigate the male species. Why not. They've controlled the world, and I am the teacher of their descendants.

What would it be like to have agency just because you were born into it? Did I mistake kindness for power? I remember my first boyfriend. He had beautiful green eyes, sunken cheeks, tan arms. I'd sit on the bleachers while he played baseball and, bored, pretend to watch his game, peeking up from the pages of a novel. I'd sneak him into my bedroom, and we'd make out, kissing and grinding against each other until we were both so turned on, we had to stop. I was still a virgin, but I wasn't ready. He complained I was giving him blue balls. Guilt-ridden, I tortured myself. Was I being unfair to him? Must women bear the guilt of a man's desire? Of course, women want it too. I wanted it. But I wasn't sure it was him I wanted it with for my first time.

On the M86 crosstown bus through Central Park, yellow and purple fall crocuses poke their heads through the ground and shimmy in the wind. It looks like a landscape painting invigorating a dull canvas. Soon there will be an abundance of falling leaves. Then snow. The museum from this view looks like a Victorian gothic estate with different rooms and wings and a grand staircase. Or even kind of French? No matter. I deem it my home. My body races. I mount the steps, sweating in my long coat. Once I enter the foyer, I see the boy-man at the membership table, and he gives me a nod.

You're here again, he says. Yeah, I say. You come almost every week? Why so often? I'm a teacher. What better history book than a museum? And I'm a poet. I come for inspiration. His face brightens. A poet, he says. I've never met a poet before. My lips widen. And then it dawns on me. Who this boy-man looks like. I proceed to the entrance to show my membership card and then to the theater of Greece and Rome to find him.

Portrait of the boy Eutyches
(A.D. 100–150, from Egypt, Roman period)

A teenage boy of mixed race, typical of the multicultural, multiethnic society of Greco-Roman Egypt. Most notable are those spectacular dark brown eyes, which follow me as I look at them. How gentle he looks. This portrait was painted on a panel that was placed over a mummy's face. The poor family, to have lost this precious boy so young. Boys were raised to be soldiers, considered more of a possession of the state than of their parents. Mothers were said to weaken them. Did I give more of myself to my son than I should have? Is this why his leaving has left me empty? Perhaps I would have been a better mother to my daughter. Sometimes I don't know what to say to my son. How to reach him.

I sit down on a bench in the middle of the gallery and close my eyes for a few minutes to calm myself. Then I hear the bleat of a text. It's my neighbor's daughter. She's been on my mind and I'm glad to hear from her. She's so bright and yet she doubts herself. Once, in high school she came to me in tears. Something had happened at school, but she wouldn't tell me. I told her that at her age I was self-conscious, I didn't speak in class, but my papers achieved high marks and my teachers gave me the benefit of the doubt. At the end of my senior year, at graduation, I was given a prize for my writing. I couldn't believe it, or accept it. That was the way I was. I thought my teachers felt sorry for me for not having a father. When I was cleaning out my mother's apartment for her move to assisted living, I found the award in a box with my school notebooks. It took me all these years to take it in, I said. You must trust yourself.

She looked at me with dry eyes and an open expression. I don't know what it was, but that story seemed to reassure her. I made tea and she brightened. She texts me that she saw a notice in *Publishers Weekly* announcing my new book and wants to know when she can read it. I tell her I will send her a copy. I ask her how her thesis is coming along. Her thesis is called "The Female Voice." She argues that we must realign the definition of authority, excellence, and scope advanced by the male tradition in literature and redefine its terms through female culture, experience, and creative form. She texts back that she received an email from her adviser and that her thesis is on track. I give her a thumbs-up emoji. My mood lifts. I tell myself that all these doubts and worries about my son will soon pass. That I am still adjusting to his absence.

What was it like when you were empty nesters? I asked Leslie Ryan at school. She's a decade older and teaches math. Her boys are close to thirty. She said it was the best time of her life. We were eating our scoop of cottage cheese inside a half cantaloupe in the cafeteria. She couldn't wait to get them out of her house. She immediately renovated the boys' room into a study. I wanted to tell her that upon waking every morning, I'm awash with dread. It's like I'm paralyzed, at the bottom of the sea, and can't rise or call out for help. To go from knowing every day, every hour where your child is, even if he may not be telling the truth, to not knowing anything about his days or nights? I should have expected it. Leslie drinks chamomile tea before bed and brushes her teeth in the women's room after lunch, wears pleated plaid skirts and starched oxford shirts. I'm not sure she's ever experienced an emotion.

I move on to glean this magnificent statue of a kouros, or youth, from ancient Greece. His long physique and broad shoulders remind me of my son's.

Marble statue of a kouros (youth)
(ca. 590–580 B.C., Greek, Attic)

Is it because of the baby we lost that I fear something terrible may happen to you? I say, observing him. Is this why my husband asks for more from you than you can give? It's okay, Mom, I hear him say. I know I'm a goofball sometimes, but I'm fine. It has been more than two months. The longest time I've been away from you. I can't rest. Or dismiss the feeling that something is wrong. Why won't you text me? I sit down on the bench and put my head in my hands, surrounded by proud Athena, sexy Aphrodite, clever Poseidon, stalwart Hermes, almighty Zeus among them, and like the ancient Greeks and Romans, they have become my monitors. *Please protect him. Keep my son safe.* I look again at my kouros. The gods act quickly. They do not abide human pride and arrogance. When Niobe boasted of her twelve children to Tito, who had only two, Apollo and Artemis, Apollo killed her six boys and Artemis murdered her six daughters. And now she is turned to stone forever weeping. I will never boast of you, I whisper. I will never kill out of envy. I continue my search, strolling in and out of the statues of the gods.

Bronze statuette of Neptune
(early 1st century A.D., Roman)

Neptune, like so many other male gods, is a rapist. I must sit down. The wind has left me. I can barely stand to look at this vile creature. A burst of fear adrenaline floods me. In Greek and Roman mythology, the gods are forever plagued and be-sotted by female beauty and in constant pursuit to temper their lust. Women flee and the gods deceive, shape-shift: Zeus as a swan to conquer Leda, to Europa as a bull. No, it wasn't like that. I shake my head. He cared for me.

Neptune, ruler of the sea, who lived in the bowels of his father, Cronus, until he vomited him up. Neptune, with his arm held up as if he has a right to victory. I detest his bearded face. I detest his very stance. Demeter tried to fend him off, turning her-self into a horse to escape him, and to outrun her he morphed into a stallion. Neptune, your body too lean, almost Christ-like. Nothing like a stallion. I do not desire you. You can lower your fist. An image bursts forth of the Visiting Poet with his thick fingers and that scarf around his neck. Pheromones spill-ing out of me, in his presence, like those wild nights as a teen-ager. I remember the day I found him in the library in one of those leather club chairs with a book in his lap, staring blankly outside the window. He looked lonely. A bit lost. I went to say hello and he brightened. He volunteered to tutor Malcolm, who was failing fifth-form Spanish, during study hall. I was helping Mohammed with an essay. After the bell rang and the boys fled, he invited me for a Starbucks around the corner. At one of the crowded tables, he put his hand under the table and moved my knees to one side, to make room for his long legs, and then he cupped one of my knees for a few seconds. I could barely breathe. I look at Neptune's muscled abdomen. No, it was a gesture of tenderness, I say to his driving eyes. I pass the boy-man at the membership table as I ready to exit. What have I discovered? Nothing. He's texting on his phone, looks up to see me. There is no one in line. *What is it?* his expression says back. Just like the way my son could always read me. I could never hide from him. *Nothing, absolutely nothing.*

## THE VISITING POET

Once he brought to my classroom a beautiful poem about grief my student James had written, told through a narrative of his mother watering her houseplants. I told him that James had lost his grandfather on 9/11, and his father died of cancer when he was thirteen, and it touched me that the Visiting Poet had taken an interest in him. We exchanged exercises for our poetry students. I had forgotten the unclouded joy a friend with similar interests and mutual respect could bring. He eyed me when we passed in the corridor of the academy. He seemed to always find me in the lunchroom. When I filled my cup of lukewarm coffee from the teachers' lounge, he poured in the milk. One sugar or two? He left notes on top of books he presented on my desk for me to borrow. Look at page 31. It was a copy of *Metamorphoses*. Let's discuss. The notes made my stomach drop in anticipation of what was inside; of course, it was the myth of Echo and Narcissus, because we'd argued over it. I said that Narcissus rejected sexuality because he could only love himself; the Visiting Poet defended him. Who if not ourselves is going to love us? he said, and we laughed. I forgot how much I missed laughing. I began to look forward to the notes. So much so that I wanted to savor the unknowing of these notes, when I found one on my desk, just to continue to feel the adrenaline running through my body, just to remember that I had feeling. I had an instinct. I was no longer numb. My husband was either running with our son or working late at the lab. He brushed a kiss on my cheek when he came home and mumbled a few words at dinner. I knew all his stories. He knew the ones I shared with him. We were so familiar to each other. I took a long walk through the halls of the school, through the foul-smelling gymnasium with its waxed blond floors, and sat on the bleachers alone to hide a smile that crept into my face before returning to class and struggling over how to excite twenty-two high school freshmen in a discussion of *The Odyssey*, a poem that had possessed me for years. One of his notes came with a xerox of "Anecdote of the Jar," one of my favorite Stevens poems, how did he know. "It took dominion everywhere," his note said, quoting one of the lines scrawled by a fountain pen in handwriting that was slightly shaky and for some reason broke me.

Eventually I gave him an early draft of *The Rape of the Swan* to read. I don't remember if that was the title at the time. It may have just been *The Swan*. The working title for ages. We were in the teachers' lounge, and he had the manuscript in his hand.

He'd taken it with him over the long weekend. I was uneasy and itching to know what he thought about it. I hadn't shared it with anyone yet.

We lounged on the pea-green leather couch. Stuffing was coming out of a crack in the seam. I'm curious, he said. Why do you write? He crossed his legs in a feminine gesture, reached his fingers to his broad forehead to push back his hair. That's a strange question. I don't know, I said. It should be simple, shouldn't it. I've always wanted to write, ever since I can remember. It was a desire unnameable. A need. To be able to express oneself in language. The magic and mystery of what might unfold.

So you do it to satisfy a longing? He looked into my eyes with what seemed like genuine curiosity.

Maybe. I thought about it some more, and then it came to me. I told him the myth of lusty Pan and the wood nymph Syrinx from *Metamorphoses*. How she wasn't interested in his advances. He was half-goat. He chased her, and she ran away through the wilds till she came to the waters of Ladon, and there she begged the sisters of the stream to change her so that Pan wouldn't find her. Pan thought he had her, but when he went to grab her, instead of the nymph's body, he held reeds from the marsh, and while he pondered it all, the wind in the reeds gave out a clear sound. He was transfixed. "Hoc mihi colloquium tecum manebit," he said. "For me this will remain a conversation with you." I paused. Writing a poem is like that, I told him. A private conversation you hope the reader will follow. Yes, why not. To satisfy a longing, I said. Sure. To inspire. To release the numbness. To feel alive, and then my cheeks grew hot. Was he mocking me?

It wasn't enough. He persisted. So, your swan . . . at dusk . . . The act of writing is to yearn desperately for it, even as the swan disappears into the darkness. Is that right? Is that how the poem becomes the manifestation of yearning? He turned to me, searching. Is that what you see in it? I said, unnerved. What was he after? What about you, I said. Why do you do it?

My reasons are not as complex. It's a drive. I write for power, he said. Yeah. I write for rage. He got excited and stood up. I look for inspiration outside myself. Not like you. I don't delve inside. His head nearly touched the low ceiling in the teachers' lounge. Yes, I write for fame too. I'm not afraid of it like you are, he said, sitting back down. You cloak fear behind modesty. He moved to the edge of the couch to be able to look at me more deeply.

I felt small next to his hulking body, his thighs the circumference of a sapling, those monstrous hands. I moved an inch or so away so as not to be further encroached. I had never thought of it that way before. Was he right? Or was he teasing me? I couldn't quite figure him out or know what to expect, like a day when the snow threatens, clouds weigh in, and you don't exactly know what will happen, will the snow be light, or heavy and wet, or maybe the low clouds were only a ruse.

This poem you've written is different from your other work. It's more ambitious. You've subverted the self in the image of a female swan, hidden away for a lifetime but never once forgotten. The warmth of his breath on my cheek, its whiff of coffee as he spoke, forced me to turn my head. He was right. I've always hidden. Even hidden, perhaps behind my husband, my marriage. From coming forward as a poet. I was always tentative, even despite my ambition. I looked out the window. It was too bright. It hurt to see, and I turned away. Maybe it's why I fumbled around the Visiting Poet. He saw things in me I couldn't see. Maybe it's like that for everyone: people see in us the things we feel we've worked hard to hide. I wanted to get up and retreat; I felt exposed. I didn't want to ask, but I needed to know. He had read my poem and had said little about it. So, what did you think of it? I finally asked, straightening my trim shift over my knees, before we had to go to teach.

Your poem, it says, I have loved this self all my life and will continue to love the self she is to my dying day. No one will stand in my way, he said emphatically. Why do you say that? I asked. I had no idea what he was talking about. Because all poets are transparent. Your swan is longing, he said. It's very compelling, and then he gave me a smug smile. It isn't finished, I said. I want more to happen. It will, he said. And then he paused. Our process is different. You find your way through multiple drafts. My books come quickly, in a burst of inspiration. I rarely revise, he said. My publisher has been putting pressure on me to get a new book out soon. He says he has a vacant spot on his list next fall, but I've got nothing. You can't rush the process, I said. It comes when it's ready. I suppose, he said, and then got up to leave.

I followed and watched him greet James in the hallway. He put his arm around the boy, a foot taller, and the two walked into his classroom together, engaged in conversation. That night, as I lay beside my husband in bed, thoughts of what he said, quandaries of what he intended or did not intend, drifted in and out of my consciousness.

## APARTMENT 9B

My boy has been assaulted. Knocked unconscious, having gotten in a brawl with a group of locals congregated outside the bar at the college. They were taunting two girls and my boy had come out of the bar, witnessed it, and told them to lay off and one of them clocked him in the face and in the gut. The call comes at three in the morning. We quickly throw clothes in a bag and head out in the car to the airport. The anxiety and the free-floating feeling that something is terribly wrong is a mother's sixth sense about her child being in danger. I knew it. Dionysus, the god of debauchery, is flirting with my son. In some depictions of him he is a youth with long effeminate hair; in others he is old and bearded with grapes in his hands, temptation in his eyes, lust in his countenance.

What kind of boy gets into a fight like that? my husband says once we're on the road. It is before dawn. Still black out. No wonder he's flunking, my husband says. What is he doing in a bar at two in the morning? He's not flunking, I offer. He's hurt. As we drive, the sky begins to open with light. Zeus is watching from the heavens. Protect my boy, please.

## THE COLLEGE NEAR THE CHURCH
## OF THE NAZARENE

On our way to campus we pass the meth houses, miles of cornfields stretching into the distance. Churches of the Nazarene. A sign in front of one of the churches. Bible study on Sunday, racial reconciliation on Thursdays, AA meetings Monday and Wednesday nights. We drive up the long, winding path to his dorm room and find him curled up in bed. My husband switches on the light. Our son's eye is bruised and closed shut. How did you get here? he says, as if he's forgotten he had called us. Blood is on his pillow. His hair is damp. A cut above his eye is still bleeding and needs to be stitched. He's clutching his abdomen. I smell alcohol on his breath. I look at the desk stacked with his textbooks and notebooks and am momentarily cheered. His legs poke out from his blanket. When did he get all that leg hair?

My husband asks him what happened, laying a hand on his shoulder. He tells us that a group of his friends decided to go to a raunchy townie bar after last call at the college bar. Men who once worked at the mostly defunct Mercedes factory, or in construction, go there to get trashed. My son said that two guys were taunting some girls and he stepped in. *Fucking faggot*, they called him, pointing a finger into his college letter sweatshirt. Motherfuckers, our son says, still intoxicated when he tells us what happened. Sixty thousand dollars a year for all this? I think.

That was stupid, my husband says. You don't go into a place like that. What did you think was going to happen? Fuck, Dad. Do you want me to lie? my son says. You do nothing bad. You're perfect. Fuck you, Dad, he says. Tears in his eyes. My husband softens. He apologizes and tells him that it's okay, that right now we need to focus on getting him help. We drive him to the nearest hospital. The gash above his eye requires more than twenty stitches. In the ER, he's lightheaded. He rises to go the bathroom, faints, and loses consciousness. More tests, an MRI, blood sent to the lab. His spleen is damaged and is causing internal bleeding. He's put on an IV and given blood.

My husband's right. He *is* flunking. His reading for philosophy is dense. I couldn't read all the works on the syllabus in one semester—Plato, Aristotle, Hume—on top of his other courses, his track-and-field practices, nights at the bar, weekend parties. He can't handle it all. It is as if the bleeding is calling him back to reality. In my mind, the dreams I had for his college experience quickly evaporate. Those were my dreams, not his. Perhaps a mother isn't supposed to know her son's dreams. Or perhaps I am making a judgment. Getting ahead of myself.

He's a boy who has newly found his freedom, I say to myself. My husband wants to find out who did this to our son and press charges, and I leave it to the two of them to sort it out.

While he's sleeping, I take the car and drive back to his dorm room to collect a few of his clothes, his robe and toiletries and books. It's good to have a break. To walk. The air is crisp, the campus in full autumn foliage, leaves falling in slow motion on the stone pavement, the pathway umbrellaed by rust-red and flame-orange trees. It was just one bad night. A misjudgment. The gothic buildings with lead windows and towers poke the sky. In front of the library, a statue of Athena. She's everywhere. After I gather his things and put them in the car, I walk to the town square for a coffee. Parked on the sides of streets are mostly Chevrolets and pickups. On one corner, a Walgreens. On another a Burger King and a McDonald's. Compared to New York, it's like a ghost town. I walk down another street and past a liquor store and a laundromat and a small market, a rundown seafood place. I keep walking. There's a crumbled-down building with a few people hanging out on the porch. It looks like it was once a hotel. A handful of poor souls dressed in what look like rags falling from their skeletal bodies, smoking cigarettes on the dilapidated porch. At the end of the corner a man with rotted teeth is begging for money; I give him change from my pocket, ashamed. Closer, he's a teenager, thin, with wrinkled skin. I quickly walk past, find a Dunkin' Donuts and go in. No people of color in this town. Inside, a woman with her toddlers sitting at one of the tables feeding them donuts and little cups of Sprite. Two construction workers size me up. Dressed in my black New York jeans, sweater, and a black puff vest and black boots, I must look to them like an alien from another planet. I buy a cup of coffee and begin walking back through town toward the college. On the street, a group is handing out leaflets. I take one. Something about a meeting at the church. And then I understand that these people are white supremacists. There is a wrapped white-and-red peppermint stapled to the leaflet as if to sweeten the racism. The juxtaposition of the townies and the privileged college students with their books against their chests—I don't understand our country anymore.

I'll take a leave from school, rent a house in town, help him with his coursework, put him on a schedule, check in with him, but I know I can't save or protect my son. I can't bribe him. I can't lock him in his room. He's got to find his own way. Back at the hospital, while my husband goes for a snack from the cafeteria, I tell him to stay away from town. He agrees, says they shouldn't have gone out to the bars. A girl from school was raped, he says. She was assaulted in her dorm room by someone from town. Now the school's on lockdown. Some days it feels like a prison. We were restless, it was stupid. What about your classes? I ask. He tells me he's doing well in econ. In computer science they're making their own video games. His is based on *Beowulf* and his professor is into it. You used to read it to me. I smile.

He's in the hospital for a few days until his blood pressure stabilizes. After he's discharged, we check into a hotel an hour away from the college to rest and regroup. It is the three of us again. All the angst of the last weeks slips off my body like water. My husband softens. He goes into high gear; he's a fixer. We tell our son to come home for the rest of the semester and start again in January, but he's adamant. He wants to stick it out. We encourage him to drop his philosophy class and focus on his other courses. In private, I ask my son if he wants to quit track. He isn't ready, he says. We order room service, turn on the television, all three of us lying on the king-size bed like we used to, watching a movie of our son's choice. My husband goes to the candy machines and scores with M&M's and Twizzlers. My husband and son are stretched out on the bed next to each other. With their hairy legs and long limbs, it's hard to tell them apart. The movie has ended. My son and husband have fallen asleep. Why wasn't this enough? The light fades out the window. I close my eyes praying for sleep before the rosy face of dawn appears. In *The Odyssey* she stretches out her fingers at least twenty times.

## APARTMENT 9B

He'll get thrown off the team. He'll flunk out. I'm telling you. He won't make it. He'll either kill himself or get arrested, my husband unloads, once we're on our way back to New York. If I defend our son, it will cause an argument. I'm tired of trying to reassure my husband. I too am afraid of Dionysus. I face the window and let him rant. There is no comforting him when he's in this state. I want to tell him that human development,

per Freud, is built on the conflict between tension and pleasure. That our son has not found his balance. That by overin-
dulging him, doing everything for him, we have frustrated his
desire to achieve the next stage of development, but now is not
the time. My husband's face. The skin under his cheekbones
pulses with rage. The Minotaur. I want to touch his arm, to
soften him, but I refrain. I remember the statue of the kouros
at the museum. Tall and strong, a symbol of male youth just
entering the body of a man now able to join the brotherhood of
men. Despite what's happened, I have faith in my boy. When
you know a person, you can't turn away from what you know.
He'll be the end of us, my husband says.

We park the car, walk silently toward our building, past a gut-
ted brownstone ruined by fire, a car alarm blaring, underneath
a block of scaffolding in which a homeless couple has made
their bed out of boxes and blankets, it isn't fair. In the second
year of the Peloponnesian War, during the classical period in
ancient Greece, a plague broke out in Athens and wiped out
one-third of the population, and people begged for food and
water. Here, the war is capitalism. I'm glad we live in a prewar
building, a chance to hold on to the past, rather than in one of
the hideous new structures that line many of the streets con-
necting with Broadway. Once inside our apartment, I feel as if
I've entered a sanctuary, though in my state I have no sense of
relief. Drained, I go into the bedroom to change for bed. Minutes later I hear my husband in the kitchen. Goddamn it, he
says, son-of-a bitch. No doubt he's dropped something on the

floor. He can't bear an imperfect universe. I go into the kitchen for a glass of water. My husband has already retired to our son's room. I turn out the lights. It's dark. The radiator spews out heat, groans, hisses. I go past my son's room. The door is halfway open, with the lamp lit on the bedside table. My husband at the foot of our son's bed holding the trophy our son received when his team won the state high school championship in track and field and our son in sprints and hurdles came in first. It's a statue of Achilles. Achilles: strong, brave, honorable, saved, almost, by his mother's protection. He turns the trophy in his hand and the light picks up the bronze before fading into darkness. My husband places the trophy on the bed and puts his head in his hands. I see the scar on his face.

## MY NEIGHBOR

A knock at the door. My neighbor doesn't look good. Dark circles under her eyes. I invite her in and make a new pot of coffee. But it will have to be quick. I have a ten o'clock class. What's happened? I ask.

She's in a furry pink robe tied at the waist and matching slippers with feathers at the helm. I feel suddenly hemmed in, dressed in my black velvet blazer, starched white blouse, and tight slacks. My neighbor unloads, as if my kitchen is a confessional; she moved into her own bedroom of their three-thousand-square-foot apartment, she tells me. I'm so depressed. It's come on me like a weight. I didn't realize what it was. Why it's been so hard to get out of bed. At yoga, during Savasana, my teacher placed his hands underneath my head to elongate my neck. I started to cry. No one has touched me so tenderly. After class he said I've been harboring grief in my body. He's French, she says, and a scandalous smile creeps into her teary face. I left the studio, and it was like something cracked open. I began to sob and couldn't stop. My husband has been making me sick. I'm so lonely, she says.

The amazing renovation in your apartment. All those architectural plans. New furniture. All the years in which architects, construction workers, interior designers traipse in and out of the hallway. You seemed close. Days we'd find you arms linked, the twins, in the playground, and we'd drink our coffee and watch them play. All your holidays.

She tells me since the twins have been gone, her husband only complains about money. He barely looks her way, even when they speak. She's moved into her own room to figure things out, she says, perching on the bar stool. I look at her closely. Something is different. She sees me peering into her face. She pushes back from her forehead her long hair sculpted into waves that flow past her breasts. I had my eyes lifted. Why? I ask, alarmed.

My eyelids were sagging. I miss my old face, she says. You better get used to it, I say, and we both smile mournfully. Didn't your husband notice? I inquire. He never notices anything about me, she says.

When the children were small and once every few weeks we joined them for dinner, a pizza and salad delivered in, my friend wore tight blouses that exposed her cleavage, her nails painted in the latest color, hair painted with highlights. I was in yoga pants, sweatshirt, and Uggs that made my feet look like a bear's paws, my hair pushed off my face in a high ponytail. I had no time for getups, manicures, hairdressers. Occasionally I caught my husband gazing across the table at her breasts, like the pink blush of hydrangeas—I couldn't fault him, they're impossible not to look at. Occasionally, my neighbor rose from her chair and rubbed her husband's shoulders. Sometimes she cocooned in his lap, at their house for dinner, the children running in and out of the living room. There was a period when it sometimes pained me to be around her. My son always going to her apartment. Those low-cut dresses, showing off her big breasts, all the questions she would ask, what was I teaching, reading, where did I get my pearl earrings. When we first met them, we thought they were sexy. The sexy odd couple, we called them. She was always touching and stroking his arm, and I saw my husband sometimes looking at her with a strange contradiction of dismissive lust. There was one night where we'd gone to hear jazz with them, something we rarely did. The kids were small, she was bragging about her son and his soccer game, wearing one of her skintight animal-print dresses. I think it was zebra. Both her twins are alive and thriving. Her daughter is brilliant. She and her husband didn't have to pinch pennies like we did. Her life seemed carefree, unencumbered. We got home drunk on champagne and my husband wanted to play a game. I was the neighbor. I was supposed to come into the bedroom wearing the black negligee—I still had it tucked in the corner of my drawer, a gift from my wedding shower. I didn't buy fancy negligees or lingerie. I thought they were a waste of money. I slept in T-shirts. I went ahead with my husband's game. He called her a chatterbox in private, and now I was her.

He doesn't like it when I speak, she says. She's leaning over my kitchen counter waiting for the coffee to finish brewing. Her legs are bare underneath her robe, and one of her legs is crawling up the other, like tree pose. She has beautiful legs. Imagine what it is like to live with someone who won't speak to you? He says he speaks to people all day at work. He's tired. He comes home and scarfs down his tea. The chicken cutlets I prepared just the way he likes them. They disappear from his plate within minutes. I've just tucked my napkin in my lap, and he pushes his empty plate away, retreats into his little theater to watch sports and binge on crisps. He says he's entitled.

I pour coffee in her cup and shake my head. Is that the bargain you made? I ask. She doesn't understand the question. That he makes the money and you take care of the home? It's what he expects, she says. But that doesn't mean he gets to ignore me. Of course not, I say. What about you guys, she asks me, how are you doing? We're good, I say. I don't mean to withhold. I just don't know how to begin. Her twins—her son is playing soccer at the University of Wisconsin, and her daughter is studying literature and philosophy at Stanford. They're both in their third year. I can barely get out of bed, she continues. In the afternoon, she must take a lie-down that sometimes stretches into the early evening. I thought it was my fibromyalgia she said, but it's my husband. I've hired a life coach. She does Reiki. Have you heard of it? She's helping me discover where my energy is blocked. So many changes, I say. What has he said about your new bedroom? He doesn't seem to mind. The bloke still thinks he gets bedroom privileges, she says, and gloomily shakes her head.

How are the twins? I ask. She says that her daughter is struggling. I tell her my son is too. That I'm worried about him. Maybe we spoiled them, she says. Maybe, I say, or maybe the struggle is good. Life shouldn't be perfect for them. I've seen what that's like with some of the boys I teach at school. You know what my daughter's like, my neighbor says. She's so hard on herself. If she doesn't get all A's she thinks she's failed. She's so anxious. I'm worried she's falling into one of her dark funks. She sent me a terrific paper, I said. It was influenced by Judith Butler about the double bind of gender, the punishment for transgression, and the desire to be free. I knew in the paper she was trying to work something out about herself, about her own gender identity, but I didn't mention that to my neighbor. I thought it would only upset her. Why are men such fucks, her daughter once texted me, after listening to a tedious and pompous lecture by one of her male philosophy professors. I love this girl. I know she is going to be exceptional. She reads her life through books, I say to my neighbor. She's nothing like me, my neighbor says. Sometimes I wonder where she came from.

I gave her my copies of *Little Women, Jane Eyre, Wuthering Heights*, all the novels I adored as a young girl. In high school she sometimes came over for tea after school and she shared some of the books she'd discovered, experimental and cultish works by Sophie Calle, Jane Bowles, Anaïs Nin, Kathy Acker. Occasionally she complained that her mother was suffocating her, that she couldn't wait to get away to college, but I never told my neighbor. My neighbor asked me once if her daughter made me feel sad over the daughter I had lost. She makes me happy, I said, and then conceded. It's bittersweet. Maybe we're supposed to not understand them, I say. Maybe that's the point. When they're little we think we know them because we've objectified them from our own life view. Maybe we must see them for who they are now, I say. Or who they might be, I think to myself. Who she might be, my daughter. My neighbor nods. Everything is changing, she says. Maybe that's why I feel this way.

I look at the clock and begin to pack up my papers and books into my work bag. I'm sorry you're suffering. Do you think it's because the twins are gone? I say, as an afterthought. Is this when it all started? Maybe. I thought it would get better, that we'd spend more time together, get closer. Now the bloke's taking up fishing. You're lucky. Your husband loves you, she says.

## WEEK 7

It's like he's taken it hostage. My son's bedroom. I want to keep it sacred just a little longer, a shrine to his boy-self on the floor playing with his action figures, listening to the sounds of battle coming from his mouth, or curling up in my arms while I read to him. I go in when I'm missing him, to dust, smooth out the sheets and comforter on the bed. This morning my husband has left his half-drunk water glass on the bedside table, as if an affront. I take it into the kitchen and then come back and sit on the boy's bed. If he wasn't at my neighbor's house, or doing sports with my husband, I was his playmate, helping him build Lego dungeons, reading to him, lying next to him until he fell asleep. I sometimes could not get him to leave the playground. Distracted with his friends, he could see or think of nothing else. Sometimes he'd run away from me because he did not want to go home. Then the minute we'd be in a cab or on the bus, he'd forget about the playground and his friends and slide onto my lap and rub his fingers into my cuticles to comfort himself. All these years of attending to my son, to my marriage. I wouldn't take it back, but now it feels like someone else's life.

Today the sun is out, turning frozen puddles into slush. Birds twittering in a weird chorus. *Come, come,* they seem to say, *get a move on.* Instead of taking the bus, I walk to the museum through the park and stay on the path, guided by the cacophony of birds; underneath my boots, the rot and refuge of dying leaves. Mush. Couples stroll hand in hand, children run behind them, a few lonely women walk their dogs of all breeds and colors, one a Chihuahua dressed in a dainty sweater, more fitting for a child. Bicycle riders whisk past; one nearly knocks me over. Skateboarders. Teens with buds in their ears talking into the air. A couple pushing a baby stroller with a black mini poodle inside, its tongue hanging out. When did this become a thing? So much life. It won't last, of course, the sun eventually shifts into a dark corner. I exit the park at Fifth Avenue, and there she is. Magnificent. The slow leafing of those London plane trees on the south side of the building. The air fresh from the park. I slowly climb the museum steps. Near the top, I pause and sit down. It's too much. My husband weighs on me. How I've disappointed him. I feared for years that I was not exactly what he had bargained for. He's a man of reason. Practical. Lives in the present. I try to keep my obsessive nature under cover, not to divulge too much. Not to share my anxieties and worries. He isn't one to ask questions. To probe. To analyze. The past doesn't interest him. Occasionally, I would prod, asking about his childhood, his family, to understand him better. In a box in his closet, along with his trophies and diplomas, are a few black-and-white photos, crinkled at the edges. One with his sister and parents on a picnic table. His father looks like a kid wearing a baseball cap and holding a can of beer. I wonder what it was like for him, always having to temper his father's rage, pulling him out of fights when he was drunk, fetching him from the corner bar, comforting his mother. Once he said his father nearly killed his sister after he caught her smoking a bowl in her bedroom. I can't imagine what it must have been like. To be the sane, sturdy one during a storm. I never knew his father. He died of lung cancer before we met.

I show my membership card and, before going to the gods, remember the work of Giovanni Battista Galestruzzi, the plates he made of the myth of Cronus and Uranus. Imagine having to cut off your own father's manhood? In one plate, Cronus is castrating his father. I pull it up on my phone and ask the boy-man at the membership table where I might find it.

The Castration of Coelus (Uranus) by his son, Saturn (Cronus);
Coelus seated at left, Saturn at right, Gaea standing in the background,
after Polidoro da Caravaggio
(1640–60, Italian)

Ouch, that hurts, the boy-man says, looking at the photo. This one I don't know. Go ask at the information booth. There is a long line snaking for membership behind me. I say thank you and retire to the information station, where an attendant in a yellow cardigan set, a bit too bright for my mood, plugs the name of the piece into her computer. I'm sorry, she says. It's not on view. That is quite an image.

Uranus was afraid his sons would overthrow him and hence tried to prevent his offspring from leaving Gaea's womb, but she wanted them out. When Uranus tried to make love to her, his son Cronus castrated him with a sickle and her children spilled forth. In Greek mythology, sons and fathers are always at war. In *The Odyssey*, in the guise of Mentor, Athena tells Telemachus that it's "rare for sons to be like fathers; only a few are better, most are worse." But aren't all sons in competition with their fathers?

Is this what's going on between my husband and son? Is he subconsciously trying to arouse his father's anger by doing stupid stunts? Does he feel he has to outdo his father, to become a man? I decide to go back to the Greek and Roman galleries.

I go to the terracotta cases. Athletes running a footrace, identical in shape and stride, so that it seems as if these many athletes are all one being. My son and husband ran together in matching pants and jerseys, my husband only a few inches taller. My boy hated getting up for practice, running sprints, climbing up and down bleacher stairs, while my husband relished it, but once on the starter blocks after the pistol sounded, he flew out the gate, knees in the air like a gazelle, effortlessly leaping over hurdles, knowing when to add the speed and power. Other runners are

Terracotta Panathenaic prize amphora
(ca. 530 B.C., attributed to the Euphiletos painter)

taller, with more muscle in their stride, more determination, more frustration when they don't make their mark, but my boy has grace. For a moment, I'm dumbstruck. I see it now more clearly. My husband and son trying to beat each other. My poor husband, militant toward his boy's coming of age. Still waging war with his own father. Still trying to outrun him.

Ha. Look. A boy riding a rooster. Like my son on the playground. Always goofing around to get attention, to deflect. His third-grade teacher told me she had to look away when he performed stunts on the jungle gym. A daredevil, she called him. But he always landed on his feet. Why though? Why doesn't he

take himself more seriously? I've been so enamored with him I
hadn't noticed.

Terracotta plate
(ca. 520–510 B.C., signed by Epiktetos)

Now that he's left the comforts of boyhood and is entering the
thickets of manhood, I sense he's conflicted. He wants to do
well, find a passion, have a family, follow in his father's footsteps, but he also gets distracted, worries he won't meet his father's expectations, likes to blank out on alcohol or god knows
what, testing the limits. How long will the war persist? The
two so tangled up with each other.

I continue. Oh. How sublime. Eros, son of Aphrodite, primordial god, a child of Chaos, who blessed the union of Gaea and Uranus and the universe was born.

Bronze statue of Eros sleeping
(3rd–2nd century B.C., Greek)

In the face of this bronze baby is the sweetness of a boy's love, untouched by brutality, sleeping the sleep of boyhood like my son used to do. But this Eros, also, is intoxicated by the sheer bliss of love, the warm bath of its aftermath feeding him like a soporific drug. He's a toddler, but he's also an adolescent, but somehow also a baby. A conflation of baby sleep with postcoital sleep? Strange, a baby deemed the personification of erotic love? Because the impulse is instinctual, the way a baby reaches for his mother's breast? Or cries in a fit of obstinance? This Eros fills me with a rare burst of joy. Yes, these men and boys are all babies at the core; I'm surrounded by them, at home and at work. No wonder the world is in such a torturous, tumultuous state. They haven't learned how to square with their emotions.

Bronze statue of an aristocratic boy
(27 B.C.–A.D. 14, Roman)

All boys, boys who are not gods, boys who are mortal and fragile, look like Eros. This boy—the plaque says he resembles the young princes of the imperial family of Augustus, but he may have been the son of a member of the ruling elite or an important Roman official—has Eros's face and figure. He is excellent. And maybe it is this light, but it looks as if he has shed tears. I'm filled with pity for the sex whose members always feel they must outdo or perform, hide emotions. It's so tiresome. Or maybe his heart's been broken.

I thought you'd be here, the boy-man from the membership table says, towering over me with his big thick glasses he pushes back with one index finger. He looks like a kouros come to life with broad shoulders; the shape of the letter *V* forms from his shoulders to his hips. In this light, he looks like nobility. You usually come on Sundays, he says. Yes, I say, and nod.

After a while you get to know the regulars. There are the photobombers who stand in front of the paintings, unaware of anyone else trying to look, he says. The sleepers who find a quiet bench and sleep sitting up with their eyes closed. Artists who come to draw. See that man over there, he says, pointing to a young man with dark skin who is sitting on a small stool with a sketchbook on his lap drawing baby Eros.

And then there's me. The strange woman in the museum, I say. The boy-man at the membership table laughs. Is there something you're looking for? Something I can help you with today? he says.

We're studying *The Odyssey* in the class I teach. One of the assignments is for my students to write an essay about the relationship between Telemachus and Odysseus. I give my students essay questions that interest me, otherwise it's too boring, I say. I wonder why Homer thought that sons are rarely better than their fathers? Freud thought the dynamic between mother, father, and son to be indicative and reflective of all the passion and aggression in Western civilization. Of course, myths were at the root of his argument. It's something I've been thinking about. I have a son. He's a bit younger than you. I worry about him. The male species needs to evolve, I want to say, but I keep quiet.

Come, he says. We walk out of the entrance hall. I follow through the maze that leads us to the gallery that holds nineteenth- and twentieth-century European paintings and sculptures. I will never be able to navigate this museum. It's like a corn maze, I say to make conversation. He laughs. Here, he says.

*Oedipus and the Sphinx*
(1864, Gustave Moreau, French)

What a strange creature, with a face and torso of a woman, eagle's wings, and a lion's body. It's weirdly erotic, I say. And look, at Oedipus's feet, her victims.

Poor Oedipus, after learning he had bedded his own mother, blinded himself and was swept into the earth to become its guardian, the boy-man from the membership table says with his arms crossed against his chest. One's mother, he repeats, and shudders. Those ancient poets, he says, and shakes his head. How did they come up with these stories?

Do you think all boys fear killing their father and marrying their mother? I ask. Maybe, the boy-man says, and laughs. There were times when I wanted to kill my father. And your mother? You know the saying. About guys marrying their mothers. He pauses. Why are you worried about your son? I pause to think. Maybe because he's a riddle I haven't solved yet. Maybe mothers aren't supposed to solve their son's riddles, he says. Eighteen? He's still a kid.

I hear the voices speaking to me, I want to tell him. The chorus. In Greek drama the chorus comments on the actions of the drama. But I keep quiet. Instead, I consider the sphinx, her wings raised as if she's about to wrap them around Oedipus before he guesses the riddle. Her paws pressed against him, clawing his chest and thighs. She wants him. She won't turn away. She's not afraid. He looks at his watch. His break is over.

He walks me back to the Greek and Roman galleries, because otherwise I would not find them, and we say goodbye. Passing through the Temple of Dendur, I see the sphinx again, this time rendered in this gentle figure, the face of both male and female and the body of a lion. Guard of the temple, protector of Queen Hatshepsut, guardian of my lost twin.

Sphinx of Hatshepsut
(ca. 1479–1458 B.C., New Kingdom)

Here are the sexes, human and animal, combined in one. *Nemes* headcloth, soft face, tender eyes, dignified nose, closed lips, arms in sphinx pose. Centuries of stories, myths, in which the male holds the power, starts wars, makes something explosive happen, in which women either serve, are containers of consumption, or stand in the shadows. That painting of the sphinx clinging to the body of Oedipus. What does she want from him? To not guess the riddle? To devour him?

The chorus intervenes: *What if women no longer desire to satisfy the privileges of what the patriarch has built? They've been telling and writing the same stories for centuries. What if a new story begins with gentleness, negotiation, intuition, femininity, how would the dynamic shift? What would it look like if all along we had not been brought up to please one sex over the other? How would it level the dynamic between father and son?* I want to touch the sphinx's gentle golden paws, but I know the rules.

## APARTMENT 9B

*Hera, goddess of marriage, truest of wives. You, whose mother-milk sprayed from your breast to form the Milky Way. You who held marriage holy. For what? To turn women against each other. To hold dominion over Zeus, who is eternally unfaithful. There are desires one can't contain. They pull. Contort.* This is how it begins, with voices that come forward like a winding cord that has been knotted and no longer wishes to be constrained, eventually to be transformed, one hopes, into a piece of enchanting music. Mornings, just upon awakening, still in bed, when the noises of the ordinary world have not yet taken hold, they chirp in my mind like the earliest of birds in a sanctuary.

My husband has come out of the master bathroom, bare-chested, minty smell from the shower on his skin, white towel wrapped around his waist, like an ancient Greek with soft curls and broad shoulders, as if to announce himself in my myth-making. I'm quick to hide my notebook for fear of his condem-nation, *You're in your own world*, but he doesn't glance at me. And yet I feel linked to him, entwined. I'm sure he wishes for a different wife. More like his longtime girlfriend. In one photo, in the box he keeps on top of his closet, they're on the beach at Coney Island, and she's in a bikini. Another their college graduation. What was lacking in her that he liked about me, or vice versa. It was a puzzle I was never able to solve, why he fell in love with her, who was so different from me, and on oc-casion it crept into our marriage. I knew that she emailed or phoned him every year on his birthday, and he did on hers as well. Every year she sent a Christmas card, a photo of her and her husband and their six children all wearing the same khaki pants and polo shirts. I wonder if my husband is jealous of the husband, if he would have been happier living in a suburban house in Westchester with six children. It appears as if age has treated her well. She looks almost pretty in the latest Christ-mas card. As soon as he leaves the bedroom for the kitchen, I take out my black moleskin notepad again. *Zeus, lord of heaven and earth, do you see how she suffers? What has she done that you too have not partaken of? If she has consorts, she is not alone.*

I smell the freshness of brewed coffee and am lured toward its dark scent. I wander into the kitchen, still half in dream, pour myself a cup of its thick brew like a stimulant from the gods, put a slice of whole wheat bread in the toaster, open the refrigerator for the apricot jam. Do you mind? my husband says. I stand in the way of his ability to pour himself another cup of coffee from the coffee maker on the other side of the counter. There is only room for one of us in our galley kitchen. I take my coffee and toast to the table with the newspaper and watch him master his breakfast. He cracks two eggs sunny side up in a pan over a brush of olive oil, sprinkles pepper onto the yellow eyes so that the pan looks like a face full of freckles. Sits at the kitchen counter on a stool, away from me. I try not to look when he takes his fork and stabs the center of the eye. After he finishes, he takes his plate to the sink, grabs the sports and business sections of the paper, tucks them into his briefcase. Suited, shaven, prepared for the day. Where's the kiss he used to press on my cheek before he left? The pat on my butt? The heavy metal door of our apartment slams shut like an affront. It's been years and still no one has bothered to fix it. I go into my son's room, seeking the company of his ghostly shadows, but instead I'm confronted by my husband's computer on the bedside table luring me toward it like a jealous lover.

I open the top and it blinks on. I look at his history. Perhaps all men watch porn. This is something we have not talked about. This is something that no amount of coaxing will induce us to put into words. Fantasies are myths too and surely as powerful as reality. Why should I deprive my husband of his dreams? Of his fantasies? It would be like chaining him to my ankle. I don't want him chained to me, or me to him. Still, I shake my head. Porn. There is something ugly about it. And marriage. In ancient Greece marriage was a social responsibility, less about personal relationships and connection, at least for the upper class. Plato, in his *Laws*, said men must consider the state over their own desires. If a man was not married after thirty-five, he would be subject to fines and dishonor. Women were second-class citizens, though Plato, later criticized by Aristotle, believed—how kind of him—that women should be included in all meals. In Homer's epic, his male heroes are allowed to marry only once, by law, but are allowed concubines.

What does the Russian bride look like? Is she really my husband's virtual bride or concubine? Maybe just a peek? I go into his history, tap on the link. A small icon shows the thumbprint of her face. A strange configuration of beautiful and menacing, with big features, long wavy coils for hair. She, this creature, who is she, blinking, as if in invitation. Perhaps the Russian bride wants more from my husband than I know about. It must be nice to turn on one's email and know that a sex slave is waiting. Does she wear a negligee or panties and bra? Is she naked? What words does she say to make him come? I click on it. There's a password required to enter further into this fantasy. I close the laptop. It's too much.

## MUSEUM

I climb the steps, dodging the smokers, a woman reading, a couple of hipsters in black caps with the flap facing the back of their head, sipping their coffees, a few stragglers alone. Some who stare forlornly out onto Fifth Avenue. I enter the museum without stopping to see the boy-man at the membership table. I'm too eager. Too in want. The face of this Russian bride. Yes. That's it. With her long unruly coils, she reminds me of the face of Medusa, the woman who turned men to stone. I want to understand more about the many paradoxes of desire, of marriage, among the societies of the Greeks and Romans, the gods and goddesses. Last year there was an exhibit at the museum about only her. *Dangerous Beauty*, it was called. I remember going to see it with Leo Lazlo, the head art teacher at the academy. He is pleasant company, even though he is prone to lecturing. In the museum alone there are sixty images inspired by different interpretations of her, cameos, paintings, sculpture, a tableau on a marble floor, faces on the pillars of temples, even the logo of the fashion designer Versace. She's a hybrid of contradiction, representing erotic desire, seduction, horror, death, femininity all rolled into one being. She is also a symbol of emasculation. Medusa was the mortal among the three Gorgon sisters, and the most beautiful. Ovid mythologized her as a beautiful maiden who became a symbol of desire. Until Poseidon raped her, in the temple of Athena, and Athena turned her into a monster. But why punish Medusa and not

Poseidon? With her large head and glaring eyes and tongue, hair entwined with snakes, she became a lure and a punishment to men. Perseus beheaded her when she was asleep. In victory, he held up her head, and does so now in Gallery 548.

*Perseus with the Head of Medusa*
(1804–1806, Antonio Canova, Italian)

Oh dear lord. He's beautiful. It isn't fair. He holds out Medusa's head, neither in disgust nor in love. It's too horrible. He cut off her head! He looks so serene, too serene, after what he's conquered. I close my eyes, but it's too late. It pushes forth. I must sit down. Like Perseus, the Visiting Poet is tall, with a head of thick curly hair the color of slippery dark coffee beans. And eyes that change color depending on the light. I look up at

Perseus, holding Medusa's head with that same smile. Perseus crept up upon Medusa at night and instead of peering directly at her, out of fear of being turned to stone, looked at his shield, its mirrorlike reflection, and in his trickery swiftly lobbed off her head. Still, he could not cut off her power. It remained steadfast, strong enough that he gave the head to Athena to use on her shield as protection. I glance at his broad frame and scan the strange smile on his face, as if it is my head that he holds. I imagine my hair coiled with hissing snakes as I look into the suffering eyes of Medusa. There's that wry smile on Perseus. Why do you smile, after you've maimed her? Did you want to unfurl violence upon her because her beauty undid you? Because you could not control either her or yourself? Yes, her power remains. You can't take that away from her.

Two teenagers linking arms walk in, snap me out of my thoughts. *I hate you, I love you, I hate that I love you,* they sing, lyrics from Gnash I recognize from my students. I laugh. *Yes, I hate you, I love you,* I sing silently to myself. An aching desire to see Heracles takes hold. He's always there waiting for me, like a good friend. I see a few stragglers have stopped to admire him too. I creep around Heracles to avoid eye contact. His tight buttocks, thick and sculpted thighs.

I halt in his presence. The marble bench is cold, hard but invites me. Heracles's sinews and muscles in his legs, arms, his clenched jaw as if he's wired. If one can love a statue, then I am in love with him, the same way in which I am in love with my

Marble statue of a youthful Hercules
(A.D. 69–96, Roman)

husband for the very thing Heracles represents, his strength. He can't contain his love. I know this, but it does not make it easier to bear. Once after watching a film in which a man struck a knife into another man's throat to protect his wife, I asked my husband if he could do that. Yes, he said, if someone was threatening my family. My husband has always been my protector. I go soft when I overhear him tell our son he loves him, or pats him on the shoulder, or listen to the two of them from another room laughing over a silly movie. He's a man of few words, but he's emotional and nobody's fool. I stare into Heracles's eyes, but they remain inanimate as stone. *It is not a crime to feel. To follow your instinct. Guilt is a tremendous burden.* His eyes become animated. Are these his words, or my own? Or the chorus? I don't know the difference anymore. It is a whisper now in the gallery. So quiet I only hear my breath. We're alone together. Heracles could hold me in the cup of his hand. A wind slips under my coat, lifts my shirt. Heat rises in my chest and tickles my genitalia as if I am being kissed. Heracles's stunning, muscular chest, thick alabaster thighs, scrotum, and nub of a penis. The wind pushes against my hand. *She seeks union, solidarity.* Is it the chorus again? I look up at Heracles, but he has turned back to stone.

I'm too much in my head, "building that terrible acropolis / Of deadly thoughts." The Greeks believed solitude is dangerous. We read *Medea* in my AP English class. The boys were enraptured. *She killed her children, she killed her children, man,* Hamilton had repeated. Sometimes even Hamilton surprises me. "Great passions grow into monsters / In the dark of the mind; but if you share them with loving friends, they remain human, they can be endured," the chorus implores Medea. But whom can I trust? Whom can I talk to? Yes, thoughts turn into monsters.

The gallery now abruptly fills with people. Why are they entering my space? A gloriously tall woman wearing leggings with thighs so thin the wind slips through them, a man with a bald head and long beard—how has this become in fashion—stroking it as he peers at the statue. I look up from my folded hands and see the boy-man from the museum membership table standing over me.

I thought I'd find you here, he says. I saw you come in. I wonder what I offer, a woman in midlife still clinging to her youth wearing black jeans and boots, hair in a ponytail on top of her head and a scarf tied around her neck. I have given up the idea of weekly blow-dries. Too expensive, and I find I do not like being in costume. I take off my oversize black-framed glasses out of self-conscious modesty, rub my lips together to make sure I put on lipstick before leaving the house. My mother never left our house without her lipstick, and I have followed her instruction. I touch the corner of my eyes to make sure I removed the bed crust. This one is said to have been evacuated from one of Nero's Roman baths near the Pantheon, he tells me. I turn my eyes downward. I don't want Heracles to know we're speaking of him or that he was evacuated from the baths.

He killed his family, I say. How could he live with it? Why do you come here so often? he asks again. As if he too can see that I've turned strange. I told you. To study the history of civilization. I'm a teacher.

But why? he asks me. It's my place, I say. I like the marble steps. It calms me down, being here. I rub my lips together and brush my hair back from my forehead. Today his eyes look like the color of precious opals. I offer a half smile. And you? I ask. Is this your home now too? He nods. Today I am practicing stillness, he says. He tells me he's training to be a museum guard. He completed his first aid and CPR training and now is in the process of getting his license. Another week, he says, smiling. And then I get my promotion to guard. Well, good for you, I say. Are those the requirements? He tells me that you must be physically fit to be able to stand for a long time. He stands up tall, as if ticking off that box. Good hearing, vision, and strong sense of smell to protect the museum collections from fire. Medical training too. Did you know that a hundred thousand people a year faint in museums? This I did not know. I ask him about the art, and he tells me he's learning the entire collection. And all the exit signs.

I think it's absolutely wonderful to be a museum guard and stand before these antiquities. What made you want to become a guard? I ask. He said he grew up across the street from the museum. My mother finally threw me out, he says, laughing, so I came here. Fair enough, I say. I like the way he smells. It is musky and deep, like fresh soil in the garden. A lock of hair has fallen in front of his face. I want to push it back, and almost do, like I used to do when my son was studying at our table, but I must not. He is not my son.

Did you know Modigliani's elongated necks and almond-shaped or slit-like eyes were inspired by the busts of Egyptians he saw at the Louvre? he says. I did not know this, I say, but now that I do, I see it. I want to tell him that he looks like many Egyptian and Roman statues standing guard, but I don't want him to think I'm being fresh. I'll let you get back to work, I say.

Marble head and torso of Athena
(1st–2nd century A.D., Roman)

There she is, Athena, with her discerning, troubled gaze; I've come to imbibe her strength and wisdom before I leave. She's the goddess who appeals to Zeus to help Odysseus return home and free him from Poseidon's fury. She knows something I don't yet know. Clever goddess, she turns Odysseus into a beggar when he finally returns home to claim his home from Penelope's suitors and test her love. Warrior and wielder. I retire to the bench. It was as if he held me prisoner, like Calypso held Odysseus. I tried, but I could not escape Athena's shrewd eyes. She's trying to tell me something. I tour the gallery until I find her again. Here she is with her owl in her hand about to fly, it is sacred to her, symbolic of her wisdom. Her toes turned up are so alive. "You did your best, you tried," the chorus says, "but you are human. The heart is a riddle."

Bronze statuette of Athena flying her owl
(ca. 460 B.C., Greek)

What happened? I plead. She's strong, with her helmet flipped up on top of her head. Zeus's favorite child, born dressed in armor. Clever. *Art over life. Imagination over reality. One kind of love over another. It's not a sin, to struggle, to not yet know.*

*Mortals are weak.* She's also the goddess of time, about to release her owl and let her fly. It's not enough. I want more of her. I go to the case that holds the Greek vases. I'm convinced that if you studied all the Greek vases with their painted compositions that reflect Greek culture—there are 174 at the Met alone—you would experience the breadth of Greek and Roman civilization played out. But I do not have time. My time is running out. How long will my husband be able to bear our exile before he casts me aside?

Terracotta lekythos (oil flask)
(ca. 490–480 B.C., attributed to the Brygos painter)

This vase is terracotta with red figure. Here Athena is warrior with a spear in one hand, a helmet in the other, owl over her shoulder. The owl that sees in the dark is always on Athena's blind side so that she'll always be able to see the truth. A wash of poverty floods me. We all feel poverty at the feet of greatness. *Take on my plight*, I say. To preserve the order of mortals, Athena takes on Odysseus's. She's his patron. She holds domination. I tell my students that it is Athena who finally brings Odysseus home. That battles were fought by their predecessors. That women too held power in ancient civilizations, though mostly they were not mortals. She was not one to be toyed with. I glance back at the boy-man from the membership table. I will not bother him. He is practicing stillness.

## CLASSROOM 2B

At a far-too-early faculty meeting, chaired by Miss Hughes, the school's guidance counselor, agenda: to-dos if a student seems depressed or suicidal. A recent suicide in one of our sister schools has us on edge. A senior jumped out the window, ostensibly for failing French but of course it was deeper than that. I look out for any signs of trouble in the personal narratives they write. That poor girl. Her parents. We must do more to respond if we sense a student is struggling, I say to the faculty. Really? Mehta responds, in his holier-than-thou voice. Isn't our responsibility to the text?

It's amazing, how the relics of another era forever rear their arrogant heads. He's been teaching in my department for forty years. Looks at my breasts when he speaks to me, a strange sneer on his face. Hair greased back, troubling long Roman nose in the air. Boys, depressed? To him, depression is a female condition. I'll never forgive him and Lacy and how they gaslighted me early in my tenure at the academy. Jealousy, an unconscious fear of losing power, threatened, these are the only motives that come to mind for such unnecessary cruelty. It was just after my first book of poetry won a prize. I had been reluctant to share any news of my writing life with my colleagues out of fear they would think I was shirking my responsibilities at the academy, but once my first book was taken, I felt I could come forward. Both Lacy and Mehta were pure academics. They didn't have any knowledge or regard for contemporary poetry or even fiction for that matter. Later I found out they got a copy of my book and behind my back shared it with the dean. They took issue with my use of the persona poem in which I'd imagined the voices of girlhood. One poem, "Virgin Spring," was about the experience of losing one's virginity; another, "The Wrath," was about a young girl getting her period for the first time. They suggested that the poems were too graphic and explicit and that parents might not approve of the content and should the boys get hold of it, it might overexcite or trigger them. Thankfully, Fitz, the dean at the time, defended my work and the book, impressed by the endorsements it had received and the notices in literary journals. At the time I was in my late twenties and I looked to the senior faculty for approval. I wanted them to respect my work. It was something never spoken about between Mehta, Lacy, and me, but it hung in the air, and by being wounded, without knowing it, I had given over my power. Once the book began to get positive notices, after parents congratulated me, Mehta and Lacy did whatever they could to talk over me in meetings and demean any of my suggestions for improvement of the curriculum or my recommendations to make the department more current. When I filed a complaint with the head of school, he called me into his office and told me it was pot wash! Pot wash! I'd never heard the term before. It was dirty water to be rinsed away? A sexist term, as if I were a scrub maid? I didn't understand they'd been threatened by me somehow, that I seemed to represent someone foreign and hence not to be trusted. And I'm not sure why I felt I needed their approval. Because they had more pedigree than I had, having gone to fancy boarding schools and prestigious colleges. Because I had been raised by a hippie mother and had grown up outside the status quo that I had wanted in? Because I hadn't yet known how subconsciously I had accepted the ingrained lie. I gradually recognized that small boned and feminine women weren't always taken seriously or deemed intelligent—that one had to push through the stereotypes to prove oneself, and worse, be on guard of men who felt they could dominate and undermine by making demeaning comments cloaked in humor or playful banter. I gradually began to see that those impulses were sadistic and cruel, and my former respect turned to disdain. My opinions, my confidence, and my abilities blossomed under their dismissiveness. Why did I stay, all these years? Because of my devotion to the boys, I suppose. Because of my fear of change? Would my marriage have survived if I had pursued academic positions outside New York, where my husband's work life was fully ensconced?

Our responsibility is to teach, Mehta regurgitates, in the glib tone that makes his students want to put tacks on his chair and scrawl derogatory remarks on his classroom door. We're not babysitters. For god's sake, I wish he would retire. I can't bear his condescension. Once, after I published a poem in *The New Yorker*, he snaked into my classroom and with that same sneer said, So now it's decreed. I didn't know what he meant. It appears we have a famous poetess in our castle, he said with his nose in the air before he walked out. Was it an attempt at an apology? Or smugness? Of course, no mention was made of the poem itself.

It is our responsibility if something should happen to one of our students under our watch, Dick Phillips, head of school, says in reproach. Report any student you feel is in trouble to Miss Hughes. Mehta concedes, says that that's what he meant. That it was not his place, that it was for Miss Hughes to manage. *Manage?* Miss Hughes distributes a pamphlet of signs to watch for, and the meeting is dismissed.

After the meeting, I retire to my classroom. At my desk attempting to prepare for class, I can't let it go. I march into Mehta's classroom. You're an ass, you know. He looks up at me, bewildered, Dumbo ears pinking, and then I walk out. Why hadn't I said it before? Students thunder in, some with heavy backpacks slung over their hunched shoulders, others looking at their phones, a few still half-asleep. It's hard for them to settle. They fidget and twitch, uncomfortable in their almost-bodies-of-men not meant to conform to small desks and hard chairs. Not meant to sit all day. They talk loudly, a few gathering around Hamilton's YouTube video on his phone of god knows what until I call the class to order.

Today we're discussing duty. Agamemnon commanded Odysseus to journey to Troy to bring back his wife, Helen, who was abducted by Paris at the start of the Trojan War. Odysseus, not wanting to leave his wife and Telemachus, his newborn son, feigned madness to get out of his duty. Agamemnon said if he refused to honor his commitment, he would have his son killed. Homer pitted Odysseus's duty to his country against that to his son. Why? I ask. Nigel waves his hand as if he's flagging a cab. He's a forward on the hockey team. Poor Nigel, with a bad case of acne, and braces. I want to tell him that it will soon pass, his skin will clear, and his teeth will be beautiful. Because duty for one's nation is above the family, he says.

But isn't protecting family a duty as well? James asks. Odysseus is gone for twenty years, leaving his wife and son to suffer. His mother is alone, James says. His brilliant eyes could light a house on fire. Waiting all those years and allowing those suitors to destroy her home. In *The Odyssey*, men govern, fight wars, wield political and personal power. The epitome of a patriarchal society. Women are nymphs or handmaids, wives destined to the hearth, or so beautiful they start wars. To become a man, we rescue our fathers. Isn't that what Telemachus feels he must do? Fidel joins. If you think Odysseus is worth rescuing, Mohammed says. He's left his son for twenty years. Does that make him a hero? His coming home makes him a hero, Fidel argues. There's that line in *The Odyssey* about nothing being more delightful than when a man and woman see eye to eye and keep house. Homer believed in the family.

It's Athena who makes him a hero, James interrupts. She disguises him as an old man. It was her ploy. The women in *The Odyssey* are the heroes. Some claim that *The Odyssey* was written by a woman. Maybe Telemachus is the true hero, Mohammed says. Isn't *The Odyssey* saying that, to become a man, a boy must rescue his father to free himself of the burdens of his mother? Yeah. That's what I get out of it, Fidel says. I agree with Mohammed. Telemachus is the hero.

Hamilton's slumped in his chair, texting under his desktop. Is Odysseus a hero, Hamilton? I ask. Tyler needles him with his elbow. Hamilton quickly picks himself up, hides his phone. For seven years he's trapped on an island with a nymph who has sex with him every night. I guess you could call that heroic, he retorts. The boys howl. Ha, says Tyler, his wingman, always in Hamilton's shadow. The two came to choir rehearsal drunk and were suspended for a week. My son tells me that there is a nurse on the Upper East Side the uber rich call to attend to hangovers.

Yeah, but Odysseus weeps for home. It's one of the major themes. If he can't return home, his family will be destroyed by the suitors. Family is what keeps societies in order, says Mohammed. So then, is the nuclear family worth our investment as a society? I rise, doing my teacher thing. Or do we have to change the rules? I lean on my desk to will their attention. There's always more to consider in *The Odyssey*, an oral art passed down by bards. What looks like the crushing rule of the gods reflects our human inner turmoil.

If the nuclear family is worth saving, roles between husband and wives, between partners, must evolve along with our changing society. Marriage should be time-limited. Or, like, be renewable by both parties, like a driver's license, Nigel remarks, and then smiles proudly. He's so thin and tall, I worry that his pencil legs will collapse when he runs track. That's genius, Hamilton echoes. Yeah, Tyler agrees with a big grin. The bell rings. Go, get out of here, I say, laughing. The boys collect their notebooks and books and rush out of the classroom.

## STARBUCKS

I go to the Starbucks on Lex to hide out between third and fourth period. I'm checking the final proofs of *The Rape of the Swan* in one of the lounge chairs in the corner, sipping a cup of chai latte, admiring the old-style Le Jeune font. In the fourth crown of sonnets, the interloper lurks in the grasses, the female swan protecting her eggs. She stretches her neck toward him, fans her wings, liking the attention. My face prickles, at my own words and what they signal, by my attempt to locate thought, by the insular nature of my investigation. I read that if a swan's mate dies, she or he too could die of a broken heart. My desire was to locate the depth of this natural attachment. When swans fuck, the male swan gets on top of the female, rides her, nips at her neck, his webbed feet at her torso, pushes her face underwater, nibbles further at her neck, and then a long calm ensues, a purring noise like the sound of a whimpering child. I witnessed it several times on my walks around the lake in the park. My face warms in memory of what I've sought to immortalize. I've quarreled with myself, misjudged myself hundreds of times during the hundreds of drafts. A writer is not always the best judge of her own work. Familiarity blinds. Annie on her potter's wheel in the academy's basement. First, she makes a hole in the middle of the mound of clay, then pulls and extends the walls into the shape she wants, whether a vase or a cylinder. Sometimes it wobbles, sinks, and caves. Other times it forms almost silk-like in her hands. I've watched her pull up what looks like perfection, and then smash it down like a pancake on the wheel in her attempts to master the shape. I look at my pages again. At the beautiful, brilliant font and the tiny ornament between sections, and as I read my words, I remember the shifts and turns each poem took, thought swirling like a snake in the grass. A few more weeks and it will be bound. And reviewed in *The New York Times! Please, please don't let it be Pynyon.* He eats women poets for breakfast. I pick up my latte cup and notice the logo. It's supposed to be a Siren, but it strikes me now as the head of Medusa. Why hadn't I noticed before? Maybe it's a bad sign. It's always there in the back of my mind, this feeling that something ruinous is about to happen. I look at my watch. I'm late. I take my coffee and head back to school.

I teach three more classes, chaperone two study halls throughout the rest of the day. I stay late in my classroom reading and taking notes. The sky from my window darkens. It always depresses me, as if all energy fades with it. It's nearly five and I wish only for another day to pass. For some signal to direct me. I go into my drawer, take out the box with the onyx black-swan charm the Visiting Poet gave me before he returned home to Ohio, and I release it from its white pillow of cotton. Was it all a dream? I gather my books, turn out my classroom light. In the lobby, I bump into Miss Reynolds with her brown paper bag, the top folded over in her hand, where she carries her extra sandwich, banana, and cookie she takes from the cafeteria for her dinner each night. Sometimes Miss Wallace gives her an extra cup of hot soup in a paper to-go cup. Once I saw her take a few rolls of toilet paper from underneath the sink in the bathroom and put it in her tote bag. She lives in a studio apartment she's had for fifty years. I wondered why she had to steal toilet paper, until one day she told me that her ill sister, Agnes, lives with her too. Something about a breakdown when she was in her thirties. She can no longer work. For Christmas, Miss Reynolds was my secret Santa. I bought her two scarves: one for her and one for her sister. We invite both to our Thanksgiving dinner every year.

Miss Reynolds is always the last one to leave the building. You're here late, she says. Grades are due next week, I remind her. I ask about her sister. She's the same, thank you for asking, dear, she says. She asks me about my son. My husband. All is quiet on the western front, I reply. She asks if I've spoken to the Visiting Poet since he left. What a fine fellow. You must miss him. The two of you became so close, she says. A tremor trills through my body. Excuse me, Miss Reynolds. I've forgotten a book I need. I tell her I'll lock up. And then I nearly sprint up the stairs, three flights to my classroom, out of breath.

I turn on the light and sit at my desk. He's everywhere I look. Hovered on this desk. Lumbering in the halls. On my desk is the volcanic desert rock with its hues of purples and reds, and little hints of white and crystal he gave me at the conference in Taos. I use it as a paperweight. I pick it up, look at it, feel its edges, like rock candy you could chip a tooth on, and the memory rushes forth like water letting out from a stopped-up dam.

## TAOS

I was invited to a poetry conference in Taos, New Mexico. It was December, three months after the Visiting Poet had begun his yearlong stint. My husband and son were going to a track-and-field competition that weekend in Albany, so I was free to go. The Visiting Poet was also invited to attend.

At the conference hundreds of other poets and writers congregated, like salespeople touting their chapbooks and slim volumes, even though we could expect to sell only a handful of books. How pathetic, the lack of an audience for poetry beyond the teachers and professor-poets. The Visiting Poet and I laughed about it. Douglas Crane is giving the keynote, he said. When isn't he giving the keynote? And Hugh Pynyon, I said. Will he be invited? Doubt he'd show, the Visiting Poet quipped. He keeps a low profile. So he doesn't have to come face-to-face with anyone he's trashed? He's an equal-opportunity hater, I said, and laughed. That's what one of my poet friends from grad school calls him. He decimated every one of her books. He's not so bad, the Visiting Poet said. He tells me that Pynyon was a visiting professor for a semester when he was in grad school. That he was supportive of his work. They're pals. They played poker every week with a bunch of other guys. I bet you got drunk and dished women, I said, rolling my eyes. He looked at me and smiled. Yeah, I thought so, I said. Do you like his poems? I asked. Not for me to judge, he responded with a grin.

The Ramada was old and drab. Outside our doors, plastic chairs to sit in the sun. Coffee from machines. At this conference, unlike in the rest of the universe, poetry was flourishing. The shabby bar where the lectures, presentations, and panels were presented was dark and smelled like beer and cigarettes. We ventured outside to take our break. My eyes hurt from the brightness. At night, a country band played. There was dancing. The wine terrible, the margarita too sweet, and still we imbibed.

We sat at the same table at meals, took afternoon walks through the brush and cactus, jaunts into town where in the shops turquoise and beaded jewelry were under glass and I helped the Visiting Poet pick out a birthday present for his wife. On one of our walks, he told me that she volunteers at the town library and nature center where they live. She's a composer. They met at an artist residence. She complains she no longer has time for it, now that the girls have been born, but it isn't that. She's lost interest. She's lost her ambition. And she resents me for it. She's not thrilled that I've taken the position this year at the Academy. She doesn't understand that the epicenter of our world is in New York City. That it's good that I'm here. For us. For my career. To get out of fucking Ohio. Epicenter, I said, with a bit of a laugh. Well, my editor's there, he said. And there's you. We spoke about monogamy, problems with our children, gossiped about certain poets at the conference. Then he asked me what one word I would use to describe my marriage. It was terribly hot in the desert. My mouth parched, lips dry, the sun, with nowhere to hide, seemed to penetrate even my sunglasses. I thought for a moment, my hand over my eyes to blind the rays and further protect myself. He was being provocative, but I enjoyed the game. Sublime, ecstatic, erotic,

I laughed. Come on, seriously, he said. And then I asked him what his word would be.

Oppressive, he said. It sounds like a cliché, but really, when you think about it, marriage is nothing more than a shifting exchange of trade-offs, he said, looking at the dry and dusty ground, and then up at me with intensity. His white linen shirt drenched with sweat, his cheeks red with the heat, his purplish-blue eyes like the color of a bruise, catching the light.

I told him I thought there was more to it. To have someone who cares about your well-being. Who's there for you. And yes, there are practical considerations. Duties. That if it's going to work it has to be a team effort. The dust was everywhere, in my eyes, my nose, my throat, there was nowhere to escape it. My damp cotton dress stuck to my body. My thighs were dripping with sweat. I don't know why I was arguing for marriage's virtues when I felt so unhappy then. It was after our son had recovered from getting sideswiped and my husband and I seemed never to be on the same page about even the simplest of things, like whether one of us had to be home late and who was making dinner. It seemed I was always in the doghouse. Late from class. Nothing to eat in the fridge. My mind drifting. In my own world, yes. But wasn't that inner world worth fighting for? To wall off from the rest of the world in order to create. To be who we are meant to be. To become ourselves fully. Isn't that the only way to some form of Elysium, not in the afterlife, but in the present? Yes, I'm selfish when it comes to my work. But isn't my husband?

What does the scientist say? he asked. Does he mind that you go away, alone to conferences to taunt the rest of us? No, I said. I suddenly felt protective of my husband. Why should he? He goes away to conferences too. Why should there be a difference? It's too hot outside, I said, and ventured into one of the gift shops and left him on the sidewalk.

When I left the gift shop, he was coming out of another shop. He unveiled a sparkling volcanic rock with jagged edges from a brown paper bag. He said it contained seven minerals. One of the minerals gave off flames of fire. Another, amethyst, contained dangerous beauty that would be absorbed to the field of the user. One would tap into passion. Another held creative energy. I held the rock in my hand, the minerals like stars in a dark sky, and warmth radiated. It's for you, he said. I'm sorry for being a jerk before.

You're forgiven, I said. Marriage is hard. It takes negotiation, respect. But there's dignity to it. To commit to someone above anyone else, to pursue common goals and a common lifestyle. Of course, at times, it can be deafening, but isn't loneliness more so? You're generous, he said. You really do believe in goodness. I'm not sure. We're a miserable society, I said, surprising myself. In general, I've found people to be disappointing.

But you're good at heart, he said, his hands in his pockets. Am I? I'm not so sure, I said. I didn't feel that I was good. I was always disappointing my husband. And I found that my tolerance for some of my colleagues was waning. I had to stop myself from rolling my eyes in faculty meetings. I wanted more. Yes, more recognition for my work, my accomplishments. I was restless. Angry. On edge. But I was a good mother, a good wife, friend, at least I thought so. I had wandered slightly off the path, turned my ankle on a rock, and he pulled me back. I shook my head at my clumsiness, and we laughed.

Back from our walk, drenched from the hot sun, we said goodbye and headed to our separate rooms before dinner. I peeled off my clothes and lay on the lumpy bed. The desert sand had made its way into the roots of my hair, pooled into the pillow. I felt sand between my toes and stuck to my armpits. The air conditioner spewed out hot, dusty air. I looked at the rock on the room's desk and its sparkling minerals radiating, almost vibrating with strange energy.

My phone buzzed. It was my husband. *All good over there?* he texted. *We just arrived at the hotel. Hope your accommodations are better than ours. No such luck,* I texted back.

I remember feeling guilty that for that entire day, so absorbed in catching up over coffee with other friends from graduate school, attending panels and readings, I had forgotten about them. I read from the first crown of sonnets from my manuscript of *The Rape of the Swan* with two other poets and afterward was flooded with attention. The Visiting Poet had stood in the back of the room while I read with his arms crossed over his chest and a smug sort of self-satisfied look of ownership on his face. I felt more myself than I had in a long time.

The last ones at the bar that night, the Visiting Poet and I walked back to my shabby room at the hotel. We stood outside and smoked a cigarette together. And then he took out a spliff. He said he subscribes to medical marijuana for his sciatica. Though I was never a pot smoker, I took it from him, pressed the soggy spliff to my lips. He took it back, sucked it while gazing into my eyes, and grinned. I grinned back. What was I doing? I said good night, lightheaded from the pot, still buzzing from the excitement of my reading, and ventured into the dark, damp, and moldy room with the moist gray carpet. After I closed the door, I intuited him waiting outside it, or maybe I'd imagined the heat of his body against it. His breath. His broad stature. I was so high, I sank down on the thin mattress to contain myself. The springs screeched and cried out like the Harpies. The hotel room was spinning. The guest chair in the corner, a depressing brown thing, shape-shifted into some kind of demon as I looked at it. Coyotes howled in the brush. Creeped out, I rose and opened the door for some much-needed air. The Visiting Poet was smoking a cigarette, waiting, quietly, steadily, as if he expected me. I told him about the coyotes and the strange demonic shapes, and invited him in.

We lay down side by side on my bed. I was dizzy from the combination of alcohol and cannabis, the oppressive heat. It's hot as fuck, the Visiting Poet said, and we laughed. I knew I should not have a man in my bed, but we're friends. We teach together. And I didn't want to be alone in a strange hotel room. I pointed to a spiderweb in the corner of the ceiling, the spider dangling from a thread, and we laughed again, and that's the last thing I remember before I fell into a deep sleep. Sometime into the night I felt his body touching mine and I was aroused. I turned over, looked at him, and he kissed me. It didn't feel wrong, I don't know why, but I convinced myself that I was entitled— it was just kissing. I hadn't quite known that platonic, affectionate friendship could take on an aspect of greediness. We kissed some more, and then he lurched over me. I thought he was going to bang his head on the thin headboard, and gently he pushed back and curled himself behind me, his trunk-like legs dangling over the queen-size bed, and then, exhausted, we slept again until the sun came up and he crept out of my room.

After he left, I couldn't go back to sleep. My clothes smelled like marijuana, and the low ceiling with its water-stained linoleum tiles was oppressive. My lips and cheeks burned. I felt strangely not myself. I had enjoyed kissing him, and liking it made me uncomfortable and uncertain. I didn't want to get out of bed. I didn't want to return home. I didn't know myself anymore. It was so hot and just seven in the morning. I couldn't breathe; still, I wanted to stay in that damp hotel room and to not think about anything more. The room was spinning, I was nauseous, and then it all surged forth. I stumbled into the bathroom, vomited into the stained toilet bowl. Just that one time, I told myself, afterward, looking at my face in the distorted mirror. I was always a good girl, too good, compensating for my mother. Her sexuality overwhelmed our home. Her suitors coming in and out, staring at me when I developed breasts and a figure. It frightened and disgusted me, to be looked at in that way by men two decades or more older than me, men my mother desired. Wasn't I allowed to be bad for once?

Though we took the same cab to the airport, we didn't speak about it, only words about our travel. If we spoke, then what happened had happened. It was like a private code. All through the flight home, though we didn't sit together, he was with me when I closed my eyes. I felt his long breathing in my ear, like a tick squirreling in deeper, and my skin prickled. He'd invaded my being.

I hold the slippery fine-grained rock in my hand with its clasts of other rocks melded together; the bedecked crystals give off demonic energy. I'm seated at my desk. It's a few minutes after seven o'clock. I should have texted my husband that I'd be late. I lay my head down on top of my crossed arms. I don't want to get up to go. It was a kind of strange death, giving in to the will in his impervious eyes the color of dark berries, his scent, his touch, his increasing demands for my attention. Yes, his demands. Sitting in that lawn chair outside my door, waiting for me. Always by my side at the readings. And the drinks afterward. It's all coming back to me, even as I try to shut it out. Aggressive emotions, untamed ambitions, sexual advances— it is not as if they are evil itself, but an inclination. But once unleashed, harder to restrain. Is desiring someone else when betrothed to another evil? Untamed desire, is that also evil? Gods, answer me. I pick up my head and hold the rock's jagged edges. *Don't berate yourself. You're human, you're not one of the divine.* The chorus again. There are moments when reason fails, when pleasure reads like self-hate. I should have protected myself, stayed shored within marriage's mysterious island.

## MUSEUM NIGHTS

The sky is dark. It is emptiness incarnate. Not one star. No moon. On my shoulder, the satchel I carry, heavy. Inside, the foul matter (as the publisher calls it)—my original manuscript, the copyedited version, the marked-up page proofs offered back to me by the publisher now that the book has been printed and the publication inching forward. An exploration of motherhood, monogamy, and survival mirrored through the lens of two swans I observed for two years in the lake in Central Park. When it was cold and wintry, they ducked into the water and then rose into the silvery air, one reaching out his wing and covering the other in bondage. In summer, they whistled with their necks stretching into the sun, the lake black against their frilly bodies. The musty, dewy smell of grass. When the pen sat on her nest to protect her eggs, her cob hissed to fend off other waterbirds. I rewrote the ending the last weeks before the final pass was due to the printer, just after the Visiting Poet had returned to Ohio. There was no magical scarf like the one given to Odysseus when Poseidon waged war, to throw into the sea to keep me afloat. No prize in remaining timid. Only words to exorcise.

I instantly hate it. My book. It's like a teeming thing. With a mind of its own. A two-headed monster. A hissing snake. I take out the envelope to toss it, all those pages I've read hundreds of times, in the garbage can overflowing with empty bottles, leftover sandwiches, random trash, and then I succumb to reason, place the foul matter (a fitting term) inside its envelope back into my satchel.

It's getting late, but it's Thursday and the museum's open until nine. It's my favorite time, when crowds are thin. I should go home, but I can't. I have come here tonight for a reason. I miss my husband, but I no longer understand what's become of us. I'm tired carrying my heavy satchel from school up Madison and then onto Fifth, but I persist. I know I'll find the answers if I don't give up. I climb the thirty-two stairs, counting to calm my nerves. Inside the foyer, tall pillars, high sturdy ceilings, as if Atlas is holding it all, everything made of marble and stone. A gigantic statue of Athena in the great hall assaults the passersby; she weighs three tons and is ten feet tall, so you have to crane your neck to see into her eyes. She's wearing a helmet with a shield down her back and a long robe tied around the waist. *Be careful*, she says as I pass by. Why is she instructing me? What is she afraid I'm going to do? I want to scream to hear my echo. To hear my voice, but I refrain. An idyllic palace, idealism incarnate, as youthful as adolescence.

The boy-man at the membership table in white shirt and dark jeans gives me a big smile, his teeth white against his skin, beneath his glasses, luminescent turquoise eyes, one of which I now notice has a freckle in its iris. I am interested in knowing more about this young man, what his plans are for the future. I wonder what my son will do. What profession he will take up. Who will he become? For now, I am content to receive the boy-man's youthful smile, flip of a raised chin.

I proceed to the Temple of Dendur. On my way, I pass a statue of a striding man directly outside the temple in the Egyptian wing. A striding man? *To stride* means to walk with long, decisive steps, someone who has made progress, reached his stride. Where is the striding woman?

Statuette of a striding man
(ca. 1919–1878 B.C., Middle Kingdom)

Broad shoulders, narrow waist, muscular and purposeful limbs of an athlete, refined eyes and mouth. Bemused. The look of a man one trusts, just, moral, puts one foot in front of the other. A gleaming spark in his half smile. He reminds me of my husband. There is a young woman with long red hair dripping down her back, wearing all black, seated on a stool with a sketch pad on her lap, bringing him to life with her pencil.

The museum plaque:

> The impression of utter perfection conveyed by the small image is based on its even proportions and the balance between the forward movement of the left leg and the slight upward lift of the head. With these formal qualities, an attitude of equilibrium is expressed, which ancient Egyptians considered ideal human behavior. "Patience is a man's monument, quietness is excellent, calmness is good." These and many similar admonitions were taught to the aspiring member of ancient Egypt's elite.

I desired to marry a man of ideal human behavior, even if rough around the edges. I looked for him in each boy-man I went out with and found him, to my surprise, in the guise of my husband. Did these ideals and expectations morph from this ancient civilization? We met at party where I went with my roommate to husband-hunt. That is what me and my

roommate called it, late Saturday afternoons when we were in
our SRO wrapped under a blanket, watching a movie like *Love
in the Afternoon* in sweaters and leggings, admiring Audrey
Hepburn's dark hair wrapped like a crown of femininity on top
of her head. Sometimes one of us had to convince the other to
go out to a party or club, hoping we might meet someone (this
was before dating apps!). Our biological clocks ticking, longing
for a steady partner, children. Tired of parties, always the same
losers on the make, the same conversations about who was getting published, or getting laid, the petty gossiping, tired of our
lonely Bohemian poverty, we longed to begin a REAL LIFE. It
wasn't husbands per se we wanted, for then we did not know
what to be husbanded meant. *Husband* is also a British word
for manager, the archaic definition "a prudent or frugal manager." We did not want managers; we'd had enough of them at
our institutions. We were tired of our own self-centered exis-
tence. This party was different; it was at the home of one of our
colleagues. His wife had completed med school, so the party-
goers were unlike those we usually trafficked in, artists, poets,
writers, who in the male version were for the most part gay
or career- and self-obsessed, which left the need for a partner
negligible in comparison.

For a year I wasted my time dating an uninteresting yet
good-looking history teacher. At dinner when he delivered a
dissertation on Stalin and the repercussions of his regime, my
eyes glazed over and I had to call myself to attention. Though
he was handsome, his smile revealed his upper teeth, two

bicuspids next to incisors shaped like spikes, while his lower teeth were tiny in comparison. I did not inquire about why his lower teeth looked like baby teeth, but his smile made me uncomfortable. What did I see in him? He drove an old blue Alfa Romeo convertible and once took me out of the city for a ride. It must have been the convertible that convinced me that he was worth holding out for. In my delusion, I pictured in my future long windswept drives through the countryside, stops at flower markets and cafés, walks in unnamed gardens. After I slept with the history teacher, who was less passionate than I had hoped, he confided that he was in love with someone else who wouldn't have him. I convinced myself that he thought he was in love with this person because he feared intimacy, only to discover a year later, still dating this man, who bored me, who was always sulking, that I was wrong.

My husband, who was not yet my husband, was sheathed modestly, jeans, Timberland boots—it was winter—and black turtleneck. It turned out he was not in love with someone else. I liked my husband's warm eyes and sincere smile, not a smile that is in love with itself, or a smile with spikes and baby teeth, but a smile that mirrored a delight in what he was seeing, like a radiant cone of light drawing you to its source. The scar along the curve of his left cheekbone manifested in a vulnerable stalwart countenance and made me want to touch it, but I refrained. My husband who was not yet my husband said he had never met a poet before, and somehow the fact that I was a poet delighted him. He tried to impress me by telling me he got A's in English in high school and that he used to take his elderly English teacher to the theater because she did not have a driver's license. I decided that I liked this person who confessed to good grades in high school and was chaperone to his English teacher. He had finished medical school and was beginning a fellowship in infectious diseases. I asked him about the origins of the Hippocratic Oath, because upon meeting him, I connected it to ancient Greece and one of Hippocrates's essays was part of the syllabus of a course I sometimes taught. He said the oath was thought to be written by Hippocrates, but it could have been written by one of his students. The gist of it is to act ethically and morally. I think there are like twelve different aspects to swear by. The first is to swear by Apollo. Ah, I said, the god of healing. So did you swear by Apollo when you got your diploma? He smiled and said, Are you really interested? I nodded, because I was, finally, and that was the beginning. I decided I liked this man instantly. He was a master of ethics and morality, a healer, and I was a poet of the ephemeral, and a teacher, and for a while, in our unknowing, it was bliss.

Women in ancient Egypt were only considered to be women once they had a child. I too wanted a child when I met the striding man who was not yet my husband. He had further elicited a surplus of oxytocin in my brain that triggered my desire. I longed to abandon my adolescence (even though I was in my twenties) and be dipped, as it were, in the ancient sea and become a woman.

I did not know how I felt about marriage, whether I ultimately believed in the institution, raised in an era when so many marriages of my mother's generation were breaking up, when male and female roles were clearly defined, and women suffered over loss of identity. My mother found herself desperate after my father left and she had me to raise on her own because she could not make an adequate living trading in retail and selling decoupage boxes at street fairs. She kept waiting for a new man to fill in, but he never came. In graduate school, my teachers—two married poets with a small child, they seemed the perfect union—broke up over one's fling with a student. Many of my mother's friends divorced because their husbands fell in love with younger women, and they were abandoned without having made their own livelihoods. And in the marriages that lasted, it seemed as if the women were living in wallpapered prison cells. Marriage did not seem to be the answer. I was looking for someone to share my life, to have a family, a home, whatever that meant. I respected my not-yet-husband's vocation. A man who believes in ethics and in healing others. Who would not want such a man of high moral distinction and goodness? We made an ideal partnership, we told ourselves then. I will educate and create, and he will heal the broken. That was what I was like then: I believed in purity, goodness, loyalty; I was naïve in my innocence. We were in love and hastily took up nesting like my swans.

The museum is oddly quiet tonight. Or maybe visitors have flocked to the exhibitions. This time of evening there are few children, more grown-ups with arms linked strolling the gallery. I wander away from the striding man into the temple. The sphinx, with the head of woman and the body of a lion, greets me as I enter. God and guardian, male and female, prominent cheekbones, flawless nose, almond-shaped eyes, cascading headdress. My mind and body quiet. No matter how crowded, there is always space in this vast gallery to breathe. Outside the windowed wall, with its pattern of small rectangular glass as if to mimic a pyramid, the light has faded.

Sphinx of Hatshepsut, detail

The Temple of Dendur
(completed by 10 B.C., Roman period)

Dark purple hues color the view from the open windows that face the walkway to Central Park. Images of my son's previous selves float like ghosts in and out of the temple. Its base holds representations of the lily pads and papyrus that grew along the marshes of the Nile. The temple was built just after the Romans conquered Egypt. Wars were fought. Sacrifices made, laws broken. The rituals of marriage and childbirth performed. As I enter its clay walls, the temple becomes more real and less artificial. I am greeted by the priestess.

God's Wife Tagerem, daughter of the priest Imhotep
(ca. 300–250 B.C., Ptolemaic period)

She is not immediately apparent; you cannot see her until you walk through the walls of the temple. She is enclosed in glass, and light shines like a halo over her divinity. She "embodies the perfected ideal of the female form attained in the early part of the Egyptian Ptolemaic period." Her legs long, shapely under her see-through gown, her belly soft, round, waist narrow, arms proportioned to her body. Who would not want such loveliness?

Commissioned by Emperor Augustus of Rome, the temple was built by Petronius, the Roman governor of Egypt, around

15 B.C., and dedicated to two deified sons of a Nubian ruler, and to the divine king Osiris and his sister, Isis, whom he later married and who was worshipped as the ideal mother and wife. An ideal mother and wife in earliest civilizations sacrificed her own intellectual, political, and artistic potential to reside solely in the home, and hence, without her own independent financial means, she was at the mercy of the patriarch. I am not an ideal wife or mother in the Egyptian sense, nor did I ever want to be. To take care of oneself, to be mistress of the self, is the only way to be free in any relationship. My husband too wanted a partner and not a domestic servant. We were each content to attend to our own vocations to provide the means for our family, and both of us wanted to bring forth children. On one of the walls leading to the temple is a marriage contract made out of papyrus.

Marriage Contract
(380–342 B.C., late period)

It dates back to the thirtieth dynasty and is written in Demotic, an Egyptian script. In ancient Egypt, there were no religious ceremonies for marriage. The families worked together to arrange the marriage and establish the bride's price, and the

groom's family offered gifts to the bride. Infidelity was considered taboo, especially for a woman because the bloodline
was passed through her. In one recorded government case, a
woman was put on a stake outside her home and burned to
death for besmirching her home. In another she was cast off in
the river to drown.

We have our own marriage contract stored in a drawer with
other personal documents. It is written in light blue and gold
ink and bears our signatures, signed in a state of devotion and
bliss before our wedding ceremony. Signing it, I understood
that my beloved belongs to me and I belong to my beloved, and
that the contract was sacred. Stability, loyalty, love, kindness,
equality. It is not something to venture into lightly. We do not
hang such a document on our walls. It is personal. It is not a
work of art to be displayed. I sit down on the bench to steady
myself.

I go to the dark waters of the Nile surrounding the Temple
of Dendur. I take a penny from my purse, throw it into the
waters, and make a wish that I might not burn or wander and
become water whose course is unknown. It is only now that I'm
beginning to feel the repercussions I've tried to push away. I
drop in another penny, this one to wish for the safety of my son
and to pray for my daughter's soul. Children were considered a
blessing in ancient Egypt. They were called "the staff of old age"
because they took care of their parents in return for birthing
and caring for them.

One of the oldest known medical papyri in ancient Egypt records practices the Egyptians undertook to determine fertility. To predict fertility, a woman was to moisten barley seeds with her urine every day. If the seeds grew, she would bear a child. I imagine these women, watering the seeds with their waste, praying for a seed to sprout. Such was the hope for a child.

I became pregnant a year into our marriage; we hadn't planned it, and hence we deemed it *bashert*, our destiny. Ten weeks later I began to cramp. Black blood clotted in my panties. The cramps, extracting tissue in my blood, grew more severe. I hid in our living room, curled into the sofa. My cheek retained the print of the sofa's tapestry pillow. There were more miscarriages. In ancient Egypt, miscarriages were thought to be the fault of the woman's body. She either lifted too much or didn't eat enough or had a fainting spell. In the modern world, a miscarriage is deemed *unviable*, another word I do not like, a word that caused distress when it was repeated by my obstetrician. Unviable. As if my body didn't want it. As if it didn't want me. As if it were destined. Would my husband stay with me if I could not give him a child? He never said it, but I couldn't blame him. I knew he wanted children. This dread became my shadow. I who only thought marriage was for childrearing.

After each miscarriage, I came here, to the temple to mourn and pray. In Japan, they have cemeteries for babies who have died from miscarriage. This was my cemetery. I look into the black waters, the pennies at the bottom that represent so many wishes and lost desires.

I sit at the edge of the pool facing the temple. Each brick is meticulously wedded to the one before it and behind it. The temple walls are inscribed with images of kings making offerings to deities by performing everyday rituals such as bathing and eating, pouring milk, and burning incense. Rituals of family life that were said to keep the kingdom in order and allow people, while in the temple, to be closer to the gods. There is something to be said for rituals, to organize life and society, to share in duties as a means to ward off lack of power, laziness, despair. Suffering. Perhaps in the modern world we ask too much of marriage. A friend says that every now and then, when at odds with her partner and in doubt about whether her marriage will prevail, she goes to open houses in Brooklyn. She says it comforts her to know that there's a way out.

The Temple of Dendur, detail: Augustus (*right*) offers jars of wine to the deities Harendotes (*center*) and Hathor (*left*)

The temple's terrace overlooked the Nile. I like wandering inside, gazing at the intricate Egyptian hieroglyphic writing, which contains something like a thousand different characters. Language as symbol. Inside the enclosure, I'm reminded of the biblical stories. They come to life here amid the reeds and the clay walls and the beautiful priestess behind glass. The story of Pharaoh (as he is called in Exodus), who was threatened by the Israelites and so made them all slaves and decreed that baby boys must be murdered at birth. And the story of baby Moses and his mother, Jochebed, who put him in a basket in the tall grasses among the papyrus growing along the Nile to save him. Jochebed watched from the long reeds as the basket with her baby drifted in the current. To hear her baby cry without being able to soothe him must have been torture. Pharaoh's daughter, coming for a swim, seized him from the basket and took him in to raise him as her adopted son. Baby Moses would not be nursed by any of the Egyptian maids-in-waiting, so Miriam, Moses's older sister, asked Pharaoh's daughter if she might procure a Jewish nurse for the baby. Pharaoh's daughter agreed, and Miriam brought her own mother to act as Moses's nurse. Sometimes love is rewarded in the small act of being able to nurse one's own child. I move out of the temple and sit down on the corner of the Nile. A few couples stroll in and out of the temple, but so close to nine o'clock, it is almost empty. *Don't weep, you can't control destiny*, says the chorus. I don't want to hear it. To remember.

*The ghost of one's earlier life, can it ever disappear?*

Remembering is painful. Loss blinds the light. My body aches with it. Mostly I tried to steel against it, with a new baby to care for, to feed, diaper, to slurp little spoonfuls of tasteless oatmeal in his mouth, one cannot dwell. Most couples would not have survived it, my obstetrician later told me. I stare into the dark water. My son was born first, brought in a basket floating down the Nile of our desire. When we saw him for the first time, we couldn't believe he was real—that is how far out our longing had taken us until the basket reached us. The two of us had grown to live so close to disappointment that when beauty awoke us we couldn't see it right away. Twenty-eight minutes later, I began to push again. Our baby girl. So beautiful covered in a sheen of blood and mucus. I looked at my husband, his wet eyes gleamed. But before we could hold her, she was whisked away from us and taken to the ICU. Minutes passed in agony while we marveled at our baby son with his soft plump skin and almond-shaped eyes. This is what binds us. This is where we became one. My obstetrician came back into the room with a grim expression. Our daughter was having trouble breathing, every part of her little body hooked up to machines. For one full day she was ours. Within the next twenty-four hours, I held her fingers, kissed her head, I couldn't take my eyes off of how perfect she was. I watched her tiny chest puff up and down, the liquid moving through an IV into her veins, studied the heart monitor, praying. What happened is worthy of a Greek tragedy. Imagine, unable to breathe oxygen to sustain life. Could one day be a lifetime? We must share our boy's miraculous arrival with our grief over the loss of our baby girl.

I don't know why or by whom we were being punished. It is God's wish, the rabbi expounded in synagogue when the rivers parted, or Abraham was forced to sacrifice his child. It is because you are strong and can handle it, my mother said to console me. I did not want to be strong.

I perch on the slate edge of the pool made to mirror the Nile. I'm still angry. I look at the temple, pale yellow in its glow. In ancient Egypt yellow represents what is indestructible, eternal, the color of the sun, color of gold. The sun dies and is reborn each day. Deep into the pool of water pennies tossed out of regret, sorrow, desire. I take another penny from my purse, close my eyes, and make a wish.

The skin on my hands is dry, cracked from wringing them. In the water's reflection I see my slacks skating down my hips. I run my fingers through my hair; a few strands come loose in my hand. I've lost my breath and can't calm down. I don't know what is happening. Breathe, breathe. *Regardless of how we try to thwart it, truth pushes against us. It is our ghost. The ghost of one's earlier life, can it ever disappear?* I don't want to remember, but now that it's there, I can't push it back. I was on bed rest for the last few months of my pregnancy. I was supposed to leave the couch only to go to the bathroom. I was thirty-six weeks along, and I couldn't take it anymore. It was summer. The air coming through the open window intoxicating. My husband was at the lab. All I wanted was to take a short walk, pick up a corn muffin, come back home, bathe in the fresh air. It would

be like going to the doctor's office for a checkup. How could
that short time make a difference? I held the bottom of my
abdomen to protect my womb as I walked. Birds were chirp-
ing, it was August, a wash of flowers in the beds beneath the
trees on the sidewalk, and it seemed a sublime time to soon give
birth. After being shut away in a studio apartment with only
one window facing west, I felt as if the sun were blooming on
my face, my skin. The corn muffin tasted better than any muffin I'd ever tasted. The next morning, I woke up and got out of
bed and my water broke, gushing down my leg. I thought, it's
time, the twins are coming, but quickly fear won out. In the
cab, my husband clasped my hand. At the hospital my obstetrician was reluctant to deliver the babies, it was too early, he was
concerned their lungs had not fully developed. He said that
the amniotic fluid replaces itself, that two days, even one, could
make a difference. At night in the hospital, when my husband
had left to sleep, I knew something was wrong. I was still leaking fluids. Another two days passed this way as I lay in the hospital bed watching soap operas to drown my fears. Was it my
fault? Taking that walk. I asked every doctor, nurse, resident
who came to examine me. They all said it could have happened
regardless. Even going to the bathroom or lying down, especially with twins, could have started the process, that I wasn't
to blame, but I didn't believe it. My uterus crushed my baby's
lungs. No wonder my husband holds me in disdain. If I still
feel the loss, the grief and shadow life, so does he. I'm sure of it.
I killed his baby girl. No wonder I am vile. Hate myself. I can't
change what happened, nor can he. I would blame myself too,

if I were him. I sit on the edge of the Nile looking into its deep, black waters. I look at the temple and console myself with the ancient Egyptian belief in the survival of the soul after death. There's more coming. I feel it. I don't know what it is, but I know that every act has a consequence. The gods don't let us off lightly. And I know this too, suddenly, here in the temple, surrounded by the hieroglyphics, the rituals of family, society, that even if I've been cast aside, bewitched, that all I've ever wanted was a family to behold.

## WEEK 8

I awake to find a bouquet of red tulips in a vase on the kitchen counter. Yesterday I baked a lasagna for him. I left it on the counter like a love note. I made the lasagna the way he likes it, with crispy cheese on top and tomato sauce simmering and thickened for hours. This is how we speak now, in gestures—sometimes words are inadequate. Early in the morning, he's packing his suitcase for his midyear infectious disease conference in Chicago. I watch him meticulously roll up his T-shirts, workout clothes, socks, underwear, jeans. He takes out a suit, tie, two dress shirts covered in their cellophane wrap from the cleaners. He finds satisfaction in organizing and getting the best value out of space in his suitcase. Watching him, I am flooded with a wave of separation anxiety. Though we rarely speak, I don't want him to go. I go to his drawer and take out one of his sweaters. I tell him it is going to be cool in Chicago, and I fold it into his suitcase. For a minute our eyes meet. I ask when he will be back. He says his plane is due in time for dinner on Sunday. His eyes scan my body, still in the T-shirt and panties I wear to bed, and I suffer an ache of desire.

It is so very quiet without his large heavy steps. The sound of the TV as he views his sports and news. The feel of him in a room with me, watching me even as he ignores me. At night witnessing the sliver of blue light from underneath my son's bedroom door, the glow that comes off his computer. I imagine the call of the sirens, their enchanting songs enticing men toward them. What *do* I desire? I look out the window. The sun is a blinding shield.

After discovering the fridge is grim—a bag of flour on a shelf, a few shrinking lemons in the bin, and a theater of old condiments in the side door—I slip out to the greengrocer on Broadway to buy a few groceries for the weekend. I bump into my neighbor at the cash register. She's thrilled to see me. It is too early in the morning to be assaulted with hugs and kisses, but I must succumb because friendship is not to be taken for granted. We walk back to our building together, her arm locked in mine. I don't mind the questions today. *How's my son, have I seen any good films, what groceries did I buy.* It reminds me that I still exist. I've been dying to talk to you, she says when we get to our floor. We step off the elevator and she asks if she can come in for a few minutes for a chat. Of course, I say. I'm happy for the company.

She takes off her coat revealing tight blinding yoga clothes of bright pink-and-orange design while I pour water for tea. Her perfectly shaped locks flow to her shoulders. I touch my hair, ashamed, because I can't remember if I washed it, and she stops for a moment to look at me. Are you okay? she asks. You look pale. Have you lost weight?

I've been tired. Parent-teacher conferences at work, prepping for class, nerves about my new book coming out. Missing my son. Poor you, she says. I don't know how you do it all. You need to take better care of yourself. Not push so hard. I'm excited for your new book, she says, and smiles so brightly that I am cheered.

We sit at my dining room table covered with stacks of student papers, my computer, books. I push it all to the side, pour her tea from my teapot, offer her a muffin from my grocery bag. I can see there is something different about her. She sips her tea, takes a pinch of muffin from her plate. Smiles.

I can't hide anything from you, she laughs. She's fallen in love with her French yoga instructor. The yoga instructor is in his thirties. She was complaining of a sore neck. Her sacral chakra, the one at the physical center, which controls sexuality, desire, he said, was blocked. He asked if I had difficulty allowing myself to be sexually and emotionally intimate, she said. Well, that's a come-on if I ever heard one, I say. And we both laugh. It feels good to laugh again. You think so? she says, her eyes brightening. I want him, she says. I would keep him trapped with me on an island if I could. Ah, Circe. Her beauty will turn them all to swine. I can't tell if I'm jealous or appalled. Along with practicing yoga she's also practicing meditation and other newly discovered acts, hoping to find her ananda, her divine bliss. Really? Sometimes I can't tell if she really believes what she says.

He's gorgeous, she says. It's like he could read me. See what I've been feeling. How lonely I've been. Now I understand why she sprays herself with lavender and vanilla oil. Why she moved into the guest bedroom. She showed me the bedroom a few days ago when I came over to see if the finished books I've been waiting for from my publisher had gotten mixed up with one of her packages. The bedroom is feminine, with pale pinks and a white lace throw over her bed, and a white dresser with a vanity mirror; it looks like a bedroom for the kind of daughter she might have wanted.

It's wonderful to be adored, she muses, her face lit up like that of a girl who has just been given one of those big lollipops or a spray of cotton candy at a state fair. She says the sex is so good that sometimes she has to tell him to stop, she can't take it anymore. He lives in Brooklyn. In a railroad flat. We had sex on his couch, his floor, the bed. I've been so sore, she says, and laughs again.

My friend offers too much information. Now images of her with her French yoga instructor have seeped into my consciousness.

He's in his thirties and she's more than a decade older, with two children and a husband. It will get complicated. He'll get tired of my neighbor. Soon enough the yoga instructor will want to consider sex with another woman, I know the type, but this is something I can't tell my friend. I don't want to burst her cloud of newfound glory. Let her enjoy it. Let her turn him into a hog.

Of course, already I'm worried about my friend. Her husband, even though he ignores her, and is angry and withdrawn and hunts pheasants for sport, is basically a good man. And I love her kids. I don't want it all to fall apart, but this is something I can't say to her. It will sound selfish and judgmental to deprive her of bliss, even if it will be short-lived. Once something happens it cannot be undone. The institution of marriage is not to be toyed with. Of course, it doesn't always endure, but we must respect it. Or maybe not. Maybe it's the cause of ruin and despair.

My neighbor stops talking, realizing she's dominating. How are you guys doing? she says. She admires my husband because he doesn't sport all weekend with his buddies. Because when my son was little my husband woke up early on the weekend to go to the bakery and brought us back muffins, fresh donuts, and coffee. She'd see my husband take my son out on a run or to the park, while hers, she said, was changing into his outdoor gear. She's told me I'm lucky that my husband does what she calls "chores," which means that he too makes dinner or sweeps the floor. I tell her that he's good. He's at a conference, because to reveal more would feel like its own form of indiscretion.

I look at the stack of papers on my desk because, for now, I've had enough of my neighbor. I'm not used to seeing her transformed by ecstatic sex. She gets up and puts her teacup in the sink. Off to yoga, she says, and gives me a hug before she leaves. I don't know whether she means she's actually going to yoga or if she's going to Brooklyn to her yoga instructor's apartment, but I refrain from inquiring. After she closes the door, I still smell her lavender oil. I collapse on the couch. Am I jealous that she's ecstatic over an affair with a yoga instructor half her age?

Thoughts of the Visiting Poet press into my consciousness. After Taos, we grew closer, laughing off what had happened by the bizarre circumstances that night. Sometimes he'd come into my classroom just to chat. After the Greek play, we ate the leftover pomegranates sitting on my desk, and sucking the pearl-like seeds. Sometimes we went for a quick coffee at the Starbucks around the corner.

We occasionally went to poetry readings together. Once he took me to a party on the Upper East Side. In the living room, original art by Matisse, a Giacometti sculpture in the corner, and since we were on the penthouse floor, a view of Central Park that nearly made me faint. I watched the Visiting Poet mingling and, so as not to crowd him, talked with a few people

I knew and then stood by the window to admire the view. He came up behind me and offered me a glass of champagne, thanked me for being his date. We spent the remainder of the party drinking champagne out of long flutes, looking at the art, at the view from the window, gossiping. In the cab home, I was a little drunk. I tried to steady myself before getting out of the cab. Walking into my apartment, my son at the dining room table doing his homework, my husband making dinner, I was flooded with guilt. You look a little tipsy, my husband said. He kept looking. I slipped into the bathroom, like a teenager hiding from her mother, splashed water on my face. Had he caught the excitement, the new life in my face? But he never said anything, never challenged me. I wandered into the kitchen to begin making a salad. I meticulously dried the lettuce, cut up radishes and carrots, sprinkled in walnut bits and some crumbled blue cheese. He looked at me. Why all the fuss? he said. Is there something wrong with my wanting to make a nice salad for my family? I said. It's just a little out of character, he remarked. I turned my eyes away.

I decide to take a walk in the park. It's late afternoon, that time when the sky is folding from blue to dark blue, the light fading but not yet fallen into blackness. I pass the bench in front of the massive weeping willow where the Visiting Poet and I sat months ago before we'd gone to the mansion. I'd forgotten about it. Thoughts, memories, they are not orderly, they come back without will or reason. It was a late-March afternoon. A Monday. Sipping tea in the teachers' lounge. Everyone seemed to have already departed. The halls eerily quiet, without the herd of rambunctious boys stomping the stairs. All outdoor sporting events had been canceled due to rain. Our shoulders touching, sitting next to each other, my body buzzed with sensation.

He abruptly stood up, tall, as I recall, tall as an aristocrat with that lilac scarf twisted around his neck in his tweed jacket, to stand by the window. It's getting dark, he said, and then came back to sit next to me on the couch, close enough that I could smell him, that odd mix of cologne and damp wood. Thick thighs covered by his large hands and hairy knuckles. His expression grave, his darkness suddenly all-consuming.

I asked him about his weekend to break the uncomfortable silence. He told me it wasn't good. He stood up and returned to the window, his back to me. The rain had stopped. He asked if he could walk me home through the park, that it would feel good to walk. Of course, I would walk with him. He didn't know many people in New York, and those he knew were casual acquaintances. I have many acquaintances but few real friends, and those I have, I truly care for. I wanted to help, to be there for him. We looped slowly following the park's path near the lake and the fountain, past a cold burst of forsythia, crimped and crude, like someone flamboyantly dressed in need of attention, the greenest of grass taking on that new spring glow. The air smelled good, like it does after a rain. It almost devours you. The trees releasing their earthy, piney scent. Occasionally our shoulders brushed as we walked. And then, I began to feel myself disappear. It was something that happened when I was with him. It was like I lost all identity. Sometimes I couldn't feel my feet on the ground. I was airless, unable to think or concentrate. A thin butterfly flitting into the sky.

May we stop here, for a moment? He was always polite, almost formal at times. We approached a bench at the Cherry Hill Fountain, and he took out a pair of wool gloves from his pocket and wiped the corner of the bench so we could sit. I felt myself disappearing again and peered into his face so as to force myself to pay attention. He smoked a cigarette. It was lovely looking out at the weeping tree with its stout trunk and arrowlike leaves, dripping with water from the rain. Sometimes it was more pleasant not to speak, to sit, to be, to take in.

I hope it's okay to confide in you. I feel I can say anything to you, and you'll listen, he told me. He said his wife had visited over the weekend. He described it like a death march. Always waiting for the grand finale. Even the sex is no good, he said, and laughed. The weeping willow stood across from us, a stout widow cloaked in mourning clothes; her girth blotted all else, as she does now. Of course you can talk to me, I said.

Sometimes I can't breathe. Knowing exactly what she'll say before she says it. The same look on her face when she's disappointed in me. The same arguments. Sometimes just her footsteps on the wood make me cringe, he said. No wonder it's

not working. He laughed again and his cheeks turned pink. I
offered that he should resist that feeling. You must be braver,
I said, because suddenly I was afraid for him. The words surprised me. Where had they come from? Is that how I felt,
what I told myself so that I could endure the claustrophobia,
the all-too-familiar responses and gestures, the dismissiveness
from one's spouse I sometimes felt in my marriage? What I
imagined all married people must feel at one time or another.
No one can know what it's like once the curtain of marriage
drops and the union becomes its own microcosm. No, you
don't get it, he said. It's not working.

I didn't know what to say. What he meant, exactly. What
wasn't working? The marriage? Or the sex? He took my hand.
I don't want to think about it, he said. Thank you for being
my friend. His hand was cold, wet; in his, my hand felt small
and weak. I couldn't remember the last time my husband had
taken my hand. The dripping branches of the willow tree, so
magisterial and protective, invasive in the fading light; my
eyes gazed to the puzzle of clouds in the sky, and a cool wind
swept in as if in mourning, the crowns of daffodils bowing
their heads in bereft ceremony. Shimmering the rain off their
nakedness. I stood up. I was beginning to feel it again. That I
was disappearing. He stood up too. The trees were still mostly
bare, but you could see their tight nipple-buds against the
grandness of the weeping willow, and it was chilly. I have to
go, I said, looking at my watch. I'm late. I kissed his cheek, and
he kissed mine.

I reached up to the weeping willow and pulled off a small leafy handful and took it to my nose. I'll never forget that smell it released after the rain, so earthy and rich, and then I walked away. I almost stopped to go back to him, I felt he needed me, and I felt sorry for him, but before I could turn around, he came after me. Wait, he said; he took my hand and pulled me back toward the weeping willow and kissed me. I don't know what came over me. It was as if I'd drunk in the beauty of the cool grass in his kiss. With you, it works, he said, pushing his groin against me.

Once I got home, I took off my wet coat and pulled off my boots. My husband, in the kitchen, grilling peppers and onions, a rich, warm tomatoey smell in the air I had come to associate with home. I felt my cheeks. They were hot. Our son was in his room, battle sounds from *Game of Thrones* through our thin walls. An overpowering sensation of love swept through me. I looked at my husband, like a god mastering the tools of the kitchen. He knows, I thought, of course he knows.

The weeping willow is massive, overtaking with its drooping branches. It's not a tree you can sit under. There's no place to go, branches drape to the ground. You feel trapped in her girth. She looks mad, shape-changing in this late October light, drooping and hunched over, like a woman who will never be able to stand tall. I can't bear it. A couple stroll past hand in hand. Two women walk by engaged in lively conversation. And here I am alone. Shutting myself away in my own machinery of thoughts. Suddenly, frighteningly, it's making sense. Trying to pull me away from my family, burdening me with his loneliness. His impotence. Always appearing in my office, in the teachers' lounge. And that kiss beneath the willow's immensity. These drooping shaggy limbs, a cascade of tangled hair one can never forget or undo. My body is cold. I wind my scarf tighter around my neck. An image of him, huddled in the library with poor lovely James coaxing poems from the gentle boy. Nearly every day dropping by Miss Reynolds's office to share a few kind pleasantries to cheer a lonely woman. No, he was good; he wasn't bad. That laugh, what was it, the laugh of self-loathing? But then, why not a word? I follow the path, through the dips and curves in the park, filled with dread. The wind kicks in. It is a monster, nearly blowing my scarf away. I can no longer deny it. All the way home, as the sky darkens to ink, it strikes me with clarity. I lost my compass. My beam. My lighthouse.

## APARTMENT 9B AND THEN THE THEATER

I run a bath. I can't bear to think about it anymore. In the tub I look at my body, which appears to be floating away from me in defiance. I've neglected it. Even masturbating has lost its charms. Flashes of my neighbor and her yoga teacher absorb my thoughts. Memories of my husband coming home, still in suit and tie, propping me on the countertop, nuzzling my neck. The power of authority in the way in which he touched me then, authority without words, without demands, without remorse or guilt. His masculinity so foreign. Am I emasculating to my husband, in my dearth? Does he sense that sometimes he's not enough for me, as I know I am not enough for him? I can't be, if he turns to the Russian bride for his needs. Maybe he's having a fling at the conference. No. Tonight, I will not dwell. I am taking myself to the theater.

Red dress, heels, lipstick, dressing up for only myself, and out the door, I treat myself to a cab. There's so much life outside, cabs zooming down the avenue, people walking arm in arm, the bright lights of the billboards, they seem to all call out to me. So much to see and do. *Be a player, not a witness*, I hear. Who is it? The chorus or Zeus, who has contempt for all women? He's unfaithful to Hera, has consorts, changes into animals, birds, to fornicate, rape. Or maybe it's Aphrodite, goddess of beauty, calling out to me to enjoy myself, to relish in my womanhood, my femininity.

I step out of the cab, join the crowd in line for my ticket, find my seat. A woman dressed in a beige shift with matching patent-leather heels and a clutch purse sits next to me. What is it like to be a person who is color-coordinated? She too is alone. A couple moves into the seats in front of us; he is exceptionally tall, and in a southern accent that surprises me, the woman beside me asks the man if he will switch seats with his wife so that the tall man is now in front of me. The request takes me aback, because now this man is blocking my view. The man turns around and suggests that the two of us switch rows with him and his wife so that both of us can see, and the generosity of his gesture touches me. Once we are in our new row, the woman turns to me with an apology in her sheepish smile, her dark, made-up eyes gooey with black mascara. She asks me why I am here at the theater without a friend or partner.

I am treating myself, I say, as if I need to justify going to the theater alone. I am too, she says, and brightens at the idea that something she regrets is now acceptable. Where are you from? she asks. I tell her that I live here in the city. I live in Charlotte, she says. I have lived everywhere. My husband. Every year, we move somewhere new for his work. Then her eyes mist. Not anymore, she says. We're getting divorced.

I flip through the theater program. The play is *Blackbird*. I've wanted to see it for months. I'm glad I've come alone. It isn't my husband's cup of tea. He grows restless in the theater, his legs cramped in the narrow rows. Part of me is sorry this dialogue has begun because I can see that this attractive woman is lonely and wants to talk, but another part of me sees something disturbing in her cloudy eyes that I don't want to be near. We are sitting so close together, our elbows nearly touching, that it would be impolite not to inquire further. How long have you been married? She tells me twenty years. I nod. Me too, I say. She looks at me and I can see that her eyes have welled up.

He's leaving *me*. It turns out he's been planning it for years, she says. I tell her I'm sorry. I ask if she has children. No, she says. We don't have children. That will make it easier, I fumble, but the minute the words are out of my mouth I regret it. It's not easier, she says. People don't like women without children. They think you want to take their husband. Why would I want their fat bald husband when I already have one? Why would I want yours when I am married to the boss? she says, with sudden hostility. Her eyes flitting back and forth look insane.

It's a relief when the curtain drops. The distraught woman next to me has already asked the couple behind us if she can buy them a drink after the show. I fear she will turn to me next. Throughout the first act I put up an invisible wall between us because I don't want this woman to ruin the experience of what I'm witnessing onstage, another drama, this one between a man who got himself sexually involved with a twelve-year-old and convicted for it, and now they are meeting again for the first time in over a decade in the office building where he works, and understandably the dynamic onstage is tense. When the show is over, I'm shaking. It has undone me, the wire of sexual tension pulsing on the stage. Once the applause has died down, I flee from the theater and then once in the cab I'm ashamed of myself for not having said goodbye to the woman who sat beside me. I'm suddenly worried that my husband has been plotting too.

When I get home, it's late. I'm tired. I change out of my clothes and collapse on my bed. I look at the nightstand and there, tucked in the tower of books, is *Denying Heaven*, the Visiting

Poet's early volume. I read it years ago, when it was first published, before I knew he would be coming to our school, stirred by the intensity he brought to his encounters, the exoticism of some of the work's setting. I flip it open. The poems, though technically skilled, now read as sentimental, sinister, dated. Women serve as vessels to provide a lofty lyric intensity. "Village girl, carries / the weight of history in her arms / heavy breasts / her skirt catches the light, and takes down the sun." Village girl? Where did that come from? And another, more sinister, a poem called "Garden Party": "Come, have a seat in the garden, I'll play the part. You take off your clothes / I'll take off mine. / You'll find nothing inside." Maybe I'm being too harsh. But it's true. Every encounter a come-on. The fancy party in the penthouse, that time under the weeping willow. Which came first and when is unclear. One evening I was working late in the classroom. I was packing up my books into my backpack. You're still here, the Visiting Poet said. His eyes were glassy. I smelled alcohol on his breath. Do you want to get a drink? he asked. I told him I couldn't. That I'd promised to make dinner.

You're turning down a drink with me to make dinner? he said. I remember he looked unbalanced and steadied his hand on my desk. I don't have my family here, you know. I get lonely. I told him that it must be hard, or something like it. What's hard is that you're ignoring me, he countered. I had never seen this side of him before. He was usually lighthearted. Playful. Funny. I told him I wasn't ignoring him. His behavior took me by surprise.

Let's fuck then, he said, just like that. And then he took my hand and tried to pull me into the cloakroom. I told him to stop. Was he serious? And then I laughed and told him we weren't going to do that. He looked at me halfway between a laugh and a scowl. I'll never forget that look. Of course we're not, he said. I was joking. He stumbled again. You go make dinner and I'll call my wife, he said, and quickly left the classroom. You go make dinner and I'll call my wife. The words trembled in my mind. Had I gone too far without knowing it?

I remember after he left, thinking to myself, Why not? I'd been fantasizing about him since Taos. I'd retrace in my mind that night together, how we had laughed at that spider, and fallen asleep and awoke in each other's arms, and when I remembered our kissing, I languished in it, my cheeks grew hot. I don't know why. How to explain? When we think we are content, we discover we don't know ourselves, our own nature. I needed time to think. I almost went back to his classroom and tried to find him. To ask him how he felt about me, what he wanted. But then if I went back and made love to the Visiting Poet, I would have to remember it every day when teaching. And what if that one time leads to another, and another? I couldn't do it. I did not have the sustenance or constitution. I did not have the courage.

Walking home from school that evening, I kept repeating it over and over: *You go make dinner and I'll call my wife.* It was late and the trees bowed down before me as I walked briskly, the sky darkening, night descending. Did he expect me to be responsible for him since he was alone without his wife? He'd been drinking. The next day he came into my classroom to apologize. He brought me daffodils. It was in April and they had just begun to bloom. He told me that it had been hard. Being away from home. That he'd felt lost. Lost, I thought. It was the last thing I would have thought about him. But maybe it was a performance. I couldn't quite read it. I accepted his apology and thanked him for the flowers. Shall we have lunch today, then? he said. I'm not crowding you, am I? After he said it, I realized how much I looked forward to our lunches. You know, you're ruining me, right, he said, with a half smile. Or something like it. Something charming and seductive. Heat crawled up my neck and made me feel clammy. It was a feeling that happened around him. I remember that day, especially. We had lunch—we brought buttery grilled cheese sandwiches from the cafeteria outside and sat on a bench while the traffic on Madison Avenue whisked past both looking at the trees across from one another on the avenue, how in the wind the branches moved toward each other and then apart. There was a moment when we both stopped, with our sandwiches in our hands. We turned toward each other. It was longer than I'd ever looked, and I felt uncomfortable, but I couldn't turn away. It was as if I'd been bewitched.

I flip through more pages of his book. Scenes from *Blackbird* bloom in my mind. The play's left me shaken. It wants to convince us that a man having an affair with a twelve-year-old is a twisted but convincing love story. No, I won't read his words. I won't think about it any longer. What's wrong with me? It's over. And then the note slips out. I'd forgotten I'd hidden it there. He'd slipped it underneath my door after he, after he . . . I don't know what it was. It was terrible. I can't think about it. I won't. I tuck the note back inside the book and force it into my nightstand drawer. I don't want to remember it. But I can't stop the images from coming forth.

That bronze statue of the satyr propped on his side and wagging his penis blooms forth. I nearly bumped into it on the Homer Tour with my students. The museum houses 140 images of this creature, friends with Pan and Dionysus, whose craving for sexual pleasure is strong enough to make flowers and plants come forth in a forest. No. My head aches. I must pull myself together before my husband returns tomorrow. *Oh what have I done, what have I done.* I can't stop the thought. This is why I can't make love to my husband. I'm so ashamed. Behind the window in my bedroom, caged behind the iron bars of the fire escape, the sky is completely black. It has lost all meaning. It is the hour of unreality. I can't hold it back any longer. Something terrible has happened and I don't know what to do.

### MANSION

I agreed to go to the mansion, though it was a horrible place— owned by Roderick Fitz, the former chair of our department, who now teaches only one class because he does not want to be relegated to the life of leisure he had been granted. It was April. It was the coldest month.

At the academy, it was a rite of passage to get an invitation. For years, I was excluded. Snickers and gossip ensued among the faculty as the holiday weekends approached, everyone wondering who had gotten the invitations that year. After a decade of teaching, I was invited for the first time. It rained all weekend, and the days were spent in the grand room doing jigsaw puzzles, playing rounds of chess, drinking hot toddies or sherry. I was invited a few times after that—the last time I had to lock my bedroom door because Ian McFarland, professor of mathematics, twenty years my junior, drunk, tried to play footsie with me underneath the dinner table and patted my ass while I was clearing dishes. When I confronted him, he said he was just playing. Play with someone else, I said.

An inheritance from Fitz's ancestors, the mansion had a rich and tired look about it, as if it had once been grand but now was half-asleep. The pillows on the couches worn, the curtains faded, the forlorn portraits of the ancestors peering every which way so as to make you feel you don't belong. Spiderwebs in the high beams. The heavy dark furniture, the dusty antique rugs, the creaky staircases reminded me of the damp smell of a dingy bed-and-breakfast where I was put up at one of the university towns in which I traveled to read my poems. One of the sleeping rooms, called a dormitory, had four twin beds meant for children. The male guests slept in the dormitory together, grown adults having to dress in the open space; the women were privileged with their own private rooms in alcoves on the third floor.

Fitz is in his seventies. Though most of his friends from Harvard had become bankers or lawyers, he had stumbled into teaching at the academy, where he was once a student. He will only write with the gold pens residing in a marble holder on his desk; they look like daggers when wielded to sign a reimbursement slip or a recommendation form. He wears a hankie in his lapel and eighteen-carat gold-rimmed spectacles. He is uninterested in a single thing about my personal life, but he's kind. And has always been my champion at school. Because I will listen, he comes to my classroom, pulls up a student desk, tells me facts about his multiple obsessions—hunting, wine, food, history, while I try to hide my yawns. Men talk and women listen. I was raised to be polite and serve my elders. If Fitz traveled to a city or a continent, whether Paris or Africa, it was like he was the first person who ever visited, and when he returned I endured the details of his itinerary, what he saw, ate, drank, where he stayed. He seemed to go on these journeys for only one purpose: so that he had topics of conversation at his fingertips. It took me years to realize that members of the ruling class do not ask questions, or divulge. Perhaps that is why none of the faculty speaks about the fact that after his first wife died two years ago, Fitz married a woman nearly thirty years younger.

I agreed to go to the mansion again for one reason only—the Visiting Poet was going as well. We'd become close by then. He was curiously fascinated with my work. We were intellectual equals; both of us had for years made literature the staircase in which we climbed. He confided in me his worries about his own work. You're lucky, he had told me. My poems were getting attention in a few of the more mainstream publications, and he noted it. No one wants to read work by middle-aged white men. It's as if we're the villains for crimes we haven't personally committed. It's a sort of fantasy, isn't it? For women, he said.

Fantasy? Don't you think it's time that women received the same recognition as men? I said. What I mean is, it's a problem, for someone like me. Poor you, I joked. Are you afraid of women coming into power?

I'm not afraid of you, he said. Your swans. It's ambitious as hell. You know that, don't you? It's visceral. Compelling. Raw. I wish I could write like that. I'm empty. I'm up for tenure this year. I need to get back on the stage. It's been a while. I haven't written a word all term. What about the poems you showed me? That lovely villanelle? I asked. He said he wrote those poems in the summer. That he hadn't written a word in New York. He gave me a searching look. He said he hadn't found his subject yet. That he wanted to do something grand. Unforgettable. Dangerous. Like your long poem. His second book won a big prize with a substantial purse. But his last book had gone unnoticed. I knew what it was like to feel empty, and I sympathized.

At the mansion, we sat at opposite ends of a long farmhouse table at a grand lunch of cold cuts, rye bread, pickles, olives, cheeses, and salad. We did not speak but were in keeping with each other's every move. We had a glass of wine. He might have had more. When he drank, he became different. His eyes landed on my breasts and moved up to my eyes, and I put my hand to my neck and chest. As soon as I got up to go to the bathroom, I turned to see his eyes bleeding into my back, watching me walk. I didn't like it when he drank. He became menacing, angry. When I went to get a sweater for a walk he cornered me in the narrow corridor to my room and with his hip playfully nudged me against the wall. What are you doing? I joked. You're coming with me, he said, and took my hand.

We made a milk run in the late afternoon. We drove one of Fitz's old Mercedes-Benzes from his garage. The minute we left the long circular driveway and turned down a winding road, the Visiting Poet pulled the car to the shoulder. You're radiant, he said. I had to stop just to look at you. You're nuts, I said, and laughed. He raised my dress above my knee. Just a peek, he said, and smiled. You can't do that, I said, shook my head, and took his hand away. He put the car in gear and drove off.

I'm sleeping in a dormitory, he said, in reference to the mansion. We're in a boarding school novel, and we both howled with laughter. You know, Fitz is a bit of a prick, he said. Showing off his old family money. His wine cellar. I think his nature is good, I said. He wants to share it with us. That's ridiculous.

He wants to rub it in our faces. Make sure we know who's superior, he countered. I didn't like what he'd said about Fitz. Fitz is one of the reasons why I've stayed at the institution all these years.

Is that what you really think? I looked out the window and along the drive at the other mansions, with their stone walls and crumbling facades. He thinks he's better than us plebeians, he said with a sneer. I don't think so, I said. And then I asked him what was wrong. I could tell he was troubled. He told me he'd applied for a big grant and didn't get it. He said he deserved it. Of course you do, I said. I'm sorry. I mean, we all do, don't we? I'd applied for many grants and fellowships over the years and was most often rejected. He said he was counting on it. He needed it. You think because you need it, it should come to you? Come on, I laughed. What arrogance.

He steeled himself. Of course I'm arrogant. How else to live with the foolishness and meaninglessness of living? It's all bullshit. Arrogance is valuable. Without it, I would not be who I am. It is not a crime to be arrogant, he spat, not in his own defense it seemed, but as an accusation against me. I deserved it, he said again. Men are born to feel entitled. Arrogance is entitlement, I said, a shield against true feeling. Is that what I lack, he said, and then squeezed my thigh. I'm feeling a lot right now.

We were quiet. I looked out the window the rest of the way to the store and let him sulk. On the drive back to the mansion we passed a serene lake, its grounds surrounded by another mansion; perhaps it was private. We exited the car and sat underneath a stand of dogwoods just beginning to flower into their umbrella of pink, though surely we were trespassing, and we watched two swans with their long, seamless necks parading in the lake. I was deep into the writing of my long poem by then and had been struggling with the ending sequence, and finding the pair of swans in the lake then, at that moment, felt weirdly clandestine. Yeats's "Leda and the Swan" came to me. The sonnet as a form was constructed for themes of love, but in "Leda and the Swan" the subject is violation. That subversion of the form is brilliant, I recall I said, or something like it, as the light played fancifully, sneaking in and out of the tree branches, their leaves curling to receive it. The swans flirting with each other at the lake. The tulips and daffodils waving in the breeze.

Why a violation? Yeats wants it double-edged. Leda is enjoying the abduction, he said. Really? *The great wings beating; the staggering girl; the dark webs, her nape caught in his bill; her helpless breast. Strange heart beating.* Doesn't sound like my idea of pleasure, I said.

He put his hand on my heart. It was beating quickly. Then he ran his hand up and down my arms. Look, you have goose bumps. Come closer, he said, and put his arm around me. He leaned into me, that *shudder in the loins*, he said, and then placed my hand on his erection. What are you doing? I said, and pulled my hand away. I smelled the wine from lunch on his breath. I told him to stop. That he was being ridiculous. We're talking about a poem, I said, to deflect and not to insult him. I laughed again. I liked that he was flirting with me. But I was also uncomfortable. He was taking it too far.

A faint sweetness was in the air like the smell of a slowly dying flower giving off its last burst of life. White and purple water lilies gone to bed by the bank. Everything too bright to temper. Are we? he said. I know what's underneath that lace-collared dress. He traced the buttons with his finger. You think because you dress like a prim schoolgirl that you're not sexy. You're sexier, he said. Is that what I dress like? I said. I think you're a little drunk from lunch. That's what I think. He told me it was a turn-on. A disguise for my hotness. I was flattered, but I pretended not to be. Told him he was delusional. He moved closer to me, leaned over. Yeah, he said. I feel it now. How hot you are. There was more of an edge to his furtive banter. Stop, I said. I'm being serious. I'm interested in what you have to say about the poem., I said.

Zeus is indifferent, he's turned on her after he's had her, and then he drops her from his beak. *Mastered by the brute blood.* Do you think a woman wants to be mastered? I asked him. I was curious about what he thought. What I might have missed. Maybe, he said, and smiled. He said it was a black swan. An event has happened, its effect is profound, and yet in hindsight it all makes strange sense.

Is that what you think? That afterward Leda's transformed? That she gains power after being raped? You know the lines: "Did she put on his knowledge with his power / Before the indifferent beak could let her drop?" Yeats believed it was possible that humans could take on godlike power if gods interfered. I get that. But he raises it as a question. Maybe there's another meaning. Zeus took *her* knowledge. That's what I think. You're ridiculous, he said. Why are you taking the poem so seriously? Come here. And he put his arms around me again. He turned my face toward him, with his fingers on my chin to look at me. His eyes gleamed, as if he'd been inspired. I'd seen that look before. The sun was out, and it had been a cold winter. The lap of the lake, the sound of swans ducking their heads into the water, the smell of long grass soothed me and I relaxed.

We lay down on the grass on our backs to feel the beaming sun on our face. Underneath the willows, by the lake, the swans caressing each other—it was as if the landscape had presented itself to us, as if we were in a painting. It was brilliant, the day, and despite his suggestive gestures, I was alert, alive in the present moment, a rarity for me. I had forgotten the troubles at home, my students, my work. I closed my eyes and took it all in, and he rolled over and kissed me. I let him and then rolled away from him. Someone might see us, I said, and tugged at the end of my dress to keep it from rising up my thighs. Lust galloped through me. I couldn't stop it or ignore it any longer. I was hungry. Voracious. My body hot as a furnace. But I couldn't. Not in broad daylight. No. I don't know if I could at all. If I could betray my husband, my child. Because to betray one, it would be betraying both. It was different than at Taos. What was between us had deepened. He tried to lift my dress again like he had done in the car, but I gently took his hand away. I had to be careful. I was tentative. Yes, I wanted his attention. To be flirted with. To be kissed and touched by someone to whom I was not betrothed. Maybe it would never happen again.

So that's how you're going to play it, he said, and brushed off his trousers and stood up. I don't know if he was angry. I couldn't read his face. I didn't know what I wanted. My son was still living at home. I could not imagine breaking up my marriage.

I was confused by my own desire and reticence, each as strong as the other. We drove back to the mansion wrapped in our own thoughts. I felt something change in him. He seemed to be pouting. Looking straight ahead at the road. When we arrived, he parked the car and turned to me, and I put my hand on his thigh to assure him. I leaned in and he smelled like the evergreens near the lake.

He shut off the engine. He looked solemn. I couldn't read the blankness that fell upon his face. We shouldn't do this anymore, he said. I love my wife. My body stiffened. The comment surprised me. Suddenly he was playing the faithful husband. I'm married too, I said, in case he had forgotten. We'd better get back, he said, and shut the car door, clutching the brown

paper bag filled with milk that may have soured over the hours
we had been gone.

At dinner, he chatted up Dina Weinberg, the youngest member of the English department. Sweet and good-natured Dina,
with beautiful breasts and a tiny waist you could fit two hands
around. Her skin pale without a wrinkle. I studied it across the
table at dinner. I had forgotten how milky young skin could
look. A recent college graduate, passionate about teaching,
clever, but I wish she didn't feel the need to laugh at the male
bravado and tedious stories like I had when I was her age. I
hated her squeaky high-pitched voice; it made her appear less
intelligent than she was. Why hadn't things changed for the
new generation? I encouraged her to be less timid. At faculty
meetings, it was as if we were sitting before the all-male ju-
diciary committee—they signed off on the curriculum, mans-
plained, at times made inappropriate sexual jokes. I wanted
something different for the younger female faculty and my students. I tried to catch the Visiting Poet's eye several times, to
no avail. After dinner, we retired to the living room. Almond
macaroons passed and sherry poured in dainty crystal. The
Visiting Poet sat next to Dina on the love seat, and they spoke
in animated conversation; rather, he was pontificating about
something, and then I heard him ask her about the Yeats poem
and it was the only time all evening his eye reached for mine. I
was across from them on another sofa with Fitz and his wife;
they were telling me stories of their touring of Africa, the desert. And I was annoyed by Fitz and his wife. Where hadn't

they been? Soon I saw they would bring out the photo albums, as they had done before, and I couldn't bear it. I gave one last look at the Visiting Poet still engrossed with Dina, tempting her with Yeats, for god's sake; said my good nights; and retired to my designated bedroom. I'd had enough. I had drunk too much wine at dinner, and the sherry had given me a sugar headache. As I climbed the stairs to the third floor, I felt horribly alone and abandoned. That I'd thought him a close friend. What was wrong with me?

In my room, I took off my dress and crawled into bed and lay underneath the heavy duvet in my bra and panties. I had forgotten the T-shirt I usually wore to bed. It was chilly and drafty in the house. The wind rattled the trees. Ghostly shadows painted the walls. I was cold and miserable, my head swimming in thoughts about the Visiting Poet and our afternoon at the lake, the swans that seemed now to be performing a wicked dance in my imagination. What did I want? He could be enchanting, intelligent, sexy in his own mercurial way. I thought of his strange outburst about loving his wife. His incredible flirting all night with Dina. No. I got out of bed and staggered in the dark to find the bathroom, to my toiletry bag to retrieve a Valium from my pillbox and then an Ambien. I went back to bed and turned my head into the pillow, and thankfully sleep came almost instantly.

I awoke to a weight on top of me. I was still groggy from the pills and the wine. For a moment, I thought it was Ian

McFarland trying to get into my room, and then I remembered that he had not been invited this weekend. Before I could turn in the dark to see who it was, he was fondling me. I smelled deep burgundy wine in his breath at my neck, and the smell of the evening's fire. His heavy girth on top of me, enveloping every inch of me. In my delirium, I had forgotten the evening and for a moment I was glad he had come. He kissed my neck.

I tried to turn and move out from underneath him, to see his face, but he wouldn't let me. You're not getting away from me this time, he said, his weight nearly suffocating me. Kissing my neck again, he put his fingers underneath my panties and began to touch me. You want this, he said. I know you do. Everything between us has been leading to it. I tried to move his hand. He was moving too fast. Come on, he said, it's me, and he turned me over and kissed me and it was as if I were sinking, I couldn't come up, I was drowning. Images of the evening came to me, my perception widened, and I broke from underneath the expansive engulfing span of his arms. No, I said. You were awful. All through dinner. What's wrong with you? With me? he said. You refused me at the lake. I was angry. The swans, he said. I couldn't get you out of my mind through the rest of the evening. The black dress you were wearing tonight. That space between your breasts. Right here. I wanted to touch it all night. He ran his finger along my cleavage sending shivers up my back. His hair was tousled and unruly, his clothes damp. You can't flirt with me all these months and want nothing. He smelled like cigarettes and the cold wind by the lake. His big hands on my thighs were like hot coals and he massaged them as if they were meat he was kneading to bake or roast. I tried to move away, but he wouldn't let me. Stop, I said again. What are you doing? And Dina? All night? I took his hands away and he nuzzled his long beak-like nose back into my neck. I was looking at you without looking. It was a performance. He laughed. A shadow crept into his face. Both of us were sitting up then. Do you think that when I am not looking or paying attention to you that I am not desiring you? I desire you more, he said, and he reached over and kissed me. Just this once, he said. Then we'll have it to remember. I can't leave without it. You know I can't. And then before I could stop him, he lowered me down on the bed and pinned me down with his hands. It was dark in the room. I was half in dream from the pills and the wine. I was swimming away again. I had lost all reason. No, I said, and I tried to push him away, but he kept at me, stop, I said, but it was too late. I couldn't move. The force of his body pressed into me. Those large hands pressing my thighs apart and pulling aside my panties. You want this, he said again. I know you do. And then he bit my shoulder hard, and I screamed into his chest and tried to turn to get him off me. But I couldn't. He was too heavy. He forced my back into the mattress, pinned my arms, his magnitude rocking the bed so that it creaked. In a matter of minutes, maybe seconds, before he could enter me he came on my thigh, and I felt his warm cum and his limp penis like a wobbly sausage fall off of it, and he released me. It was awful. What are you doing? I said. What have you done? I was still groggy. I reached to touch my shoulder where he had bitten me. It was sore and I could feel the teeth marks with my fingers. What's wrong with you? I repeated. I saw then that he had his trousers off. I didn't remember if he had come in my room without them, I was still half-asleep. Shhhh, he whispered. I'm sorry. I couldn't help myself. You don't know what your body does to me. I can't think straight in your presence. All I want is to fondle you. Touch you. Eat you. Stop, I said. I didn't ask you to come into my room. You weren't invited. He touched my face. Calm down, he said. You'll wake the others. Everything's okay, he said. No, it's not, I said. Come on, it's me, he said. He tried to hold me in his arms, but I wouldn't let him. And then he said he should leave, before the others got up, so they would not discover us together in the morning. When he stood, his head almost hit the beam of the alcove attic, and he ducked. He put on his trousers and looked back at me. I saw that strange sparkle in his eye from the lake. Then he kissed me on the forehead, and he left. No, I hadn't wanted it. Not like that. It wasn't fine. It was terrible. What was he thinking? I rubbed the bite mark again. What if my husband should see it? My wrists ached from being pinned down. I wanted to stop the images from running through my mind. The room had grown colder. I pulled the coverlet closer. I closed my eyes to stop the room from spinning.. The creaking windows let in a draft. The lines from "Leda and the Swan" swirled in my mind. *A shudder in the loins engenders there / The broken wall ... So mastered.* My thoughts were whirling, and I was suddenly nauseous from the overly buttered dinner and the gushing red wine and the pills.

My head throbbed. I must have fallen asleep again because when I awoke it was to the shock of bright, nearly blinding light that had crept through the curtains. There was only one thought in my head. I must leave. I couldn't bear having to see them all in the morning. To breakfast with my colleagues. To see the Visiting Poet in broad daylight. I packed my bag before the others awoke and left a note saying that I had to get back early, that my son was sick. As I was leaving the room, I found a folded note that had been slipped underneath the door. His scrawls written on the monographed notepad with Fitz's initials. I read his apology quickly and tucked it into my back pocket, unmoved. I told myself I must forget it. I must never think about it again. I was in distress. It hadn't happened. I couldn't allow it to have happened. I drove back to the city slowly, watching the sky come to life, the trees trembling in the wind. What if word got out? Every leaf outside seemed to be shaking. When I arrived home, I went straight into the shower and wept. Afterward I turned to look into the mirror at my naked shoulders. His teeth had broken the skin and left a mark. I must never weep like this again I told myself. No one. No one must ever know.

## APARTMENT 9B

Memories are like bats: they come alive in the black night, when we have taken off our armor. It's Sunday. I eat my solitary breakfast. The tulips, reds and pinks, are opening their dark throats on my table. Alas, some of the petals have already dropped. Suddenly I know where I am going, what I must do. I take my bag and go down the elevator. Outside I wave for a cab. I can't wait for the bus today. My husband is coming home tonight. I must be ready.

All this time, I've known where the painting is, what I've been avoiding. It's in Gallery 157 in the European Sculpture and Decorative Arts collection. I go directly to it. I viewed the painting at least a year ago when I began to research my long poem. It's a painting of Leda and the swan by the Italian painter Bachiacca.

*Leda and the Swan*
(Bachiacca [Francesco d'Ubertino Verdi], Italian)

Leda is naked, caressing the swan sucking milk from her nipple, her hand cupping her breast. Beneath her, hatching from two separate eggs, are plump little toddler-like babies. Not one resembles the beautiful Helen, who in some renditions of the myth is said to be the daughter of Leda and Zeus.

In Cy Twombly's incarnation, which hangs in MoMA, feathers are everywhere, and Leda is ravished. I have the postcard, among many other images, in a folder containing research for my poem. The painting is described as "an orgiastic fusion and confusion of energies within furiously thrashing overlays of crayon, pencil, and ruddy paint. A few recognizable signs—hearts, a phallus—fly out from this explosion."

In comparison, Bachiacca's version is coy. It's an unseemly, unpleasant painting. An abjection of the myth. Leda's countenance is devious, sly. She won't be a victim, and neither will I. Who cares anyway? I will not care anymore. I leave the museum in a frenzy and nearly run through the park assaulted by the girth of the weeping willow. I'm haunted by its creepy long branches, its overwhelming breadth. But I do care. Out of breath, I sit on the bench. It's chilly out and the sky is dim. I'm cold. I don't know what's wrong with me. What I'm refusing to accept.

The last time I heard from him, it was shortly before the term was over, almost a week since I'd seen him at the mansion. It was finals week. Since he only taught poetry workshop, he didn't have to be at school that week. Not having heard from him made it all worse. I was in my classroom grading. He peered in my door. I motioned him in. His walk was unsteady. He pulled up one of the seminar chairs and sat across from me, legs crossed. How are you? I've been thinking of you all week, he said. I smelled alcohol and cigarettes on him. His eyes glassy, pupils dilated, lids heavy. He drew out his words, eyes traveling down my body as if he were in possession of it. It was only noon, and he was intoxicated. Still, I was glad to see him. I thought that by seeing him I would feel right again. I hadn't been well. I'd been miserable. At home, I'd constructed an invisible wall between me and my husband, as if to protect him from me. I didn't know how to be this new person I'd become. I fluctuated from distress to anger, sometimes within minutes. Busying myself, to stop my thoughts from flooding me. I was confused and ashamed that I'd let it all spin out of my control. And that I'd violated my marriage. I blamed myself trying to numb my emotions, but it was impossible. I had turned on myself, and to hate oneself is self-annihilating. Why couldn't I accept the bargain that I'd made when we got married? We were happy. I'd never felt more safe.

I'm leaving in a few days, he said, his scarf around his neck, his monstrous hands resting on his thighs. I bet you can't wait to get rid of me, he said, and then he laughed as if he were amused, tilted back his chair, almost falling backward and then catching himself. Listen, I'm sorry I haven't been in touch. I didn't know what to say or do. It was lovely to be with you. It was great. I shook my head. No, I said. You can't really feel that way. He picked up the volcanic rock on my desk. It was very quiet in my classroom. Quiet in the halls due to finals week. The clock above my desk, like the face of Cronus, god of time and king of the Titans, a demolishing, engulfing force, ticked away each minute. It was bound to happen, he said, filling in the silence and half smiling. Was it? I flushed. Great? I mean. Great for you, but not for me, I said. It couldn't just end, with nothing ever happening, he said, touching my hand. He was leaving and as I took it in, I grew graver, my thoughts more confused. That's your story, I said. We never talked about it. It's not simple for me. I care for my husband, my family. Now it's there. It will always be there. It's what you wanted. My legs were crossed. I was wearing a trim dress, that dress with the lace collar, and my hand reached for my neck, I felt as if I were being strangled, my hair in a tight bun on top of my head. I felt my breath constrained. I looked down at my legs in nude stockings and black heels, one leg crossed over, I couldn't stop it from shaking.

He took my hand again. Don't overthink it, he said. He stood up, moved his chair around to my side of the desk, next to mine. Nothing bad has happened. It's good that I'm leaving. We both have our own lives. I'm going back to Ohio, to my wife and my daughters, and you're here. His voice was unsteady. They're devoted to me, he said. They depend on me. I looked at him scrupulously. You're drunk, I said, shaking my head. He smiled. No, I'm not. I had a beer with lunch. An early lunch, I said, and looked at the clock. A scruff of beard marked his face. Circles under his eyes. Wrinkled clothes, while he always dressed impeccably. He'd been on a bender. Maybe all week.

Come on, he said, lifting my chin. Listen. You have your husband, your son. No one has to know. Let's not make any more of it. Let's enjoy the time we had together. We're close. We're friends. We have that. My judgment told me that I couldn't. I didn't have the words. I needed to think. It's not what I wanted, I said again. I think it was, he said, and he narrowed his eyes. No, I said. It isn't up to you to decide. I had become weirdly dependent upon him for his friendship all those months we'd been close, and the uncertainty of what lay ahead, of who I had become . . . no . . . it was awful. Still, I wanted to give him the benefit of the doubt. Isn't that what women did? He picked the rock up again and held it in his large hand. The minerals flickered, and as he turned the rock, it took on more color, more heft, like a dying ember suddenly coming back into its being. I looked directly at him. He brushed his dark hair off his forehead. A few small drops of sweat formed at his temples. He seemed uncertain, shaken. He turned the rock in his hand, and then his eyes flashed, and he grinned, as if holding the rock, he was remembering Taos, the heat, the spider, the terrible wine and overly sweet margaritas, the night at the mansion. I'm sorry, he said. I didn't mean to. I was overcome. I had too much to drink. He put the rock back on my desk, then he stood up, as if he needed to bring himself back and steady himself. He was a man and I was a woman. One end of his scarf had fallen over his chest; he flung it proudly around his neck, swaggered and righted himself so as not to lose balance. *Tick, tick, tick,* admonished the clock above my desk as if to acknowledge that ordinary time is no match for how the calculations of events and memories live serendipitously in the mind, sometimes taking on more power than others. I didn't mean it to be that way. I thought you wanted it, he said. I looked at him strangely. I couldn't think. My body was frozen. I was never good at reacting in the moment. My mind didn't work that way. It was only later that I began to seethe, taking it all in.

I have something for you, he said. I would never have made it through the year here without your companionship. You've inspired me. You're a beautiful poet. Your new book, that long poem you shared with me months ago, it's brilliant. You'll win a prize. He thrust a tiny box forward into my hand. I reluctantly opened it. Inside was a charm of a swan, cut from black onyx, sized for a bracelet or a necklace. It sat diminutively in a lake of cotton. It's beautiful, I said, picking it up and fondling it with my fingers. But then, a new perception entered, and suddenly I didn't want it. I can't, I said, and put the swan in its box and gave it back to him.

You don't want to accept it? he said. I asked him what I would do if someone should ask me where I got it, who gave it to me. It suddenly seemed calculated. I don't think you want that, do you? I said. He told me that I'd given him more than he could imagine this year. He picked up the rock again. Fondling it. More than I have hoped. You can't imagine what you've done for me. You must have it, he said. It will be our secret. Come here, and then he tried to take me in his arms, but I turned from him. No, I said. Come on. Look. We're friends. We mean something to each other, he said. I felt sorry for him, so out of sorts, so pathetic, drunk before noon. I wanted to believe him, forgive him, it was better than living with it, and slowly I relented. I wanted to make *him* feel better. I took the gift and put it in my drawer. He put the rock with its cutting edges and dark minerals, as if it contained the conflicting forces of the universe, back on my desk harder than he would have done if he were sober. We'll figure it out. I'll write, he said, rambling. I will, I'll write. You'll see. He flashed me an awkward smile. I won't forget you, you'll see, he said again, and he laughed. Why was he laughing? It was the laugh of someone who is embarrassed by emotion, the laugh of self-loathing, the laugh of someone who knows he's been wrong and is covering for it, who is only out for himself, but I hadn't understood it then. After he left, I closed my classroom door. I pulled down the blinds in the window of the door. Held the desk to steady myself. I couldn't behold it all. I didn't want to. The cool minerals of the rock like the ripples on the water when the light catches it flickered in the beam of my desk lamp, the onyx swan shimmering from its lake of cotton. But wait, am I misremembering? Did I take the rock and throw it at him? Or had I just wanted to?

## A SURPRISE

Past the southwest corner of Evodia Field in the Ramble, I hear a queer sound in the feeders. I stop, out of breath, and look up and camouflaged by the branches is a great horned owl roosting on a limb at nearly the top of an oak. Athena. A thought blooms. Now I know what I must do. Out of the park, I walk the four long avenues to Broadway and stop at Fairway, rustle through the other shoppers like a football player trying to dodge my way to the finish, buy fresh Dover sole, red potatoes, the softest bundle of butter lettuce I can find, tomatoes and avocado and fresh mozzarella cheese. I locate a sprightly bunch of asparagus and then, just when I think I'm finished, I spot the dessert case and purchase two small cheesecakes the size of a cupcake, the kind that my husband likes. I carry my grocery bags home, clean the apartment. As dusk begins to assert its black magic, I prepare the consolatory meal, a rapprochement for my husband. How long has it been since I offered myself to him? What have I been so afraid of? To give of oneself is the highest form of love. A love that I've deprived him of. A love that persists even when it frustrates. Disappoints. I remove a chilled bottle of chardonnay from the fridge, open it, and imagine intoxicated Dionysus, the god of wine. I take a sip. I want to step out of myself. Become the seductress. Tearing the lettuce, I continue to imbibe the malicious and tasty fruit of the gods.

I set the table. Take out the special candles. Hop into the shower and slip into black lace panties and bra, search for my black V-neck dress in my closet, it smells perfumy, smoky, the dress I wore to dinner at the mansion. It's suddenly animated, and I'm sickened. I stuff it into the hamper, roam my closet until I find my red dress. I put on the pearl drop earrings my mother bought for me at the museum, the ones from Vermeer's portrait, and dip my toes into heels. I let loose a spray of Coco Chanel on my neck, a present from my neighbor that I save for special occasions. Put it back in the medicine cabinet and reach for it again and spray my wrists. Once released from its high ponytail, my hair cascades in snake-like waves to my shoulders. Yes, I too can be dangerous. My body races like a stampede of horses let out of the gate. I suck in my cheeks, admire myself for a moment in the mirror. Will I be able to make love to my husband again? I researched the mating habits of swans, hours at the lake in Central Park watching the same pair, on my way to and from school. They're identical, except that the black knob at the base of the bill is larger in the cob. He will forage for aquatic vegetation, like grasses and sedges, which he delivers to the female, who lays them out. She's the artist who shapes the nest, forms a depression in the center for her eggs and her body while the edges remain raised. Some swans will create a moat around the edges to deter smaller mammals from invading. The cob assumes an aggressive posture during mating season to ward off other waterbirds. Staying close and mimicking each other's movements, they court, float side by side, dip their bills in the water, preen themselves and each other, turning their necks from one side to the other as if in a synchronized water ballet. They will repeat this ritual every year prior to mating.

When Apollo was born, seven sacred swans flew seven times around the island of Delos in celebration.

The grandfather clock asserts its domain and strikes. It's eight o'clock. My husband is late. He usually texts before his flight takes off and then again when it lands. In my delirium, I have forgotten that I did not receive such a text. The sole is swimming in a pool of butter and lemon turning to a white translucent color. The asparagus is steamed. The salad of buttery lettuce made, the potatoes roasted. I am a living goddess, drunk on two glasses of chardonnay. I light the candles. I fight against my growing despair. I catch my frame in the mirror by the sideboard, blurry, out of focus, and in that moment it reflects back an incarnation of dangerous beauty, or maybe I'm already drunk. My phone begins to buzz. It's on vibrate. I check it. A text: *Plane delayed another two hours. I could have driven home by now.*

*Why didn't you text earlier?* I text back.

The kitchen's a mess, saucepans in the sink, the chopping board filled with the ends of the stalks of asparagus, the remains of the onion I used for the sauce, and I stumble on my heels.

*I did*, he shoots back.

*I didn't get it*, I volley.

*What do u mean you didn't get it?*

He thinks because I drift off and my mind wanders sometimes that I am not paying attention. He hates when we watch television together and I read a text or email on my phone and lose my place in the drama and then ask him a question about what I have missed. He wants me one hundred percent involved in his dramas. I look at the puddle of wax that has dripped on the table, put my finger under the flame, and let the wax coat it. It burns. I search my phone, review my texts to see if he is right. If my mind is distracted. Maybe he did text me earlier. But before I can, he texts back.

*U right. I sent the text to our son by mistake. I'll text u when we take off.*

My spirit deflates as the image of my husband's impatient face comes into my mind's view. I see him shaking his head in frustration. No apology. No awareness that he has interrupted my plan, upset my mood. Undone my spell. I no longer care to make love to my husband. I make a plate and drink another glass of wine. The sole has gone soggy in its juices. The swords at the top of the asparagus are flaccid. The potatoes limp. I plate my menagerie of sole, potatoes, and asparagus for my husband and seal it tight with Saran Wrap, put it on the stove. Clean the dishes. Blow out the candles. Drink another glass of wine. It is my fourth?

I take off my dress, rub off my lipstick with a Kleenex—the red lip marks suddenly look obscene—put on my yoga clothes, and climb into bed.

I take out my reading glasses. I'm tired. Woozy from the wine. Maybe trying is not the answer, I say aloud. I do this now. I talk to myself. I thumb through my dog-eared copy of *The Odyssey* to plan for tomorrow, turning to one of my own notes in the margin. *Athena's divine female power and her trickery guide Odysseus through his journey to regain the domination of his home. Athena is Homer's grand feminist.*

## WEEK 9

I wake up in a sweat to pounding. It's so close it sounds as if it is coming from next door. I'm disoriented. A review of my new book heads the front page of *The New York Times*. *It is an abomination. A disgrace. To think an English teacher at the Academy Preparatory School could consider herself a major poet.* It takes me a few minutes before I realize it was a dream. More pounding, and that chiming aftereffect. It's excruciating. All day the construction workers, moving up and down from ropes attached to a platform underneath the scaffolding outside my window. I look at the clock. No use in going back to sleep. I shower, dress to get to school early to grade papers before my morning class. My husband's asleep on the couch with the nubby throw over his body exposing only his long bare legs with their freckles and birthmarks I have read like braille. He must have gotten in late from Chicago. Too late to get into my son's bed. His clothes are on the chair. His overnight bag in the hall on the bench. I go into the kitchen and find his empty plate in the sink. A wine stain on the counter. I creep out of my own apartment so as not to wake him.

As I descend to the vestibule of the building and exit, my neighbor's getting out of a cab. It is 7:00 a.m. She's wearing a fur vest and a fur hat. There is something in her that needs to be constantly satiated, soothed, and wrapped like an animal in its fur. I smell a hint of evening perfume, Coco Chanel (the very scent she gave me for my birthday), cigarette smoke, and a wisp of last night's spirits and activity in her hug. She kisses me on each cheek and squeezes my hand. Her hand is warm, her cheeks flushed, and another smell, nascent sex, overpowers. Yoga? I say, which is our secret word for her affair with the yoga instructor. She nods, a sleepy, mischievous look in her eyes. Ta, she says, kissing me on both cheeks. Let's get the families together over the hols, and then she dashes into the building before her husband wakes up.

On the way to the bus, I still smell her scent, a mixture of perfume and sex on my clothes. I feel complicit, knowing that she is carrying on while her husband is still asleep, knowing how sensitive her daughter is, and how she might react if she knew. She's acting impulsively. When one is in the throes of passion, it's impossible to realize the cost, how it continues to

exert itself, to cause longing and pain. Corroding other relationships, affecting even her kids. I fear that she is making a
mistake, that soon all will tumble like a building caving in on
itself. She has pushed the extremes.

When I arrive at school and log on to my computer, an email
from my publisher flashes in my inbox:

> There's a smart review published in the *Women's*
> *Review of Books*. Here's the link. And *The New*
> *York Times Book Review* has scheduled the re-
> view for next week!

There's a knock at my door. It's Lacy. He chairs our drama club
and is a senior faculty member in our department. Sometimes
he thinks he runs it. We missed you at the faculty meeting last
Friday, he says, smirking. Oh god. I forgot. I quickly cover. Dentist appointment, I say. You're looking rather unwell, he says
stroking his pointy white beard. You've lost weight. A bit pale
too. I'm fine, I say. I rub my lips together, relieved that I remembered to put on lipstick. He looks like a satyr, with his goat-like
beard sans mustache. He asks me about the book on my desk.
I tell him it's my new book of poetry. That finished copies just
arrived from my publisher. That cover, he says, picking it up.
What a mysterious self you hide in those books of yours. What
is this, your third? he says with a scowl. We missed you at the
meeting, he says, and leaves my classroom without a congratu-
latory remark. An aroma of lavender aftershave lingers.

He's written only one book to my knowledge. It's called *Utility and Delight*. It is a monograph on supernatural fiction. Charles Lacy has been teaching at the academy for forty years. He claims to have once been an actor and at the annual fundraiser performs his mastery of Dorian's monologue in *The Picture of Dorian Gray*. "Nothing can cure the soul but the senses, just as nothing can cure the senses but the soul." The same monologue every season for forty years. Each year a new generation of parents to please and stroke his coconut of an ego. He's notorious for grading papers based on use of punctuation and grammar, regardless of content. Revels in each missed comma. Mansplains in faculty meetings, sucking on one of the famous sour balls he keeps in a crystal bowl on his desk. Those sour balls. They've been in his crystal bowl for so long they've formed hair. This year Lacy came out to a class after he was offended by some homophobic jokes when he was teaching *Dracula*. Charlie Willowby, son of a hedge fund that bears his name, his father impeccably dressed, powdered, manicured, called the count a creepy homo in seminar. Lacy had had enough. He told the students how he'd been humiliated at school when he was their age for being gay. That he demanded more respect. His coming-out went viral. I was disappointed in Charlie. The boys always trying to impress each other. I was glad Lacy had the courage to come out to the class, he must have been hurt and fed up, and I knew it must have taken a lot of strength, but did he think no one knew?

Lacy's tried to challenge my course for ninth graders on modern and contemporary fiction by women. I don't get it. Is it just to claim the authority that is slowly slipping away from him as the world is changing? I've kept my own ambitions as a poet to a minimum at the academy out of fear of evoking jealousy or disapproval or fear that they'd feel I was neglecting my duties. Having been schooled by a mother who smiled and nodded when men of power spoke, who believes my father was a nameless hero, I have been a perpetrator of modesty and self-flagellation to feed the male ego, even as it has proved ineffectual. Even when the patriarchy doesn't care. The only one who has been hurt is me. No more. I put my computer on snooze and offer a silent prayer to Athena, goddess of wisdom, for a worthy review. I do not want to hear Lacy gloat. I hold my finished book in my hands, rub my finger along the outlines of the cover image of Leda and her swan, examine the spine, the binding, the beautiful typeface, and a too-often-neglected emotion of pride rushes through me.

Good morning, geniuses, I say to rows of half-asleep faces. Matt has his head on his desk and is snoring. Poor dear, I say, walking past him and touching his shoulder. Liam looks stoned and it's only nine in the morning. I wonder what makes him want to check out. I'll see if I can get him to talk to me in study hall. I decided long ago never to deride these lovely beings. My job is to give them agency. To give them a sense of purpose. Fifty percent or more living in their expensive apartments on Fifth Avenue and their palatial summer homes in Connecticut or the Hamptons. With mothers who have the time to lunch, who are philanthropists, who come to school presentations in the middle of the afternoon dressed in Chanel and Gucci and Prada that surely would cost me my monthly salary, and fathers who are CEOs in corporations, numbers guys. What vacancy in their eyes, a gateway to their empty souls. I detest their suede loafers that look like slippers, their handmade suits with gold cufflinks, their fancy Rolex watches in shiny blinding gold. Their entitlement. Every inch swaddled in overpriced paraphernalia so that they look like they might topple over. They condescend to faculty at school auctions or sports events as if we are one of their servants, then later kiss up to us to get more attention for their son or daughter. I fear for how their entitlement will shape their sons. The high-minded emails they send pressing for a better grade, the fears that their son will not get into Harvard or Yale. I could plaster the building with them. I would give A's to all my students, for having to endure their parents, if it were not for wanting to keep my job. And the boys on scholarships from less entitled backgrounds, I wonder what it is like for them, to see the lifestyle of the haves against their own?

I begin our discussion with Book Five, Odysseus trapped on Calypso's island. He wants to see the smoke that rises over his homeland, to return home to his household, to see his wife and son. He's a fighter, leader, king, lover, beggar, but also a man who cries and is homesick. Remember the first line of the poem, "Let me tell you about a complicated man." What do you think the poem is getting at? I propose. That Odysseus is the embodiment of both the male and the female? Tyler questions. Poor Tyler. His shirt always untucked, his pants too short; he's grown a foot taller in just a month. I nod. I like that, I say.

In my country, masculinity means power, says Mohammed. Men do not reveal emotion. Tyler inches up his hand.
Take Calypso, it's genius. Homer cast her to test Odysseus's
strength. She's beautiful, yeah, but she also lives on her own
island and rules. Hermes commands her to release Odysseus
upon Zeus's wishes, and she retorts that he's just jealous because she's sleeping with a mortal. She offers Odysseus immortality if he stays but he refused. You're right. Male and female
roles are more fluid in the poem. Penelope holds her own too,
James says. Fending off those suitors. Every night unwinding
her knitting to begin anew, waiting for her husband to return.
None of you want to live in a society where women are behind
a veil. In my house, my mum rules, says Mohammed. Imagine
choosing home over immortality, Reginald remarks. Human
suffering over immortality.

Home, what is home, my mind drifts. Sunday mornings,
family dinners, holidays. It all means more when everything
is at risk. I want to ask the boys what reality and identity
would look like if masculinity were not the ideal to which
to aspire, if heterosexuality were not the ideal, if whiteness
were not the ideal. I want to tell them they don't have to aspire to be Atlas holding the world on their shoulders but that
would be presumptuous and didactic. They must discover it
themselves. I drift back, look at the clock. We've got fifteen
minutes left. For homework, I asked them to write their own
contemporary myth using Greek gods or goddesses. I call on
Thomas to read his first. He's sensitive, with pale skin; dark,

spiky goth-like hair; green eyes; and long dark lashes. The world affects him. He comes to my office hours concerned about global warming and the indecency of our president. He always looks like he's about to cry. He has two mothers, one a cellist for the New York City Ballet Orchestra, and the other a chef; they live in the East Village. I've never heard him say a bad word about anyone. The other boys don't know what to make of him. They can't dismiss him; he's too full of feeling to be dismissed.

My myth is a riff on Adios, the goddess of reverence, respect, and shame, and her companion, Nemesis, the goddess "of divine retribution and revenge, who would show her wrath to any human being that would commit hubris before the gods. She was considered a remorseless goddess," he says using the index finger and middle finger of each hand like bunny ears to mimic quotation marks. He looks in my direction for approval. A direct quote he confirms. A few students snicker. At last, they have awoken. He reads a brilliant tale of a conniving candidate for president who uses tactics of lying and deceit to win the election. Through acts of trickery, Nemesis shames him for his boasting, turns him into an orange-faced gorgon, and sends him to the underworld. I nod approval. The class claps and breaks into laughter. My job is done. Class dismissed. Once the students have left the classroom, I open my desk drawer for my fountain pen. I push the box with the onyx swan—which, having caught the light, seems to be winking at me—farther into the drawer.

## WEEK 10

I trudge up the twenty-eight granite steps at the museum, stop to turn around and admire the view. There are fountains on each side of the staircase, as in the Palais Royal in Paris. Linden trees in rows. A crowd of pigeons is picking at a leftover sandwich. Someone beneath me is eating a hot dog; its feral smell floats past. Next to me a kid is devouring one of those stale pretzels with rocks of salt on top; I've heard they're baked somewhere in the subway halls, but that may be an urban legend. The scent of roasted nuts from the other vendor takes reign as the wind shifts. Next to me a group of Japanese businessmen. A few steps down a couple with arms locked making love as they speak. If there is luck to be had, it's here, on this step, and me, a resident of the museum I can leave or enter at will. The impending *New York Times* review is getting to me. *Please don't let it be Pynyon.* But the review in the *Women's Review of Books* was glowing, I tell myself. Inside the museum, I glance at the membership table. The boy-man is not there. In his place is a woman dressed in a matching powder-blue cashmere set, with bifocals dangling from a chain around her neck. The museum is crowded today. A new exhibition by van Gogh brings in droves.

I enter the Greek and Roman rooms to escape the crowded lobby. In the corner of the gallery, I note that the handsome guard is indeed the boy-man from the membership table. I smile at him. He's attained that state of solitary silence that guards at the museum have mastered. He's standing up straight, chin raised. I'm proud that he's made the transition to guard. He smiles back. I think to approach and then retreat. He's practicing stillness.

Marble statue of Aphrodite
(1st or 2nd century A.D., Roman)

Aphrodite has come from her bath. She is extraordinary; voluptuous, her body all her own. She will not be acquired or dominated or feel herself grow small at the feet of another. Shall all women aspire to her self-possession, as if she's holding something of herself within while also willing to be seen?

# JILL BIALOSKY

A drawing beside the statue shows that one arm, now only a phantom arm, attempts to cover her breasts. It's no wonder that her beauty, desirability, vanity—when she begged Paris to deem her the most beautiful of all the goddesses and offered him Helen, spawned by Leda and Zeus—incited a war.

Aphrodite was not subject to the same rules as mortals. She made love with Ares in the bed in which she was betrothed to Lord Hephaestus, not knowing that the sun god had seen them and told Hephaestus of his wife's infidelity. Enraged, Hephaestus retreated to his chambers, where he who made all the weapons for the gods constructed chains so strong they could never be undone. He fastened them on the ceilings and around the bed, and departed. Ares, like any obsessed lover, couldn't get enough, and Aphrodite, upon his entrance, invited him to her bed. The chains, like an iron spiderweb, trapped them in their embrace so that they could not move. Poor Hephaestus; revenge was not enough. He was heartbroken. Hephaestus turned to the gods for help, and upon feasting themselves on the display of the trapped lovers, they laughed at him. Oh, to laugh at another's pain! The terrible, deceitful gods have no mercy.

The museum bell sounds. It's 4:45. I don't want to leave. I want to camp here, sleep among the gods and goddesses. I pass by Jupiter, the Roman version of Poseidon, and for a moment, like the lovers Aphrodite and Ares, I'm trapped and cannot move.

Bronze statuette of Jupiter Capitolinus
(1st–2nd century A.D., Roman)

It's my husband incarnate, the do-gooder, raising his fist, commanding, towering over me, declaring his decree. Do you see that look of self-righteous scorn he casts my way? Rapidly, I feel weak, as if I too will soon be punished.

## APARTMENT 9B

Opening the steel door, I almost trip over my husband's loafers on the straw mat in the doorway. They are ancient, as ancient as the straw mat we have wiped our shoes upon for twenty years. I can barely stand to look at his toothbrush. The bristles splay open. He won't let a thin slip of soap in the shower fall into the drain. He berates me for consuming too many paper towels.

He's reclined on the couch watching the Giants game. In Greek mythology the giants are a race of men who fought the gods. In *The Iliad*, they were the sons of Gaea formed from the blood that fell when Uranus was castrated by his son, Cronus. But in this game the Giants are losing and my husband, in a ripped long-sleeve T-shirt and sweatpants, is not in a good mood. But no matter. He is entitled to his leisure, even if it causes him distress. And I have always liked the shape of his body, if only I could slip into his arms. Instead, I join him on the other end of the sofa. I prefer to look at him, rather than imagine his image cast in greenish bronze. He glances at his watch. The one with the big Roman hands. Time comforts him, the second-by-second, minute-by-minute motion. The calculation of something amounting to a crescendo. He likes its precision, how it won't betray him.

How was your day? I ask. To check in, though I can sense something has happened, just by the look in his face. He's been frustrated because a grant he was hoping for didn't come through. I wish he would talk about it. He is a man of few words. Mostly declarative, rarely ponderous. Conversation keeps a house active, sometimes I would prod, and then I stopped, and it was better, to accept.

How *was* my day? he says, looking up from the Roman hands on his watch. Yes, how was your day? I want to say, again, because I don't like to be mimicked, but I refrain because I can see that clearly, I'm right, something's happened. He stands up. Turns off the game. Why didn't you tell me? he says. His look is grave; it frightens me. Tell you what? I say. We've barely spoken. It's been almost two months now, I tread.

It's bad enough that I had to find it out from Jason at the lab. One of your fans who reads your poetry, he says sternly. Find out what? I ask. What's he talking about? The review of your book. The one you've been waiting for. That one, he says, and looks at my book with the cover of lusty Leda embracing the swan, sitting on our coffee table. It's online today, he says. Is it good? It isn't, is it? My mood sinks. I know it's a cliché, but how else to describe it? Like the bottom going out in that terrifying ride at the amusement park when I was a kid. Like a kite that has flopped to the ground, having lost wind.

Is it *good?* he says again, and chuckles. You tell me if it's good. He thrusts his open laptop at me, and I see alongside a photo of my book, a new book by the Visiting Poet. Our two photos are next to each other. That scarf again wrapped around his neck. I freeze. It can't be true. I look to see the byline of the reviewer. Of course it is! Hugh Pynyon! I give the computer back to my husband. I don't want to read it, I say. I fear I may go into shock. The Visiting Poet's new book? What book?

The swan in yours and the swan in the Visiting Poet's book— what's his name, the one from your school, he says, are in conversation, that's what the reviewer says. We were colleagues for all of last year, I say. Maybe that's what he means. He complained he was blocked, unable to write the entire semester. I had no idea he had a new book in the works. About a swan? My neck prickles with heat, my cheeks burning. Listen, my husband says, and reads from the review.

> In *The Black Swan* the poet makes evident that rape and seduction are near equivalent. The speaker admonishes the coy swan, protecting her eggs, her mate ready to pounce if the interloper comes near. In *The Rape of the Swan*, desire represents danger. The swan likes the seduction of the interloper, but she resists. It's as if the two poets were themselves entangled in an erotic encounter.

I push my body farther into the couch's cushion to contain myself. My husband continues to read from the review. I'm barely listening because my heart is beating so fast I can't catch my breath, as though I've stepped out of my body.

> Read side by side, the two books reenact a courtship. It would be unfair to liken *The Rape of the Swan* to *The Black Swan*, except for two things. The two poets taught together last year at the acclaimed Academy Preparatory and were speakers at the same poetry conference in Taos, New

Mexico. Further, there is a coy cross-referencing
in the two works that an astute reader can follow, leading the swans to a lush lake of erotic
entanglement. Unfortunately, *The Rape of the
Swan* lies in the shadow of the bigger and more
ambitious voice of *The Black Swan*, as if indeed
it wants to dominate the lesser work. As if the
author of *The Rape of the Swan* had taken *The
Black Swan* and reimagined it for her own gain.

What? I say, my voice quivering. That's absurd! I haven't even
read his book. A wave of heat washes over me. I'm unbalanced.
I can't think straight. I see in my husband's eyes that I've hurt
and shamed him, and I can't bear it.

An erotic entanglement, my husband says. And I have to read
about it in *The New York Times*. I didn't know anything about
his book, I say sheepishly. It's a review about our books written
by a misogynist, I counter. Poetry is not reality, I mutter, humbled, blackened, my fists clenched.

What's absurd is . . . this. My husband opens his arms and
points to our one-thousand-square-foot apartment, where
we have made camp for almost twenty years. It isn't working.
What isn't? I ask.

You figure it out, professor, he says, rising from the couch,
peering at me. I almost lose my breath. I touch his wrist to

lure him back down to the couch. To try to speak to him. It's the first time I've touched him in months. He flinches, and my heart lands in my stomach. Why did you want to become a research scientist instead of treating patients? I asked my husband once. Because I can't bear to see suffering, he said. Imagine, I thought, he thinks he can hide behind his microscope and never experience it. And I remember thinking he must have been so hurt, so divided in his loyalties as a child. And now, look what I've done to him. Have you heard from our son? he says. I shake my head no. Not for a couple of days. This is ridiculous, he says, though I'm not sure I understand why my not hearing from our son is my fault. I'm done, he says. He picks up his laptop, goes into the bedroom, and packs a bag. He kicks the garbage can in the kitchen and spills our trash all over the floor, then slams the door after him. No, he can't leave. Where will he go? I want to text him, urge him to come back, but I can't. I'm helpless. He's always left me helpless. I knew there would be consequences, every act is tied to another. I want to go after him, but I can't.

My copy of *The Rape of the Swan* is like a beating heart on the coffee table, the pages spilling out its blood. Minutes pass. Hours. *The Black Swan*. What has he done? He wrote his own version using mine as a template? Had he been using me all along to awaken his lust, his pride, so that he'd have something to write about, he who claimed he was blocked? Impotent. How could his book have come out so quickly? And then I remember what he said, early in the term. How he doesn't revise. How his poems come out in almost a single burst. Maybe he'd begun the book then? When I first showed him an early draft and we had talked about it. Why did I trust him? Yes, I subverted my longings into the poem, yes, maybe you could say I appropriated aspects of our involvement into its theatrics, but what he's done is unconscionable. There was always something about him that disturbed me, in spite of enjoying his company, being drawn to him. He prided himself, amid all else, on himself. It's a terrible thought to hold true. I want to refute it, maybe it's all some weird mistake, but dread won't leave. No. It's impossible. I can't put it all together. I will not allow it to be true. Pynyon has made it all up. Or maybe the Visiting Poet gave Pynyon a copy. I forgot they were friends. Playing poker, getting drunk, deriding poets with more acclaim, dishing "fuckable" female poets. This is why men and women cannot be equal. His book is about a swan? Impossible. The night is black. I feel it growing colder and tighter around me. It's like the eerie sound when the loud engine of the lawn mower finally stops and quiet reigns. And then it comes to me. That day at the assembly when the Visiting Poet gave his closing reading to the school. It was the week before the term ended. Afterward, one of the students asked why he became a poet. And, to explain, he recited the myth I told him, almost verbatim, about Pan. At the time, it didn't bother me. I thought he said it to the audience as if we were having a private conversation, a sort of intimate acknowledgment of our closeness. But no. He stole it from me to puff himself up. I can't bear it. All those questions about my work, why I write. Once he told me that my poems have a depth of experience that his work lacks. It was a poem I'd written years ago, about my grief over the loss of a child. I go to the refrigerator and find a bottle of my husband's wine, it's expensive, a French burgundy. I shouldn't waste it alone, on myself, but it's the only bottle I have. I don't want to think, to feel. My mind is racing. I drink glass after glass in a stupor throughout the hours of the night, each calculated by the chime of my husband's inherited grandfather clock, but my thoughts keep running, searching.

## APARTMENT 9B

All night the radiator banging. Battling. I awake in terror, still flattened to the couch, a panic that won't leave. I don't know how many hours, days have passed. I dreamt that my house was open with no walls. That there was a wild party in my home and my husband was not there. Couples drinking, having sex in different rooms, pilfering our wine, and stealing my jewelry. The party wouldn't end. I kept trying to tell the guests that it was over, and while some shuttled out, in each room were more guests. I employed my son to help me; we were frantic to get these people seizing hold of our home, turning it into a bacchanal mockery, out. The dream went on for hours. And then my husband came in, it was dawn by then, and all the people fled, and my husband told me he was in love with someone else. His face was riddled with trickery. It was an expression I had never seen him wear. I was wild with jealousy. I was going to lose my home. When I woke up, I realized, of course, I was Penelope in my dream. *The Odyssey*, I thought, when I made the connection, was about the pain of desertion. Of losing one's home. It is about the meaning of home.

I search my phone for a text from my husband, a missed call. Nothing. I flee to the kitchen to make coffee. I'm still wearing yesterday's clothes. Weak from lack of food. Headachy from the wine. I rub my crusted eyes. For months I've been trying to rid myself of this weight, to regain my freedom, but it's useless. My husband's gone.

I make coffee. Check my phone again to see if my husband has deigned to tell me where he has gone. If my son has deemed me worthy of check-in. There are no texts. I replay the words with my husband from the day before. I can't bear to think that my own poem has wounded and humiliated him. It's not him, it's marriage that I despise. Its constant compromise, always having to think if I've been good, if I've done enough. To think of others before myself. To take care of all my chores, responsibilities, before I can squirrel away an hour or two to write. To have to question my freedom, and of what I can say and not say in my work. I make myself a meager breakfast, a soft-boiled egg and dry toast. I can't remember the last time I ate. I stick my fork in the egg and it bleeds yellow with a speck of blood. I throw it into the trash. I look around at my bookshelves. All these books. All these spines. All these voices that have penetrated my consciousness. On one row, our family photo albums. I comb through one. Our son tearing down the slide. Running from the waves at the beach. The snow forts we built together in the park. The sleigh rides. The long nights when he would not go to bed. The moments when I caught my husband looking at me. That twinge of desire. The tears, arguments, slammed doors. I must deconstruct what has been constructed. Dismantle and forge. Tear down the walls, strip our marriage bed with its sturdy wood platform of its sheets, its ancient mattress and pillows, and shake them all out. Desire is a phantom.

I take my son's hockey equipment, his remaining pairs of running shoes, and fill the elevator to take them to our storage locker in the basement. Put my papers on the dining room table into folders and file them in a drawer, polish the golden wood of the table until it shines. I water the drooping hosta my mother gave to me when our son was born, and our daughter had perished. I've had it now for eighteen years, and miraculously it's thriving. All these years she still threatens to die, huddling her leaves close, almost caving in on herself, and then she comes to life again. The pleasure, it's insane, when white buds appear and flower.

I do the dishes and take out the trash. Anger rises. I can't comprehend it fully. I don't know what to do. I'm sweating, panting. Outside my door I see the Sunday *New York Times* on my doorstep. It's got a stain on it. Whether from the rain or a dog. I step on it and go to the trash barrels. My neighbor's puffing anxiously on a cigarette out the open window on the stairwell. She's wearing a pink Coco Chanel sweatshirt and matching running pants, her hair in a high ponytail. I know, she says, referring to the fact that I've caught her smoking. She rubs out her cigarette on the windowsill and puts the butt in the trash can. She looks at me. You look terrible, she says. I nod. One of those sleepless nights, I say. She consoles me with a look of recognition. Something's happened. I can't give up the yoga teacher, she says. And my husband knows, she says. I want to tell her your daughter is alive. Wake up. Save your family. But I don't want to be a bad friend when she's suffering. I reach over and give her a hug. The back of her shoulders and her ribs are bony like mine. Marriage, it's not easy, I say, and shake my head. I don't know how much longer I can do this, she says. There's something I've wanted to tell you. Tears well in her eyes. But I can't now. I've got to go. Her soft ballet-like shoes make little patters, almost like sighs, as she walks off, the smell of cigarette smoke in her wake.

Zeus sought to punish Prometheus for bringing fire to mortals by creating the first woman, Pandora, to deliver misfortune to the house of man. Though she was beautiful and sought-after, crafty Zeus gave her a jar. She was told never to open it, but, curious, she did—and out flew the ills of humanity such as old age, illness, hard work, so all that was left was hope. Yes, Zeus. Women are complex. We don't always listen to what we are told. We have our own conscience and system of beliefs. We can't be ruled. Our genitalia are not always our devoted guide. Some of us need more. I think of Jason and Medea, of passion, jealousy, destruction. Then, sick of myself, I retrieve the damp and bulging newspaper from the doormat, take it inside, lock the door. The book review jammed between the sports and business sections. Page 11. My photo next to the Visiting Poet's.

The review takes up two pages. *Both are book-length poems in sonnet crowns. Each poet enacts a seduction by an interloper to a pair of mated swans, with startlingly different outcomes, influenced by motifs of swans in fairy tales, poetry, literature, myth, and most notably in conversation with Yeats's "Leda and the Swan."* I skim passages. Pynyon accuses me of playing the female card to gain sympathy from the reader. He mentions my *vixen-like* author photo and writes that it is hard to imagine that I'm as immune to desire as the swan in my poem. Vixen-like? What is he talking about? In the photo I'm wearing a white ruffled blouse and a velvet jacket. Now I'm a vixen? Worse, he accuses *me* of appropriating the Visiting Poet's poem! I scan the words . . . I can't take it all in . . . *self-conscious, overly stylized . . . an attempt to give swans the same qualities as humans . . . Though technically precise, and ambitious, the poem is oddly mute. If the poet employed even a smidgen of irony, the poem may have been saved from cloying earnestness.* He describes in phallic detail, mocking me, the moment in my poem when the cob seduces the swan. *He's on top of her, he hisses and grunts . . . thrusting his phallus into the*

*vagina of the female, but good lord . . . a ruckus of flying feathers
ensues . . . Is this a tragedy or a comedy?* Oh god, it's awful.
Embarrassing. Humiliating. *In contrast, the poet of* The Black
Swan *is a master of machination. Machiavellian . . . Uses wit
like a cutting sword. Black swans are wont to cheat and are least
loyal. The poet revels in this perversion.* I scan again . . . *brilliant, masterful, triumphantly original . . . prizeworthy.* Prizeworthy? Of course. Once again, the male poet is the genius.
*The male swan desires a white swan who is already mated for
life. He moves closer to her, wraps his wings around her waist,
and in a fury of passion penetrates her . . . tears the pen apart
in a frenzy of ecstasy, leaving white feathers floating on the lake,
having her as she wanted to be had but could not face her own
unconscious erotic impulses.* Having her as she wanted to be
had? Not being able to face her own unconscious erotic impulses.
What nerve. How twisted. *After the assault, he steals her eggs
and then leaves, purloining not only her offspring but her heart
and soul. Taken together, the two books seem to ask, Who is the
true abductor, the victim or the perpetrator? Like black swan theory,* The Black Swan *has demonically left its mark on the reader.
One only wishes* The Rape of the Swan *were as indelible.*

Black swan theory. We talked about it that day at the lake.
Hadn't he said that what happened would be a surprise to Leda
afterward, that everything would be determined by the event?
That it should have been expected. What arrogance. Oh my
god, what has he done? It's all a game to him. What gets him
off. Why? To continue the pursuit. To assume his dominance,

like the black swan in his poem? Because he wanted to make sure I'd never forget? *Having her as she wanted to be had.* How could I have forgotten that men had always ruled, from the beginning of civilization, houses of worship and all aspects of government? That angry men brought our country to revolution? It was his mating dance, the cob's, not mine.

My nails are peeling. I run my fingers through my hair, a few strays cling to my hand. My muscles have grown soft. Outside it is raining. Pouring. Wind is sending branches hurtling. Pynyon read my poem through the male lens, luxuriating in the assault. Notorious for wielding his squirrely and vicious pen on women. No mention of how, above all, *The Rape of the Swan* is a nature poem. My mind is running ahead, I can't catch up. I stole it from him? Is that what Pynyon insinuated? Of course a woman would be the one to usurp. He stole from me! I should have seen it more clearly. The way he swaggered when he walked, his tweed jacket and his lilac scarf, a genteel disguise for brutality. His stoicism, his arrogance. Nothing can hurt or unbalance you if you feel above everyone else. I despise his arrogance, the fact that I will have to remain silent. Because to show hurt or anger would only exacerbate his performance. No, I won't give him that. I won't give him one more ounce of me. I will write myself out of him. *The Black Swan.* It's incomprehensible. He'd written his own long poem in crowns of sonnets, taking my themes, adopting my form? In another version of the myth of Leda and the swan, it is the goddess Nemesis who is dogged by Zeus. After Zeus impregnates her, she vanishes to Sparta and lays a purple-blue egg in the marshes outside the city. Leda finds the egg and puts it in a chest until it hatches. When Helen is born, Leda raises her as her daughter. This is the version I prefer, for to be a nemesis is preferable to being a victim, and in the final version of *The Rape of the Swan* I allude to the glorious purple-blue egg, kept in a depression in the marshes. Of course, no mention of its suggested meaning, in Pynyon's review. I hear a loud thud. My neighbor? No, it can't be. My imagination is getting the better of me. I don't know what to do. I want to call my husband. Ask him to help me, like he always does, but I can't. I go in the medicine cabinet for a Valium. I want to call my mother, but she won't understand. She can't help me either. The clock by the bedside ticks away each minute. And then I remember. I go to the drawer in my nightstand. I take out his book *Denying Heaven* and find the note tucked inside. I unfold it and read.

> Forgive me. I was drunk, I'm sorry if I was a brute and went too far. I know it's no excuse, but I couldn't control it. Our conversation at the lake about "Leda and the Swan" took over. It left me with an overwhelming desire to obliterate any space between us physically and artistically. You must know what I mean. You're my most important muse. The poem about your swans, it was a breakthrough for me to read it. It has inspired me to do something grand and operatic. I'll see you next week at school, we'll talk.

And then he signed his name with a scrawl.

It's all there in the note, written in his shaky hand. All I have to do is to send it to *The New York Times*. Take them both down, Pynyon and his disciple. Or maybe send it to his wife. The thought momentarily soothes me, and then panic overtakes again; I put the note inside my bag and grab my coat, my umbrella.

## ACADEMY

The ginkgo tree outside our building sheds its leaves all in one swoosh as I walk out the door. What sudden nakedness. Its bare branches look as if they'll break. There's a moving van parked out front. A piece of furniture, maybe part of a sectional, is wrapped in cellophane and carried by two of the movers like a corpse. A chill runs through me. My hands, my face, my bones. It's raining, pouring. Streaming in a violent downpour. I walk up the avenue. The rain is barreling down, almost in buckets. Soon there will be flooding. I've forgotten what I've set out to do. I duck under an awning for relief, to think. To calm myself. And then I see an empty cab approaching. I hail it and tell the driver to take me to the Academy. In the back of the cab, with the shield separating me and the driver, I feel as if I've been imprisoned. I crack open the window, careful not to let in the rain. And then I remember what's happened. The terrible review. It's all there in print. My husband has found me out. He knows. Of course he knows. It feels as if an elephant is stomping on my chest. I'm shaking. This is the reason the Visiting Poet hasn't been in touch. He knows if I reveal what he's done, what he's stolen, it would reveal everything. I open the door, climb up the steps, my sneakers squeaking into my classroom. I take the note from my bag, go to the copy room, and make a photocopy. Then back to my classroom, to my desk, take the onyx swan charm out of my drawer and its box. I wrap it in the cotton it came with and put it in an envelope with the xeroxed note. The note says everything. Let him think what he wants. Be frightened of what I might reveal. What I have on him. I wonder how many other women he's groomed for his muse. I seal the envelope, address it to the Visiting Poet, stamp it, and then take the rock, put it in my raincoat pocket, tramp down the staircases and out the door.

Down the block I drop the envelope in the mailbox. For a moment I feel free. He's been exorcised. I stop under an awning to catch my breath. I don't know who I am anymore. Poet, wife, teacher, mother. MOTHER. I call my son, I need him, and he accepts my call. It's a minor miracle. The minute I hear his voice, I crack. Your father's left me, I say. My hands are shaky. The rain is soaking my shoes, bleating down on the awning. He's angry at me. He can't reason when he gets that way. You know how he gets. I know I must stop. I must not pit my son in the middle, but I can't. It's raining so hard I can't see clearly. Everything's a jumble.

Mom, what are you talking about? Dad's fine. I love dad. You sound really weird. He asks where I am. I tell him I just left school and that it's pouring rain. Rainwater slips down my collar like slivers of shaved ice. He judges me. Like he does with you. Mom, jeez, calm down. Everyone knows dad gets crazy. My friends laugh. I don't care. I mean, yeah, but it's Dad. It will be okay. Dad would never leave you.

I've said too much. I'm burning down the house. I must stop. My son's voice calms me. I want to see you. I was thinking I could book a flight today. Be there for a few days. Help you with your work. A reprieve, a wave of serenity amid terror. My hands dripping with rain as I hold the phone. The rain pounds the pavement. Thanks, Mom, but I don't need your help, really. I go cold. My little boy. But I want to help, I say. He tells me he's fine. More people have come to suffer the rain underneath the awning. I make room and fumble with my umbrella, in one hand, my phone in the other. I look up. All the leaves have fallen off the trees. Mom, take a deep breath. Everything will be okay. Trust me.

Since when did my son become an adult? And then I remember, a few days before he left for college. We met for lunch. He was wearing a zip-up sweater and corduroys and seemed to have grown taller. I almost didn't recognize him when he sat down next to me. When the waiter came to take our order, he turned to me and said, Mom, what are you having, whereas before, he went first. He ordered a chicken Caesar salad with such politeness that I gleamed with pride. He asked me what I was working on. I told him about the swans and my new book. At home, he rarely asked me anything about myself. I was always asking the questions.

You're right, I say. I'm sorry. It will all work out. It was just a fight. I shouldn't have upset you. He tells me he has to go, that he'll miss lunch. I'll be fine. I'm ashamed. I stare at my phone. It is heavy in my dripping wet hand once he clicks off. I shudder from the cold.

Fuck it. I open my umbrella and run. It feels good to run in the rain, to get drenched. To think of only the rain, of running and fleeing. My umbrella turns inside out, it's useless. I dump it in the trash. The rock in my pocket drags me down. Holds me back. Along with my umbrella, I throw it into the wrought-iron trash can and through the peepholes the minerals flicker like demonic eyes watching me. *I'm done with you*, I say to them, and suddenly I feel lighter, almost as if I'm flying.

## DODGING THE RAIN IN THE MUSEUM

I reach the museum steps, where else am I to go, and almost trip. Images and thoughts run by and through my mind. Toward the steps the plazas with fountains, benches, trees call out to me. Underneath the trees, someone is playing a clarinet. Brahms, Clarinet Sonata no. 2 in E-flat. I drop a dollar bill in the clarinet's open case. There is a mime wearing all black with a sad clown face huddled under an umbrella. I walk up the steps, counting each one to keep myself steady. The steps are thirteen and a half feet high, and as I mount them, I try to gain strength. I hold my head up and imagine I'm an aristocrat entering my home and not a fallen woman.

The guard who has morphed from the boy-man at the membership table is in the gallery when I enter. He looks substantial and attentive. Like the lions at the gates of the pyramids. You're wet, he says. You got caught in it.

I'm okay, I say, but I'm not. I'm not feeling well. I'm shivering from the air conditioning on my wet skin. From my confession to my son. Because I've humiliated my husband. Outside from the windows, the sky is nearly black, the heavens in turmoil. The rain won't end. Maybe I'm walking in my sleep. A shadow of myself. I would like to ask the boy-man how he is evolving, if he did things he can't take back, but those are questions strangers don't ask of each other. The collar of his shirt has slipped underneath his jacket. I reach back to my own collar and nod; he gets the gesture and fixes it. A woman approaches the guard. She unfolds the map and points. She's lost in the museum's labyrinth. I walk away and let him do his job. I go immediately to the gods. I demand answers. I circle the gallery. I don't know how to quell my panic.

*Theseus Slaying the Minotaur*
(1843, Antoine-Louis Barye, French)

Theseus killing the Minotaur. Those thick, sinewy thighs. The body of a man and head of a bull. An apt representation. Daedalus, the great architect and engineer, built the labyrinth to contain the monster. It was so well designed that once you were inside, it was impossible to find your way out. Before Theseus entered the labyrinth to slay the Minotaur, Ariadne gave him a ball of red yarn to leave as a trail. But as in all Greek myths, victory is short-lived. Theseus had promised his father that once he murdered the Minotaur, he would change the sails on his ship from black to white so his father would know he was safe. So caught up in his desire to return to Ariadne, he forgot to change the sails, and his father, thinking he was dead, threw himself into the sea and drowned. Desire is dangerous. I walk through Gallery 157. The Greek vases and armor are under glass.

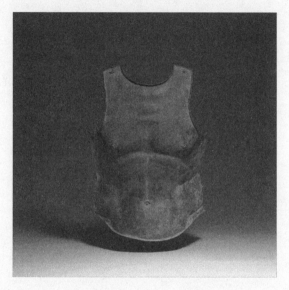

Bronze cuirass (body armor)
(4th century B.C., Greek, Apulian)

The cuirass, worn by horsemen, was a major element of a Greek warrior's panoply. This one shows the muscles of the chest, idealized in heroic proportions. Think of wearing this thick template on the chest all day. The weight of it. Looking at it causes me to sweat. This sheath of armor, like a Greek sculpture of a torso, an apt metaphor for the male fending off vulnerability, afraid to fully submit or be in the wrong, always shaking his head, superior, willful, protecting himself with his breast-plate. Hiding in the labyrinth, plotting, ready to pounce. The shields are oppressive, forbidding. I can't bear to think about it. The Visiting Poet dressed in his armor of illusion. And my husband—I should never have tried or wanted him to be any different. Who would he be without the props of his life? His clearheadedness. His stubbornness. His impatience.

It's noisy, a sea of people in the Greek and Roman gallery. I walk through the hall to the Temple of Dendur to try to quiet myself. I sit on the slate steps looking into the black marble pool. My head aches from thinking. I wish this to be a dream and close my eyes so that my thoughts might dissolve into the ether of my not wanting to ponder them. My husband's words reverberate. I don't know when to step out from my imagination, from my dream-making. And look at what has resulted. *The Black Swan?* Is the Visiting Poet sending me a message? Is his book some kind of code? Auden said, in the elegy he wrote for Yeats, that "poetry makes nothing happen." But it can divert a life. I don't know what to do with myself. The review read through the lens of a misogynist is a double assault. Denial is a powerful emo-tion, but this cannot be denied. Maybe Pynyon's right. Maybe my book's no good. Too personal, too transparent. A mockery. Imbued with my egotistical desire to reach for the ideal.

But why not? Suddenly I feel myself expanding. My arms elon-gate, my neck, I feel light, feathery. I look into the black pool of water to make sure I have not shape-shifted. I touch my neck to make sure it's mine. I look further into the black depths, and then it is Narcissus who appears. He rebuffs Echo only to fall in love with the face he sees in the water's reflection: "Unwittingly, he desired himself, and was himself the object of his own approval, at once seeking and sought, himself kindling the flame with which he burned." How awful, to love only the reflection of one-self. The Visiting Poet had argued for it when we discussed the myth. Then I doubted whether he was serious. How bewitching, the self, who tricks us into believing what we want to believe.

The sky is no longer blue. It is a wash of white clouds, and a bird flies ominously overhead. And look, now two young boys are peering into the reflecting pool known as the Nile, throwing in their pennies, making wishes. A reflecting pool holds the whispers of so many desires and wants. Copper can withstand water. It can withstand heat. It can withstand temperature extremes from below freezing to well above boiling without rupturing. But I wonder whether I will be able to withstand the disdain in which my husband holds me. I peer deeper into the black water and feel myself wanting to lurch forward like a swan, to drown. All those hours I spent on the poem. All those days trapped in my own world. *My own world.* What might I do to subvert these horrible thoughts? *The Black Swan?* How could I have trusted him?

When I was a child, I was afraid to sing. I was afraid to speak up, humbled by the power of an authoritative voice. While my mother was at work at the dress shop, she sometimes brought me to the library, where I spent my days reading. I loved the smell of books. The new ones like fresh paper, the old ones like mold and dust. Books were more than companions. They brought me the world. I became increasingly aware that the world I had grown up in was ruled by men with their locked briefcases (what was so important?), men in political office, men who were my principals, my teachers, my professors. Men I had to be cautious of when they catcalled as I walked down the street, or when I was alone on a subway platform with one who sized me up. I wonder how many men have feared being alone on a subway platform. Or feared getting into their cars alone at night. If I sat at a bar and a man spoke to me, I worried that if I was too polite, he would think I was interested, and yet I did not want to hurt his feelings. My mother told me that a man would sleep with any woman if she let him. That I must be on guard. Protect myself. As a woman, I wanted to turn heads, but only the right heads. Men were dangerous to a young girl, a young woman both in the workplace and otherwise. Always Mehta raising his voice in a faculty meeting to snuff out the females on our faculty. The gaslighting of accomplishment. My worries that they'd disapprove if my work slipped. It has taken me years at the Academy, to stand up to the male faculty, to learn that I must undo everything I had been taught to think for myself and find my own voice, my own power. Why did I care? And then, after I gave birth, I questioned whether I should write about motherhood, about the loss of a child in my work, if I'd then be considered a domestic poet. If I had a family, would that mean I didn't put my work at the center? And then I thought, Why wouldn't I reveal motherhood as a subject? Why would I be hesitant. It was powerful. More powerful than anything that had happened in my young life. Because I worried whether it would affect my career. Whether my work would be seen as lesser by critics, male poets who dominated. I had to push past those fears. A male poet, of course, would never be seen as lesser for having a family. I told my neighbor's daughter about all of this. I want her to not have to question and second guess herself like I did.

The last time I saw her, just before she went back for her senior year in college, she had grown more relaxed with herself, more confident, and her writing had blossomed, acquired a clarity and boldness of expression that took my breath away. I want your work to be noticed, to be spectacular, I told her. I was proud that she'd become a feminist, like I would have wished for my daughter. I shared parts of my long poem with her and was taken by her sensitive and enthusiastic feedback. She understood its intentions, and it pleased me that while I was much older, she had also become my friend.

I had hoped the *New York Times* review might elevate me as a poet. I subverted my sexual energy and intensity into *The Rape of the Swan*. It's my best work. I know it is. What the Visiting Poet did was an act of revenge. He took my poems, my ideas, and distorted them, made them his own, a double deceit. I hear screeching and fluttering. I look up to see a bird, it's a robin, with its orange breast and yellow beak, trapped and flying in the high ceilings of palatial ruins. Oh, the poor bird. How will she find her way out before she smashes into the glass walls? She swoops down, almost overhead, as if she's trying to tell me something. I duck. She keeps circling, tweeting, screeching, struggling to find a way out. She's desperate, flying this way and that. I take my hand to my Heracles bracelet for strength.

Figure of Isis-Aphrodite
(2nd century A.D., Roman period)

I go back to the gods. I'm at the feet of Aphrodite. Is this her work? Did she cast a spell so that I could not see the evils of desire? I hear something. Is it that bird again? That trapped robin? I turn and look. It is only the chatter of a boy wearing wireless earphones talking into his phone.

Gods and goddesses don't follow rules. They test the limits, use their powers. Deploy tricks to get what they want. Have many lovers. It is the mortals who are left to suffer. Aphrodite wears a crown that is too heavy for the weight of her body. She stands in the Egyptian room. A combination of Isis and Aphrodite. Her crown is splendid. As is her gold jewelry and her hourglass shape. Her nudity is draped in gold. Her eyes speak to me. *Don't be afraid,* they say. A draft tickles my skin. But don't you see. I've been played. *It's not wrong to be vulnerable. To be human.* I touch my chest as if to soothe myself.

Marble statue of a youthful Hercules
(A.D. 69–96, Roman)

I walk past Heracles and stop. *Help me*, I say silently. He has that lion skin slung over his arm in victory. He peers down at me. I want him to tell me what to do; otherwise, I'm afraid the walls will burn down. The house will collapse. I am told there are thirty-six renditions of him in this museum alone. I am floating in a nameless stream. It is black as the Nile. I want to swim until I've been cleansed. I want to walk on hot stones. Desire is for the young. I want to be rid of it. I feel dizzy. The last three days it's as if I've been at sea and battled wars, fought my tormenters and seducers. My head is heavy. Time has lost its accuracy. If there is no clock, there is no time. Why? I say to him. *Because he wanted you. Because he's selfish. Because he's a monster.* The swans at the lake had turned him on. He needed something to happen to inspire him. It was double-edged. He'd said it when we argued over Yeats's poem. He couldn't leave without something happening he said, it was inevitable, but then home, far from the experience, he luxuriated in the exploitation—the creative act is like an abduction, the divine overtakes you, as it had overtaken Leda. Perhaps he'd been working on his version in secret all along. Heracles, how did you survive it all? A deep pain passes into my core. *We all must bear our losses and labors. I'm not alone. Your strength will return, and you'll be stronger.* But your family. You killed your family. I can't bear to think of it. I try to stand, but I am dizzy and sit down on the hard bench. I need to lie down.

Cubiculum (bedroom) from
the Villa of P. Fannius Synistor at Boscoreale
(ca. 50–40 B.C., Roman)

I walk to this room that is belted so that I cannot enter. In the room is a bed where I imagine the gods and goddesses once made love, the bed in which perhaps Aphrodite and Ares slept. On the walls are frescos that depict Hellenistic palaces with Roman columns and vegetation. I love the blue of the cushions of the narrow bed. A room where Eros left his mark, where wrongdoings came to a head. Perhaps a room where a baby once cried, and a mother bowed her head in grief. I would like to lie down on the bed and sleep for a hundred days. It is a rendition of a bed where the ancient Greeks rested their heads. The walls are papered in murals of ancient Greece. I'm so weak. I can't resist. No one is around. I climb under the blue velvet belt-ring and go in and lie down on the floor. I look at the walls. There's Athena with her beautiful robes and her strident gaze. On her shoulder is the owl who sees in the dark with its yellow, penetrating eyes what others cannot see. I am bedazzled by this goddess who keeps mortals safe. I want her to watch over me. I close my eyes. When I open them, I'm nudged awake. I look up, it's the guard. I don't know how long I've been in here. He looks stalwart in his white shirt and blue tie and jacket. I like that he is there, guarding me. What are you doing there? You have to get up. You can't be in here. It's belted off for a reason, he scolds. I'm sorry, I say. I'm just so tired.

What's wrong, he says, helping me up. What's happened? You're pale. And shaking. You can't break the rules of the museum. I have not slept well, or eaten anything, I say. I'm sorry. I remind myself that Heracles went mad. He killed his wife and family. He suffered many labors to regain his sanity and live without remorse and regret. His grief started wars.

Come. Let's go to the atrium. The guard holds my arm to steady me as we walk. The atrium is in the sculpture courtyard designed to look like a garden. We're surrounded by European sculptures, deep urns, and vast windows. Behind pillars, standing in rows are the Greek gods and goddesses. It's as if they're lining up to greet me. They all look so real. Zeus, Athena, Poseidon. I feel as if I am floating. If sleep is a dream, then all I want to do is to dream. If to dream is to sleep, I do not want to awaken. Maybe it is a dream. All of it. *You were once. "You were never. Were you ever? Oh never to have been!" Yes never to have been.* I'm lightheaded, I say to the guard, and clutch his arm. Yes, maybe all of it is a dream.

The guard finds us a table. Let me get you some water, he offers once I'm seated. I peer at the gods. They're all chattering, ready to decree a judgment. They mock us. For what we must bear and what we neglect. For what we can't see. Our ignorance. The guard returns with a paper cone of water and I take a sip. What's happening? I ask, still looking at the gods. You're not well, he says. I try to rise, but I am dizzy and sit back again. You're shaking. Here, take my jacket, he says, and puts it around my shoulders.

Let me get you a cookie. You need some sugar. Yes, I need some sugar, I agree. I watch him walk to the counter and stand in line. The gods, they're still whispering. He returns with a big cookie and a glass of orange juice. I take a few bites. It is the tastiest, softest cookie I've ever had. I bite into a chocolate chip and then sip the orange juice, and it's as if I'm imbibing the nectar of the gods. My strength returning.

What's wrong? the guard says after I take a few bites and sips. Is it your son? I don't know. Your work? I've been so stupid, I say. Why do you think Odysseus was tested? You know, in *The Odyssey*. Have you read it? Of course, I've read it. You can't get through high school without reading it, he says. To prove his loyalty, I suppose. Do you think he was loyal to Penelope even though he slept with Calypso? If he remained true to her. Maybe. I don't know. Whom are you loyal to? I ask. To my friends and family. To my country, to my work, he says. Do you have enemies who want to hurt you? People who want to tear you down? I ask. Fuck my enemies, he says. Yeah. Fuck my enemies. I feel a quarrel beginning in my mind. What have I lost if I've been true to myself? I still have my book; no one can take that away from me. Not even Pynyon. One of the high-ranking critics of our time has deemed my poem deaf, flat. I disagree. It's a beautiful poem. It's only earnest when read through the lens of a misogynist, of a disbeliever. I look around. They're all smiling at me. I am not alone. It's Aphrodite. She's looking at me with curiosity. A new perception enters. A surge of adrenaline. To take one's poem was to take one's soul. I won't let him have it. Then Athena, looking sternly. *You must rewrite the story*, she says. *It's up to you.* I look at them all again, these splendid bodies encrypted in stone. I am in the company of gods. The Olympians.

Are you feeling a bit better? he asks.

Yeah, a bit. Thank you. For the cookie. And your jacket. Here, I say reluctantly, and stop myself before clutching it to my chest. I walk the guard back to his gallery and we say our goodbyes. When I turn back to look at him in the corner of the gallery, he has his hands behind his back. He is as still as the sphinx. As if he's always been there, in that one spot. I go back to the gallery of the gods. "For who, if I cried out, would ever hear me?" I say, but the gods are no longer listening. They are stone cold. They've deserted me.

I hurry through the long hall to the foyer and exit the museum. It's rush hour. People are running with newspapers on top of their heads, ducking under awnings for cover. Umbrellas are turned inside out. The gods are in a fury. On Fifth Avenue a stream of businessmen walk briskly by wearing rubbers to protect their shoes, briefcases in hand, determined to govern, to provide, and women stumbling in their heels in their shadow. A car speeds past and dumps nearly a quart of water on my legs. The trees on the block are cascading and shedding twigs and leaves. The rain is screaming in a violent downpour. I must think through things carefully. I was wrong to have expected my husband to fill all my needs. Wrong to think I needed more than what I have. The wind pushes against me as if forcing me to see what I've sacrificed for my vanity. What I've lost is my faithful companion. My husband is right. I've been in my own world. My way of coping for the tumult inside me. I'm the one who has changed, not him. He's always been there. Steady. My rock. The sky is crying. The trees bend to its will. It's all falling apart. I'm morphing, shift-shaping. But not because of the Visiting Poet. I did not *put on his knowledge with his power*. No. He did not penetrate me. He was not a god. The strange geometry of all that I've gained and lost is too much to consider in the pouring rain and I run.

## APARTMENT 9B

Arturo greets me in the lobby. I nod hello and briskly walk past him into the elevator. Before going into my apartment, I stop at my neighbor's door. I must warn her not to break it all apart. As I go to knock, the door swings open. I walk in and call for my neighbor. Half of the room's furniture is gone. Where is that exquisite velvet sectional sofa that was the centerpiece of the room? And that marble coffee table? Even the art she meticulously picked out by going to gallery shows in Chelsea is off the walls. Is she redecorating again? And then my neighbor flies in. She's wearing stiletto shoes and, underneath the raincoat, one of those flowing dresses, hair bouncing down her back. Arturo left the door open for me. I've forgotten a few things, she says. The bastard's taken away my keys. She stops and turns toward me. Look at you, she says. You're soaking. Do you want a towel? I shake my head no, I'll be fine. What's going on here? I say. I've moved out, she says. Is that what you meant, the other day in the hallway, what you wanted to tell me? She nods. I've wanted to tell you for ages, but I was ashamed, I knew you'd be disappointed in me. I can't do this anymore, she says. But your family, your kids, I say. What will you do? I found an apartment in the Village. All this, she says, looking around at the spacious and now half-empty villa that is her apartment. It was like we were pretending. It never was right. I'm not sure he even loved me. We got married because I was pregnant. My mother told me to stop using birth control. Why? I say. Why would she do that? Because she's old-school. Because I was in my thirties and still living hand to mouth. Because she was afraid no one would have me otherwise? I want to tell my neighbor not to go. Not to shatter her world, her kids' lives, yes children can and do survive divorce but not without consequences, to emerge from her slumber, but I can't. I don't want to tell her that I've ruined my life too. I don't have the words. What will you do? I say. The yoga teacher invited me to a retreat in Costa Rica. I'm leaving tomorrow. I mean, what will you live on? I say. A friend recommended a divorce lawyer. I'll be fine. More than fine, she says with an awkward smile. While I should be happy that she'll be well taken care of, I'm conflicted. She's well educated. Talented. I don't think her husband is the kind of man who wanted her occupation to be a wife and mother. She is clearly overqualified for it. That's why she spends her days decorating and redecorating her home, going shopping, taking yoga classes. She's turned her ambitions into their own kind of mythology, a kind of bourgeois perfectionism, even in the way she dresses. And now that she's leaving, she gets rewarded for no longer being in love with her husband. The traditions of marriage no longer make sense. I can't deny too that I find myself a little jealous of her freedom. She will not allow her desires to vanquish in middle age. She's determined to have it all. Love, passion, rapture, sensuality, a new lease on life. This happens to men all the time. I should not be deriding her for leaving her family, but I find that I can't bear to see the tie severed. I know her children. They'll always be pining for what they have lost. Are you sure? I say. She nods. Tears form in her eyes. I give her a hug. I have to, she says, I'm dying here. I understand, I say. Then she straightens herself back up. I'll be in touch once I'm back from Costa Rica. I'll be here for you, I say.

We say our goodbyes and I drift into my apartment. I'm sad for my friend. I'm sad for myself. I should have seen it coming. I've been too much in my own head. I feel an ache all through my body, as if I'm already grieving for what I've lost.

My phone bleeps. A text is coming through. Maybe it's my husband. But no, it's my neighbor's daughter. *I read the review in the NYTBR*, she texts. *You must dismiss the abomination at once. Everyone who knows your work will know the truth. I'll make sure they do.*

I feel my face break into a smile. Maybe one day, for her generation, the struggle won't be as difficult. It's up to them to rewrite the story. Suddenly the apartment is quiet. The storm at least for a moment has stopped. I can't bear the silence. The sound of my own words beating against my skull. How will I endure the silence?

When my husband proposed he gave me a glorious ring with a ruby and diamonds. It was beautiful, but it did not feel like the right ring. I thought it was too good for me. Shortly after we were engaged, I went to the Y where I swim. I asked myself whether I should wear the ring in the pool or whether I should take it off to protect it from the chlorine. I battled this thought for a while and then I put the ring in the pocket of my jeans and locked it in my locker. When I came out of the pool, showered, and changed, I put my hand in my pocket and it was gone. I panicked. I asked the few women in the locker room to help me find it. I sat down on the bench and cried with my head in my hands. The attendant said, It's happened before. The Y is also a youth hostel, some of the girls are desperate. Someone watches you, sees something they want, and memorizes the numbers as you unlock your locker. No matter. The ring was gone, and I would never have it again. It seemed a terrible omen. Maybe I hadn't wanted to get married? It hung over me. Then when I couldn't have it, I coveted the ring. I stared at women's hands on the subway, the bus, at restaurants, searching for the ring. I still remember it. Those beautiful rubies and diamonds. My not-yet-husband spent all his savings on that ring. It had been a snowy night when we first met. We left the party together and he walked me home through the park. It was quiet, the snow was falling, blanketing evergreens, falling on our shoulders. He took my hand in his, and even through my mitten I felt his warmth. It was before time, it was before we were born. The snow kept coming and I did not want it to stop. I made a wish to myself. Please, let this be the one.

Water is dripping from my hair, my clothes. I go into the bathroom to get a towel, sit on the rim of the bathtub. It's all too much. The toilet continues to run when it is flushed. The porcelain on the prewar sink has cracks. The paint on the heating pipe is peeling. The tiles on the floor are mismatched. It's a miracle. The rain has stopped. I hear a sound from outside the bathroom window. I open it and see the same owl I saw in the park perched in the tree on our block. Yellow eyes full of trickery and a solemn face, crusty and cracked, like an old woman, ancient really. Its thin and crooked beak. It is not a pretty bird. Too plump for its small feet. Its rusty feathers. Its eyes pressed far back in its head, perched upright, standing to attention. Eyes with great depths of perception to see its prey from far away. I don't trust it. *To be able to see into the night. Even when the night is black.* I turn to the mirror. I barely recognize myself. My face is different now. Hardened into itself, harder to hide behind. Angrier. My wet hair falls in viper-like spirals to my shoulders. Is this what Athena has done? She turned Medusa into a hag for sleeping with Poseidon. I touch my face. It's dry and crinkled and greenish, or maybe it's the dim bathroom light. O new day, I must coax myself into a new beginning. I have broken my own heart and, like Odysseus after the lightning bolt struck his ship, I am the lone survivor. I must build it back plank by plank. A new voice is pushing itself out of me. Wild horses spring from my neck. I will turn men who want to deride me into stone. I will no longer laugh at their jokes, smile when they mansplain. I will no longer be the passive victim. I won't be silenced. I will never be the same. A new myth is slowly unfolding. I must go where it takes me. I look at the owl again. Those eyes. What is Athena trying to tell me? I retrieve my notebook from my back pocket—it's a bit damp from the rain—and reach for one of my fountain pens. I must write myself out of my sorrow, of what I've lost. The chorus beckons.

And then I hear a noise coming from the kitchen, pots and pans making their usual racket. I step out of the bathroom. The rain has stopped. The table is set. There is a bouquet of pink peonies, my favorite flower, in a vase in its center. A stream of light floods the room.

September 16, 2025

Dear Abigail,

I hope all is well in New York and that your new book of poems is coming along. I read a handful of the new work in *Poetry*. The poems are utterly gorgeous.

With gratitude, I send you herewith my new book, *Vindication*, along with this recent review from *The New York Times*. You have been an inspiration to me and I am so appreciative.

Yours, as ever,
Amelia

Amelia Finnegan
Assistant Professor of English
Stanford University

*The New York Times*

**Amelia Finnegan Exposes Male Appropriation in *Vindication***
By Jocasta Peterson

*Vindication*
By Amelia Finnegan

September 2, 2025

Amelia Finnegan's observant, intellectually challenging essays are influenced by modern feminist prodigies such as Judith Butler, Hélène Cixous, Kathy Acker, and Julia Kristeva. It is no surprise that her most recent book, *Vindication*, is a rallying cry for the voices of female writers who have been appropriated by male writers.

Ms. Finnegan exhibits a manic curiosity about the ways in which women novelists and poets have been underrecognized, and the complexity of being a woman artist living in America at the beginning of the twenty-first century. Characterized by a sharp yet dreamlike elegance and circuitous logic, her writing is precise, hyper realized, sui generis, genre-bending, often mixing criticism with philosophical reflections. Critics have noted that she abhors and fights against hypocrisy and injustice. Ms. Finnegan has dedicated her young career to creating a female-centric approach to the male-dominated field of American letters.

Ms. Finnegan came to notoriety at twenty-three for her first book of essays, *The Female Voice*, in which she argued that we must stop pigeonholing women for not writing with the authority and scope advanced by the male tradition and focus instead on the newly prominent world of female culture and experience. She writes incisively about how male novelists and poets have been praised for establishing patriarchal ideas of "greatness" while female writers are criticized and penalized for writing about subjects that don't adhere to these patriarchal ideas advanced by white men.

*Vindication* is an urgent look at the ways in which patriarchy has dominated the mythologies of the literary arts. Basing her ideas on extensive research, Ms. Finnegan condemns male writers throughout history and to the present for their appropriation of women's voices, without acknowledgment, including the controversy concerning the poets Abigail Frost and Justin O'Donnell. O'Donnell received the 2021 Pulitzer Prize in Poetry. However, Ms. Finnegan shows by careful analysis of both works, that it was O'Donnell who appropriated Ms. Frost's book, published that same year, and demands that his prize be revoked. Ms. Frost, whom Ms. Finnegan has known since childhood, has had a great influence on her career. Other work Ms. Finnegan draws upon is T. S. Eliot's *The Waste Land*, published in 1922, two years after Hope Mirrlees's *Paris: A Poem*, an experimental masterpiece that has been mostly overlooked. Mirrlees moved in the same circles as Eliot; her long poem was printed by the

Hogarth Press. Ms. Finnegan claims it is inconceivable that Eliot hadn't read it. Many of the strategies that we regard as revolutionary in *The Waste Land*, Finnegan maintains, are already present in Mirrlees's work: the fragmentation, the disembodied quotations, the influence of jazz, the use of unconventional typography, similar motifs, length and use of notations. Virginia Woolf personally did the typesetting for both poems. Ms. Finnegan also examines William Carlos Williams's poem *Paterson* and considers his appropriation of several passages from letters and poems of Marcia Nardi. Other writers in Ms. Finnegan's cabal include Robert Lowell and Wallace Stegner.

*Vindication* has already attracted a cultish following for its subversive writing. Some critics have winced at her work, claiming that she reduces an exploration of gender to preachy treatise. But readers disagree, as evidenced by the fact that the book's title essay, "A Vindication," went viral after Finnegan posited that we have not come further as a society since 1792, when Mary Wollstonecraft argued for "women as the natural and intellectual equals of men and deserving of equal treatment and opportunities nearly a hundred years before the term 'feminist' even existed."

In response to a question about what being a woman writer is like for her, Ms. Finnegan told *The New York Times* that the very phrase *woman writer* is condescending and is exactly what her writing has been fighting against. When asked about how she felt the internet was affecting human relationships, she said, "The internet has made us a lonely, hideous society."

*Vindication*
By Amelia Finnegan
355 pp. The Feminist Press $30

# NOTES

All captions, quotations, and photographs relating to the art are from the Metropolitan Museum of Art's website, www .metmuseum.org. In the text, I've used the spelling "Heracles" for the Greek god; variants in the photo captions ("Hercules," "Herakles") follow those on the Met's website.

8 **"What I fear most"**: Sylvia Plath, "Cambridge Notes (from *Notebooks*, February 1956)," in *Johnny Panic and the Bible of Dreams* (New York: HarperCollins, 1983), 272.

28 *O love, how did you get here?*: Sylvia Plath, "Nick and the Candlestick," in *The Collected Poems*, ed. Ted Hughes (New York: HarperCollins, 1992), 240.

125 **"rare for sons"**: This and all other quotes from *The Odyssey* are from Emily Wilson's translation (New York: W. W. Norton, 2018).

142 **"building that terrible acropolis"** and **"Great passions grow into monsters"**: Robinson Jeffers, "*Medea*, after Euripides," in *Cawdor and Medea* (New York: New Directions, 1970), 120.

200    **"You'll find nothing inside":** This line is a paraphrase of "you find no one inside," the last line in Frederick Seidel's poem "The Death of the Shah," in *Ooga-Booga* (New York: Farrar, Straus and Giroux, 2006), 96.

233    **"Nothing can cure the soul":** Oscar Wilde, *The Picture of Dorian Gray* (New York: Penguin Classics, 2000), 23.

237    **"the goddess 'of divine retribution and revenge'":** www.greekmythology.com/Other_Gods/Nemesis/nemesis .html.

264    **"Unwittingly, he desired himself":** Ovid, *Metamorphoses*, trans. Mary Ines (New York: Penguin Classics, 1955), 85.

271    *You were once:* Samuel Beckett, *Company / III Seen III Said / Worstward Ho / Stirrings Still* (London: Faber & Faber, 2009), 12.

273    **"For who, if I cried out":** Rainer Maria Rilke, "The First Elegy," in *Duino Elegies*, trans. Alfred Corn (New York: W. W. Norton, 2021), 5.

## ACKNOWLEDGMENTS

I'm grateful to Helen Schulman, Rebecca Schultz, Diane Goodman, Vesna Goldsworthy, Bill Clegg, and Lorin Stein for their insightful readings and comments. Further gratitude to my agents, Sarah Chalfant and Jacqueline Ko at the Wylie Agency. I owe thanks to my editor, Dan Smetanka, for his faith, attention, and editorial acumen, and to Janet Renard, my excellent copy editor, as well as Wah-Ming Chang, Dan López, Megan Fishmann, and Rachel Fershleiser at Counterpoint Press. For my brilliant cover, thank you, Jaya Miceli. For multiple residences at the Betsy Hotel Writer's Room, where I was fortunate to be able to work on this novel, along with enjoying the sea and sunshine, I give thanks to Deborah Briggs. Huge debt goes to David and Lucas Schwartz, who have always recognized and supported my work.

**JILL BIALOSKY** is the author of six acclaimed collections of poetry, three critically acclaimed novels, and two memoirs, including *History of a Suicide: My Sister's Unfinished Life*, a *New York Times* bestseller. Her poems and essays have appeared in *The Best American Poetry*; *The New Yorker*; *The Atlantic*; *Harper's Magazine*; *O, The Oprah Magazine*; *The Kenyon Review*; *Harvard Review*; and *The Paris Review*, among other publications. Her work has been a finalist for the James Laughlin Award, the Paterson Poetry Prize, and the Books for a Better Life Awards. In 2014, she was honored by the Poetry Society of America for her distinguished contribution to poetry. She lives in New York City. Find out more at jillbialosky.com.